PAINT

THE

GRASS

Paint the Grass

H.R. BOYD

"With the new day comes new strength and new thoughts."

–Eleanor Roosevelt

Paint
the
Grass

H.R. BOYD

COPPER CROW PUBLISHING

Copper Crow Publishing

Published by Copper Crow Publishing
Bella Vista, AR

First paperback edition February 2023
Book design by Copper Crow Publishing

ISBN: 978-1-7345366-9-0(paperback) | ISBN: 978-1-7345366-8-3(ebook)

www.hrboyd.com

For Tamara,
who showed me how to be proud of my path.

For Hillary,
who dared me to believe and proved that kindred spirits do exist.

And for Jodi,
who had the strength to paint the grass after the unthinkable happened.
You will always inspire me.

ONE

IN LIFE THERE ARE these moments, the ones that mark a change, the ones that make us realize nothing will ever be the same again. I call them TP moments. And not because some of them are super shitty—though they are—and not because they sometimes scare the crap out of you—though they do—but because every single one of them becomes a turning point in our lives. For good or for bad, these moments change us. Whether we want them to or not.

And most of the time, we don't even see them coming.

They happen on mundane, ordinary nights. Like tonight.

I'm surrounded by friends on every side and completely in my element. Here at The Apex restaurant, soft music and candlelight pamper us as we begin the night's festivities. The chef's latest creation plumps the air with buttery goodness, and I swear I gain three pounds by breathing. Waiters bustle about, carrying trays of five-star food past the polished-wood bar where our party sits. We left our small town for the evening and came into the city to celebrate my husband's promotion.

I'm busy talking Jake up to his colleagues, listening to his boss's stories, complimenting the spouses on their dress clothes or their latest haircut. I laugh at jokes. I smile at vacation photos. I resist the urge to massage the ache out of my sore cheeks. I've even memorized everyone's favorite drink and order another round as we head into dinner.

Our waiter leads the way to a large table at the center of the room. As the group moves away from the bar and into the restaurant, I do a quick seat check to see who has lost an earring or left a set of keys or a handbag behind. But the bar area is clear—except for a single cell phone.

Jake's cell phone.

Not a surprise. My husband would've left his hand behind if it hadn't been carrying his drink. Good thing he has me. I lean over the barstool, shaking my head as I retrieve his phone.

When I flip it over, movement lights up the screen. His message app is open.

I miss you too. A lot. Wish you were here with me.

A text he just sent.

My lips tilt up automatically. What a funny text for him to send, I've been with him all night. Why would he . . .

I've been with him all night.

The truth of the statement hits me.

He couldn't possibly be missing me or wishing I was with him. I *have* been with him.

All night.

Then who did Jake text?

The phone buzzes in my hand and an answer to his text pops up on the screen.

And what would you do with me if I was there? 🖊

What the hell? Who's texting my husband?

My eyes focus on the name at the top of the text strand.

AP. Alex.

Otherwise known as the beautiful Alexandra Pike.

Sounds of the restaurant blink in and out as clouds of confusion fill my mind. But—Alex is just a friend. He's told me so, dozens of times. His buddy. The woman he studies with, goes running with, and apparently shares tender texting moments with.

Someone he misses.

A lot.

Someone who sends him suggestive texts with lipsticked lips alongside them.

My breath comes in shallow gasps, clearing the clouds away with a single sucker punch to the heart. I pull in air through my nose and push it out my mouth. Slowing my breathing. Trying to understand. Trying to make sense of the last five minutes of my life.

It's not possible.

He wouldn't.

The cold comes from some unseen place, pouring over and through me. Numb fingertips lose feeling as I grasp his phone in one hand. The rounded metal edges press into my skin as I squeeze it tighter and tighter still. The damning text strand, fresh on the screen.

My smile quivers and shakes until it disappears altogether.

I stumble like a blind duckling, unsteady in my metallic heels as I follow the group into the restaurant with Jake's unfaithful phone in my hand. How did this happen? My life, my entire life, has been devoted to making him happy. Especially since the boys left for college. It's been all about *Jake this* and *Jake that*. My whole existence wrapped up in helping him get his dream job. His big promotion.

I'm so blind. How could I not see? How could I not know?

"Are you going to sit down, sweetheart?" Jake motions to the chair next to him, then turns back to his conversation without waiting to see if I do.

In my dazed state, I almost walk right past him. Everyone in our group sits at the table, waiting to order until I join them.

No one notices my life snapping into sharp, jagged pieces.

My hands shake and there's a high-pitched ringing in my ears. Others glance my way, and my practiced smile lifts back into place, steadying my confidence. I inhale a slow, stabilizing breath. I can do this. It's just one dinner. Like I've done a thousand times before. I cling to my smile, take firm hold of my emotions, and sit.

The white tablecloth brushes against my lap as I glance at the back of my husband's head and wish for an apple and an arrow. He doesn't notice anything amiss. He's all ease and charisma, oozing charm as he flatters his boss's wife.

His phone buzzes in my hand, and I nearly drop it. Numb as I am, I'd forgotten it was there. It slides through my unsteady fingertips and turns face up as I attempt to stabilize it. Before I can stop myself, I read the new text atop the lighted screen.

Alex: Need to see you. How about a run Saturday morning? Just you and me. We'll watch the sunrise together. 😗

See him? But we're three hours from home. We won't be back until late Friday.

I'm breathing fast. And loud. A dragon prepping fire, ready to scorch every living human within flame-throwing distance. And my heart has somehow lodged itself in my throat. How am I going to get through this dinner? I can't swallow. How can I eat if I can't swallow?

I try taking a sip of water. And now I'm choking. Choking and not swallowing. The ever-graceful Bethany Taylor has been reduced to a hacking mess by a simple glass of water.

"You okay, Bethany?" Phil asks. My husband's boss notices my distress before

Jake does, and every face at the table turns my way. Their concerned smiles make me wish I could fade away before my humiliation becomes public knowledge.

Leaning over the table, I nod as I continue to gasp and gag. Tears wet my eyelashes, but that's as far as I allow them to go. I'm sitting at a table full of my husband's friends and colleagues. Water drips down my chin, and I'm trying desperately to control my cough. I may be a trusting fool. But. I. Will. Not. Cry.

"Next time, maybe try swallowing the water instead of inhaling it. Okay, honey?" My husband rubs my upper back with his hand, and I wish I had the mutant ability to shoot spikes out of my spine. One good shot, straight through his hand. It might make me feel better, though he deserves so much worse after twenty years of my love and loyalty.

When I'm finally in control, he turns away and focuses on his boss's wife again. Joan takes all of his attention for now. Apparently, my husband is well-practiced at charming other women.

The phone silently buzzes in my lap. Running-buddy Alex sent him a pic. One of her in an exercise outfit. The term outfit being used very loosely, of course. It's a selfie featuring a low-cut sports bra that perfectly gift-wraps her delightful twenty-six-year-old boobs.

Perhaps if the mutant spikes shooting out of my back were to cut off his entire right hand? Or both hands, maybe?

Nope. Still not enough.

I know I should put the phone in my purse. I know I should wait for a better time to deal with this. But even if nothing good comes of my curiosity— I can't stop myself.

"If you'll excuse me," I say as I stand. My chair rattles along the wood floor as it slides back, and all eyes focus on me once again. Guilt and anger mix together to color my cheeks even as my smile locks into place.

My husband absently waves at me as he leans toward his boss, falling deep into discussion about their upcoming project. The words *construction begins* and *need you there* fade behind me as I turn to walk in the opposite direction.

I push through the thick, glass doors separating the restaurant from the marble-rich lobby. The clack of my heels echoes through the large air-conditioned space as I make my way to a forgotten corner of the room. Sliding between two artificial trees, I surround myself with leaves as fake as my husband's devotion and scroll through his past conversations with Alex.

Guilt rises up, but I punch it down like bread dough, slice it into nice, manageable pieces and keep reading. It's my husband's phone, I tell myself. We've been married for twenty years, and he shouldn't be hiding things. We don't have secrets from each other. He told me so himself.

All of the texts are sweet and attentive.

I scroll back two weeks:

> *Alex:* Call me on your drive home. I need to hear your voice. 🖤

> *Jake:* I'll dial the phone as I start the car. Talk soon.

Then last week:

> *Alex:* Can you break away from your wife to spend the day with me?

> *Jake:* Of course I can. B won't be a problem. What did you have in mind? 😊

And finally, yesterday:

> *Alex:* Let's have dinner. Something spicy. 😍

> *Jake:* Sounds great. Excited to see you. Can't wait.

I'll bet he can't wait. Asshole. Bastard. Rake. Rat. There aren't any names awful enough for what he is. So, I make one up.

Fraggard! He's a total fraggard! What a fraggard he is!

A longer text comes next:

> *Alex:* Dear Jake. I'm afraid you're going to have to quit your job. Your time on the road is getting in the way of me seeing you. It's been way too long. This is a problem. Love, Alex.

I swallow the pain that bunches in my throat, but no matter what I do, I can't push away the betrayal that flays me alive. Standing here in this quiet corner, the more I read, the harder it is not to throw his phone across the room—or crush its glass face with my fashionable heels. The harder it is not to classify him as an entirely new species.

The Wandering-eyed Fraggard. Better off extinct.

The conversation continues, getting even more personal. She's going through a divorce, and Jake comforts her.

> *Jake:* On my way over. I'll be with you soon.

> *Alex:* I couldn't make it through this without you.

> *Jake:* I'd do anything to make you happy.

Then I read it. The text that shocks my tears back into their ducts, and shoves my heart into a collision with reality.

> *Jake:* I'm so sorry, Alex. I love you. You'll get through this.

Three little words bundled between such thoughtful, tender sentiments. Three words I thought were meant only for me. They burn into my tearless eyes, and the smallest of sobs escapes.

I love you?

"Excuse me, Miss." The restaurant manager peeks around the plastic plant concealing me.

"Yes?" I drop Jake's phone into my purse and step away from the corner.

"Your party's about to order." He smiles, all polish and professionalism. "Your husband wanted me to ask you what you'd like?"

I'd like for him to be castrated without anesthesia. Is that on the menu?

I clear my throat. "Sorry you had to come find me." My long hair falls over my shoulders as I nod toward the door. "I was just about to go back inside."

He leads the way to the restaurant entrance and holds the door open for me.

"Thank you," I whisper.

As I approach our table, Jake has one hand on Joan's arm, but he turns his smile to me. "Welcome back, sweetheart."

I want to scream obscenities into the crowded room. I want to grab every water goblet and salad plate and smash them to bits on the ground.

But I don't.

I won't be the crazy shrew everyone gossips about at office parties.

Instead, I take my seat, biting my lip as I focus on the menu before me. *Steady. Steady.* No one notices my distress. No one sees me in my moment of pain as I stare at my menu, seeing nothing.

How could he?

Am I not enough?

Why am I not enough?

My husband hears me sniffle again and touches my arm. Gentle. Loving. Ever attentive.

The dick.

"What's wrong?" he whispers, his face full of confusion.

18

"What do you mean?" I force another smile.

He leans in close and lowers his voice even more. "We've been married for twenty years. I can tell when something's bothering you."

"Are you sure?"

"Just tell me."

"Is this the best time?"

Every face turns toward us. Every ear leans in to listen. Every eye questions what might be wrong with the perfect couple. Or maybe they know. Maybe Jake has a secret texting strand with each and every woman at this table.

A smooth smile slips onto Jake's lips as he addresses his coworkers and their spouses. "I'm afraid Beth isn't feeling very well. We might have to turn in early tonight."

No! I don't want to be alone with him right now. "Jake, I'm fine." I reach out, but can't quite bring myself to touch him. Instead, I rest my hand on the tablecloth in front of his arm. "Really. I feel fine. Everyone will miss us if we leave." I turn to his boss. "Wouldn't you, Phil?"

"Of course. Especially your crazy stories, Beth." With one hand, he gestures toward me. "You have such a quick wit. I'll never know how Jake managed to snag you."

"I'm a lucky guy," Jake says.

All female heads tilt to one side in unison. "Ahhhs" sigh from every woman's mouth.

His kind words only twist the knife further. *Then why the hell are you texting another woman?* My smile pulls tight. Acid burns my throat, and I wish I could spit at him. Go full on llama on his ass. Spit, spit, and more spit.

This image widens the smile on my lips.

"Now there's a man who loves his wife." Joan looks at Phil. "Why don't you ever say things like that to me?"

Phil turns to my husband, his right-hand man. "Jake, email me a list of sweet-nothings I need to say to my wife first thing tomorrow morning."

Everyone laughs.

Everyone but me.

I try to breathe past the pain, through the hurt. I try to ignore the awful irony of the moment. I want to stop feeling all together.

"Beth," Joan says my name, and her sharp voice snaps me back to the present.

"Yes." I clear my throat. "I'm sorry, what were you saying?"

She smiles patiently. "Would you be willing to head up our children's hospital fundraiser again this year? We all know you're the best person for the job."

A hollow ache forms in my heart and spreads through my body with each life-sucking beat. Lub-dub. Lub-dub. The steady rhythm hints at what I really am. You-slug. You-slug.

I'm all slime and ugliness in this moment. Accustomed to being stepped on. As low as the shell-less mollusks that feed on my marigolds every summer. And suddenly, I no longer care to be me. I no longer want to be the perfect woman who always says yes.

"Um." I look down at my lap for a few seconds before I find my courage and meet her eye. "No." A small, shaky, un-Bethany-like smile quivers onto my face. "No, I won't be able to do it this year."

"What?" Jake leans toward me and wraps one hand around mine. "Come on, honey. You've got this. The boys are at college now. You have the time."

I force my smile to brighten and snatch my hand out of Jake's grasp. My husband is very successful. He's always needed at work, and he travels a lot. I stay at home and take care of everything else in our life. He has no worries at home. Not one. I even help him impress clients and coworkers on occasion. But of course, I don't have a paycheck coming in, so my life's work can't be measured properly.

An ocean of ice flows through me. Salt shrivels up my sluggish heart, and I'm even more determined to refuse. "Sorry. But I'm starting another project soon, and I just won't have time." I lift my head high, finding confidence in the simple action. "You'll just have to settle for the second-best person for the job this year."

"Jake," his boss interrupts. "Take her upstairs and show her a good time. Talk her into helping us out. Be persuasive." Phil winks at me, and every inch of my skin attempts to crawl off my body in one synchronized jolt.

With that single condescending look, I realize I'm just a tool to Phil. A tool to look good on the arm of his right-hand man. A tool who brings in clients with her bright smile and fun personality. A tool who has headed up every charity event for his company for the last fifteen years. Without pay.

I'm a tool for sure.

Appetizers hit the table, and the overwhelming odor of garlic radiating from the artichoke dip makes me sick. The dripping cheese sends bile climbing up my throat. The yeasty scent of fresh-baked bread turns sour in my stomach before it even touches my lips.

I stand without thinking.

All eyes follow me to my feet.

"I . . . I guess I am feeling a bit queasy. Maybe I will go lie down." I turn to Phil and Joan. "I hope you all have a wonderful evening."

I grab my purse and leave the hotel restaurant, not caring if Jake follows. Hoping he doesn't. I'm almost running to the elevator. The shiny silver doors are my salvation. I press the up button on the wall, slip inside, and jab my finger into the number ten as the doors close. We have a suite on the top floor. Only the best for Phil's right-hand man.

Jab. Jab. Jab. Jab.

The elevator finally starts to move, and I lean against the wall. I close my eyes, and it's as if I'm someone else looking at my life from the outside. And it's sad. A sad, pathetically perfect life. A life that doesn't actually have me in it. How is that even possible? After everything I've done. After all the hours I've spent on this earth. How am I not a part of my own life?

I'm here to bake cookies for Jake's clients. To do physics projects with our son Ryan and practice speeches with our other son Robert. To make prize-winning soups for the office pot-luck competition. To sew tote-bags for the church fundraiser and head up the *A Book for Everyone* community event. I'm here to pack the twins off to college and set up their dorm room. I'm here for everyone else. Everyone else but me.

The elevator dings and the doors slide open. I step out onto brown and cream patterned carpet and again find myself nearly running in my heels. My pencil skirt fights against the quick movement, binding my legs like a leash. I stop mid-stride, mid-hallway, tempted to tear it off and walk to my room in my underwear, black lace proudly displayed to any who might see it.

The door across from me opens, and my feet begin to move again. Two minutes later, I'm in front of our suite. I stab the card into the reader and shove my way into the room. My suffocating skirt is off before the door closes. It drops to the floor. Forgotten. I don't bother to pick it up. I don't bother to put anything else on. I stare out the hotel window, but the inspiring night sky and beautiful city lights do nothing to brighten my mood. Two lines of text parade through my mind.

I miss you too. A lot. Wish you were here with me. I love you.

Over and over and over again. In my husband's voice.

I miss you too. A lot. Wish you were here with me. I love you.

His bedroom voice. Missing someone else. Loving someone else.

I stand before the open hotel window in my underwear, listening to the voices in my head. How am I not crazy yet? Or maybe I am a little crazy.

Something I do believe about love—one way or another—it will make you crazy.

The phone buzzes again, deep inside my purse. I lift it out like it's a used tissue, pinched between two fingers, dreading what else it will show me.

Alex: What do you think of my new workout ensemble? I'll wear it for you on our next run.

Alex again. Beautiful, funny, outgoing Alex. Who drinks too much and wears too little. Alex. Who misses my husband as much as he misses her.

Hand me a sling shot and some smooth stones. I guarantee I won't miss either of them.

Behind me, the door opens, then closes again with a soft click as Jake enters. "Honey, do you know what happened to my phone? I think I left it up here somewhere."

I fold my arms across my chest and refuse to answer him. I don't even turn around. But I know the moment he notices me—and my lack of clothing.

His whistle pricks the air. "Now we're talking. Is that why you left early? You should have said something." He moves in behind me, slides his hand up the front of my bare thigh, over top black lace, and splays his fingers across the soft skin just below my belly button.

My stomach is relatively flat and smooth, but it still has a mom bump that never quite goes away, no matter how many crunches I push myself through.

I do not have abs like Alex.

Her name makes me shiver, and my husband presses up against me. "You like that, huh?"

His lips touch the back of my neck, but before he can continue, I peel his fingers away from my skin. He retreats a few steps and turns me toward him.

My emotions must show in my eyes because the minute he looks at me, both of his hands slap his sides, and he takes another step back.

"What's wrong? Now will you talk to me?"

My nose flares at the suggestion, and I shake my head. How can he expect anything from me?

"Come on, sweetheart."

I close my eyes against the endearment.

"Tell me what's bothering you." It's a command. Not a question voiced with concern. Anger drips from every syllable, and my eyes blaze open.

Then the most glorious thing happens.

I find my voice.

It's soft, yet firm, and totally one-hundred percent—me.

"I've just been up here wondering how my husband can miss another woman *a lot* while he's sharing a hotel room with me." I hold up his phone and watch as disbelief drowns the frustration from his face. "I'm wondering how, after twenty years of marriage, he can wish to be with another woman. But mostly I'm wondering how he can have such an intimate relationship with someone who isn't wearing his ring."

Then I give into my urge.

And spit.

Right in his face.

TWO

MY SALIVA SPRAYS HIS cheek in little droplets, marking the skin with liquid freckles. They trickle down his face and past his open mouth. His open mouth that has nothing to say.

Spitting is immature and probably uncalled for, but I don't stop to think about it now. "And while we're on the subject." I'm all calm and coolness. I am the yoga instructor of pissed-off wives. "What kind of a husband thinks it's okay to type '*I love you*' to another woman? A woman who is *not* his mother, who is *not* his sister, who is *not* the woman he gave a ring to twenty years ago. Who *is*, as it turns out, a look-at-my-boobs hussy who has turned a once-faithful man into the most incredible ass of all time."

I pause long enough to look at him.

His eyes widen. His nose flares. His face goes pale. He gives a small head shake and swallows hard. Ever so gently, he takes both my hands in his. "I am so sorry." He leans in and touches his forehead to mine. "I had no idea you would see those texts. Or that they'd hurt you. You know how much I love you. You're my everything."

The smashed pieces of my heart beat together all at once, and slowly drift toward the left side of my chest. Maybe he really is sorry. Maybe we can move past this.

"But . . ." He wets his lips with his tongue and lifts his head.

The fraggard just couldn't leave well enough alone.

He squeezes both of my hands. "Honey, Alex is going through a really hard time right now. She needs to feel support from her friends. And that's what we are . . . friends. Just like I'm friends with Mitch and Trent. We're just good friends. We've been friends for a while."

"Friends, huh? Remember last month when you told me you guys aren't really that close?"

"We're not close."

"You're close enough she wants you to quit your job so she can see you more often."

"Come on. That was a joke. She was joking."

"Really. Was she joking when she asked you to ditch your wife and spend the day with her?"

"Seriously? We take recurrent classes together, sometimes run in the mornings, and occasionally go out to eat. We're just buddies. That's all."

"Okay. So, do you text 'I miss you. A lot.' to all your workout buddies? And say 'Wish you were here with me' to Phil? I guess everyone at the office knows how much you miss them and love them from all the sweet texts you send out."

"You're making so much more of this than it needs to be."

"Did you just say *I'm* making more of this?" My voice is no longer quiet. "Newsflash, Jake. *I* didn't make any of this. *You* made this." I jab him in the chest with one finger. "This one is all on you." Jab. Jab. Jab.

"Those texts don't mean anything." He winces and rubs at his chest.

"They mean something to me," I say and cringe when my voice sounds so broken.

26

Jake sighs. "We. Are. Just. Friends. We've only ever been friends. And we'll only ever be friends. You are the woman in my life. The only woman."

I hold up his phone. Secure on its glowing face is the picture Alex sent him earlier this evening. Her glorious abs on full display. Her cleavage pressing out of her sports bra. Her smile inviting him to join her through the screen.

"Yeah? Well, you might want to tell that to Alex, then." I drop the phone on the floor and say the words I never thought I'd ever say in the course of my marriage. "Feel free to sleep on the couch tonight. I'm taking the bed."

WHY THE HELL DOES he want to be with another woman? Using the hotel bed sheet as a tissue, I wipe at the tears and snot dripping from my face. I've been in bed for over an hour, asking myself questions with no answers. Too busy crying to sleep. Am I not checking all the boxes as his wife? Or maybe after twenty years he's just tired of me.

Maybe I'm boring to him now.

How did this happen? I used to be so sure of myself. So confident in my marriage. But now all I can think is—he needs someone else to make him happy.

It's amazing how fast confidence drains out of someone when their husband chooses to spend quality time with another woman.

Even if I haven't let myself go, even if I'm still the same quick-witted germaphobe I've always been—it doesn't matter. I'll never be as gorgeous as Alex, or have her tomboyish charm. I'll never be able to talk engines and do ten pull-ups in a row. Besides, she's twenty-six and I'm forty-one. And I gave birth to twins! I've raised two amazing boys. Isn't that worth something?

I've given up so much for our family, why can't Jake value that? Why can't I be enough for him?

I turn over for the umpteenth time, still unable to sleep. The alarm clock flashes 2:30 a.m. Its red light seeps into the dark room, and I grab a pillow from the far side of the bed to smother it. When complete darkness surrounds me, I sigh.

Flopping onto my stomach, I bunch another pillow beneath my head, punching it with my fist. Sleep. Sleep. Sleep. Sleep. Maybe if I repeat the word enough times it'll stick, and my brain will slow down and allow me to get a couple hours of rest.

I count sheep. I do deep-breathing techniques. I imagine all my limbs, one by one, falling into a deep relaxed state. I roll onto my back and put a pillow over my face.

It's no use. The unfamiliar bed has become the mat on which I'll wrestle all my demons tonight. And I'm tapping out. I remove the pillow from my face and pull the other off the clock. Time spills into the room, glaring 3:26 a.m. into the darkness.

I roll out of bed, pull on yoga pants and the first T-shirt I can find, then shove my arms into a thin sweatshirt. As quietly as I can, I slip out of the bedroom and tiptoe through the living area of the hotel room.

My husband is snoring loudly on the sofa. One hand hangs off the side of the couch, fingertips grazing the floor. I resist the urge to step on them, to crush his cuticles into the carpet. I don't want to wake him. It's more important to sneak out in peace.

With every bit of grace I can muster, I slide my feet toward the exit, grabbing a key card and my purse along the way. My skirt's still in the middle of the floor. I step over it, crack open the door, and squeeze out into the hallway.

The harsh light pulls my eyes into a squint, and I find refuge in the darkened stairwell. I jog down the steps. All ten flights. By the time I reach the exit at the bottom of the stairs, a thin layer of sweat sheens on my freckled skin.

My thick, strawberry-blonde hair almost glows against the black glass of the door leading outside. I examine my middle-of-the-night reflection. I'm not

28

repulsive. A little pale maybe, but still not unattractive. No matter what my husband thinks. No matter who else he texts *I miss you. A lot* to.

I shove the door open and take off into the night.

Aimlessly wandering would be a generous way to describe my nighttime stroll. I'm in an unfamiliar big city in northern Montana, with no idea where I'm going or what I'm looking for. The occasional honking of car horns and the soft cooing of pigeons keeps me company as I walk along. Cool night air brushes my exposed skin and goosebumps prickle up my neck. The warm summer weather fades with the setting sun, and on this last day of August, fall temperatures fill the air. I zip my sweatshirt to insulate against the chill and head toward the lights of downtown.

As I walk, I veer to the left, following signs leading toward the park in the distance. I've always loved nature. Especially parks surrounded by city lights, where I know a bear won't eat me. Honestly, it's the trees, really. Trees speak to me. I don't understand what they're saying, but with every swish of leaves on the wind, I feel it. Comfort pours over me as I step beneath the canopy and look up.

Branches break up the continuity of the night sky, and stars sparkle through leaves like twinkle lights. I pull in a breath and slowly release it back into the night. This is what I need. To get out of the stuffy hotel room. Away from phones. From husbands. And their text messages.

I miss you too. A lot. Wish you were here. I love you.

The words bring a sharp loneliness—it reminds me of the feeling I had the day my sons left home, just two weeks ago. Another empty day for me. I walked them up to their dorm room, helped them unpack, and then drove the two hours home. Alone. My house became a foreign place. So quiet. No longer the home of the cutest-ever twin boys and their mom.

I remember telling myself, *This is an opportunity*. Then I grabbed my red leather journal and tried to write down a list of things to do. A list of what I wanted. A list of what's next for me.

Nothing came to mind.

Not one word.

The journal's still blank. Even now.

Somewhere along the way I've lost myself. I've lost my passion. Passion not only for love, but for life. Passion for *my* dreams, *my* needs, *my* wants. I'm not even sure I remember what they are anymore. Maybe that's why my husband needs a friend like Alex.

How did I get so lost?

I need to talk to Lettie.

This single thought stands out among my jumble of emotions. Lettie will make things better. I pull out my phone and check the time— 4:45 a.m. Nope. She won't be awake. My best friend is many things, but an early riser is not one of them.

I look up and keep following the path. It feels good to walk with no purpose or destination. Loud thoughts echo in my mind as I make my way through the park. I trip more than once, but my eyes never leave the sky. When I finally run out of sidewalk, I focus on the all-night diner across the street.

Might as well go in for some tea.

The diner's silver outside looks like a cross between a blimp and an Airstream camper, but the fresh-baked smells coming from inside pull me through the door. I sit at the table just to the left of the main entrance. Soft music plays in the background, but I don't recognize the song. Something written several decades before I was born, I imagine.

A server with flawless, dark brown skin and a full head of intricately braided hair makes her way to my table. Pam, her name tag says. "Can I get ya coffee or tea?"

"Tea, please," I answer. "With lemon and honey. Lots of lemon. If it's okay." A soft cry catches me off guard. Tears fill my eyes, and I don't bother wiping them away. "I'm sorry."

Pam smiles and nods, her black braids brushing across her cheekbones. "Just the tea?"

I sniff and blink my eyes clear. "Yes, please. Appreciate it."

"You got it." With a scribble on her notebook and an exaggerated hip sway, she leaves me in peace.

Sitting in this quiet little booth, I'm alone with my thoughts and emotions, which is a dangerous place to be right now. I try to distract myself by cleaning the table with the travel wipes from my purse, but it doesn't work. So, I wipe down the condiments, salt shaker, and seat, like always, but I still don't feel like me. I try to conjure up a smile, but the tears slide over my cheeks faster than I can blink them away, and no one in the restaurant will mistake my sniffles for allergies. I'm sitting in an all-night diner, crying over a little kindness shown by a stranger and a few lines of text on my husband's phone. What is wrong with me?

Fifteen minutes later, Pam approaches, carrying a small teapot on a tray. Four teabag tags dangle beneath the lid of the pot and twirl over the side. She places the tray in front of me and plinks a pair of teacups on the table as well.

A ridiculously large bowl of cut lemons lands to the left of the teapot. "Think this will be enough?"

I look up and, at the amusement in Pam's eyes, my shoulders start to shake. At first, I can't tell if I'll laugh or cry. But I'm tired of crying, and a small chuckle breaks free. It feels so good, I let go and laugh out loud until tears form in my eyes.

I'm sure the other patrons of the diner think I'm crazy.

Pam joins me in my laughter.

I've never laughed with a stranger before, and for a moment my sadness slips away. It's exhilarating and freeing to be happy again, even for a short while.

After a few minutes, I wipe the moisture from my eyes, then turn to Pam. I point to the bowl of lemons. "Thank you. This should be plenty."

She gives me a knowing look and then hollers over her shoulder. "Frank, I'm taking my ten." In an action made fluid by repetition, she pulls the white apron off her waist and sits in the chair directly across from me.

"May I?" She asks, motioning to the tea pot.

"Please." I watch as she pours us both a cup of tea. We each squeeze two lemon wedges into the hot liquid, add a bit of honey, and then sip in silence.

After a time, Pam speaks, and her voice is as warm and welcome as the tea. "You know. I see all kinds coming in here, at all times of the day and night. But I have never seen anyone with eyes as sad as yours."

I bite my lip, nodding in agreement.

"What're you doing here in the middle of the night anyway?"

"Couldn't sleep."

"Why not?"

I sigh and fiddle with my cup on the table. "It's been a long day filled with way too much emotion." I take another sip of tea, and Pam patiently waits for me to continue. "For the past hour, I've been out walking and thinking, and the truth is, I've lost something. I didn't know it was lost until just now. But..." I raise my cup, smelling the sweet citrus. "I just . . . I don't know what to do."

"Mmmmm hmmmm." It's Pam's turn to nod. "I hear that."

We sip in silence for a few minutes. One of Pam's coworkers comes by the table and asks a question. Pam's kind smile reassures the young cook as she explains how to use the new coffee maker. When the girl leaves, Pam focuses on me again.

"Listen, honey." She reaches out and covers my hands with hers. The touch of her warm skin soothes the battle going on inside me. "We've all been there. Losing things is part of life, but that don't mean we give up. We keep moving. That's what we do. We learn. We grow. We figure things out. But we don't stop living. No matter what. You hear me?"

"I hear you."

"Now . . ." Pam scribbles something on her notepad and rips off the top sheet. "I've gotta get back. This place won't run right without me." She stands and lifts the tea tray off the table in one smooth motion. "You come back and see me sometime."

"I will," I reply. "Thanks for the tea—and the company."

"Same. You have a good day now. Go on out there and turn it right around."

She sets the bill on the table and with another grand swish of her hips, disappears into the kitchen. How is it that this complete stranger, in a ten-minute span of time, saw me on a more intimate level than an entire room of my husband's friends? More than my husband has in years?

I reach for the ticket and pull my wallet from my purse. Scrawled across the pale-green paper in bright crimson ink are the words:

> No charge for the tea.
> Just remember . . .
> You have to lose something first,
> before you can find it.

When I look up again, Pam's busy at another table. Even though she doesn't charge me for the tea, I leave her a generous tip. She deserves it and so much more. I fold her note in half and place it in my sweatshirt pocket. With the taste of lemons still lingering on my lips, I call out, "Thank you, Pam."

She takes a moment to dip her head toward me, and it squeezes at my chest as much as any hug.

I leave the diner and wander through the streets, weaving down city blocks and past parks as I slowly make my way toward the hotel. My feet press against the sidewalk, each movement deliberate, each step bringing about another question.

How could I have lost so much of myself? *Step. Step.* Where do I even look to find me again? *Step. Step.* What's going to happen to my marriage? *Step. Step.*

I'm so tired of questions, but I keep walking. I keep stepping. I keep asking questions, until the sun crawls out from behind the horizon and stretches its rays into the sky.

Morning has finally come. After several hours of walking, my stomach grumbles and pulls me out of my thoughts. Visions of bacon and waffles dance in my head. I'm famished. I didn't eat dinner last night. All I've had for sustenance in the past twenty hours is a single cup of lemon tea.

How is it that I let a texting strand upset me so much? Am I not strong enough to deal with a few words on a screen?

I shake my head. Food first. Disparaging thoughts later.

Smells of breakfast saturate the air as I walk past three downtown cafés. Sugary syrups, rich sausages, and yeasty breads make everything around me smell good enough to eat. Most of the sidewalk seating fills up as the sun reaches through the potted trees and warms the morning air. I stop by a European-style café near the hotel and read the posted menu. Maybe I'll have breakfast by myself. I've never eaten alone before. It might be good for me, maybe I'll . . .

At the sound of a familiar voice, my heart jerks inside my chest.

Life moves in slow motion at times. And in this moment, I feel every whisper of wind, every quiver of my cheek, every shaky breath as I turn toward the front-most table of the restaurant.

I lose my appetite the instant I see him.

My husband smiles at a sickeningly familiar face. Beautiful Alex. His *buddy*. His *friend*. Who has stepped out of his phone screen to sit across from him now.

She has her hand on his arm and leans in close to feed him a strawberry, then whispers a secret into his ear. He laughs and tilts his head toward hers, closer still, and touches the side of her face with his hand. With one finger, he tucks a stray strand of hair behind her ear, and she leans even closer. A few more inches and they'll practically be on top of each other.

34

Before I can think better of it, I pull out my phone and snap a picture of the two of them together. I don't know why. Maybe to prove a point. Or to torture myself with it later. My shaky hands blur the picture, and I take another . . . and another. I force my fingers to stop. Shove my phone back into my purse. And step forward.

With as much confidence as I can manage, I walk toward them. Head held high and smile fixed in place. She will never see so much as a single tear in my eye.

I stand next to the table and face my husband's friend. "Alex, I'm surprised to see you here. Jake didn't tell me you were planning to come up this way. A hundred and fifty miles is quite the jog."

For a glorious moment, Alex's eyes go wide, and she has nothing to say. Score one for me.

"Beth," Jake gasps. He drops his hand away from Alex's face and leans back, putting some distance between him and his buddy.

I ignore him and continue to stare at Alex, waiting for a response.

Her face flushes as red as the berry she just fed my husband, and her lips open once . . . then twice. On the third time she finally says, "Bethany. What a surprise." She pulls her hand away from Jake's arm but doesn't reach out to greet me. Her perfectly tanned skin contrasts brilliantly with the crisp white table cloth. Nut brown hair brushes softly against her shoulders as she slowly, purposefully leans toward the man I've been married to for twenty years. "I'm headed up to the Flathead Lodge for a business meeting this afternoon, so I decided to stop off for a quick breakfast. And since Jake was here, I asked him to join me."

I tilt my head to the left and blink twice. "Isn't that nice? And since he's not here with anyone important, he of course said yes to your little breakfast date." Fire burns inside me, and I'm ready to turn this quaint, little French Bistro into a smoldering pit with just one look.

Turning away from Alex, I finally meet my husband's eyes.

Jake attempts a weak smile and squirms in his seat. "Hey, B. You were gone when I got up, so I had to come to breakfast without you. I left a note."

Something inside me snaps. "Oh! You left a note!" The fake smile drops from my face, and in my eyes, I let him see every bit of the flaming rage surging through me. "Well, I guess that makes it okay." I take a step away from him. "I guess that makes everything okay." I turn back to Alex. "Good luck at your meeting."

In what I hope is a graceful motion, I turn and walk away, swinging my hips like I'm in a runway show as I strut down the sidewalk.

A hand touches my arm, and I don't need to turn around to know who it is. Jake has worn the same cologne our entire married lives.

"Don't you dare," I manage through gritted teeth and trembling lips. "Just let me go."

His hand drops away from my arm, and I keep moving. After two blocks, I recognize the outline of the hotel in front of me. My pace quickens. I'm breathing hard as I push open the door. Full sun pours across the tiled entry, pooling on soft rugs and warming the lobby.

"Hello, Mrs. Taylor." The manager greets me.

"Hello, John. We'll be checking out shortly. Can you send a luggage cart up to our room please?"

"Of course. It's my pleasure."

The elevator opens before me, and I climb inside, still refusing to cry. Steel enters my bloodstream and pulses through my body. My emotions are sluggish and slow, but I manage to keep the tears away for the entire trip to the tenth floor.

I jam the card into the slot by our hotel room and kick open the door. I'm done being quiet. But of course, there's no one inside to disturb even this early in the morning. Jake is having breakfast with his *friend*.

With a focus brought on by fury, I stomp through the suite and into the back bedroom. Dropping my purse onto the desk, I drag my luggage to the king-sized bed. The closet door catches on a shoe, but I yank it open and pitch the offending shoes out into the room. I rip shirts and dresses off their hangers and chuck them into the bag. I'm nearly finished when I hear the door open.

"Where'd you go this morning?" Jake barges into the bedroom, bringing with him the smells of coffee, fresh-baked croissants, and Old-Spice bodywash.

"Ha!" I snap, walking out of the bedroom. "As if you have any right to ask me where I've been."

He follows me into the living area.

"Beth . . . sweet—"

"Don't. Don't even start with the sweetheart talk. I just went for a walk. I couldn't sleep."

"Why couldn't you sleep?"

I give a short, spiteful laugh. It's suddenly hot in here. Sweat beads on my face, and I take my sweatshirt off, dropping it next to my skirt. "Seriously?" I glare at my husband. "You know why I couldn't sleep."

"You lost sleep over a few stupid texts?"

"Well, at least we agree on one thing. They are stupid texts." I straighten papers on the table, open and close the coat closet door, trying to remember why I came in here in the first place. Nothing. No idea. I can't remember.

Frustrated tears burn my eyes. Maybe he's right. Maybe I'm over-reacting.

No! What if they've had sex? But even if they haven't, the words he texts her, the way he looks at her—it's not okay. I shake my head and make my way back to the bedroom. "It's obviously more than just a stupid text. You were having quite the cozy breakfast with her."

Again, he follows me. "Seriously, Beth. I woke up early, and you weren't here, so I started packing for home. I'd just finished with my bags when she called. She was driving through and wanted to stop to eat. It's not like I planned this. What's the big deal?"

"The big deal is you were having a romantic breakfast with another woman. The same woman who sent half-naked pictures of herself to you was just hand-feeding you berries while you caressed her face. And you don't see the problem? After everything we talked about last night, I can't believe you went to breakfast with her. You had to know it would bother me. Doesn't that matter to you?"

"She stopped by out of the blue and invited me to breakfast. What was I supposed to do?"

"Say no to her!" I scream at him and pace away like I'm some kind of crazed animal.

Jake stares back at me. His mouth opens, but no words come.

I focus on packing once again and jam more clothes inside my suitcase. "I'm not an idiot, Jake. Don't treat me like one. You may have convinced yourself this is just an innocent friendship, and you may not care that it bothers me, but I have eyes. I saw you touch her face. I saw her feed you. Are you sleeping with her?" My hands curl into tight fists as I turn to face him again.

"Of course not." He glares at me, disbelief clear in his eyes. "But apparently that doesn't matter. You're not going to be happy unless I cut her out of my life completely, are you?"

I refuse to answer. In my silence he continues.

"She's one of the few people in my life who actually cares about me. She calls me, not because I work with her, or because she wants something from me, but just because she wants to hear my voice. Can't you understand? She means a lot to me. I don't have many friends like her."

His words stab and stab and stab. He can't hurt me just once. He has to do it over and over again. "Oh really." I step forward, letting my pain show in my eyes. "And how many wives do you have?"

He looks at the ground, dodging my question. "Come on, B. How is Alex going to feel if I just stop talking to her? If I drop her cold turkey? Stop and think how I'd feel if I lost her. And think about the guys on our marathon team. How are they going to feel if I stop showing up to competitions?"

Even though I haven't asked anything of him, haven't asked him to stop talking to her, stop touching her face, stop missing her *a lot*—my husband knows me well enough to understand what I want. But I still stay silent.

"I didn't do anything wrong. She's my friend. And I want her in my life. You're just going to have to find a way to deal with it." He turns to leave, then stops. Hands braced on his hips, still facing the door, he whispers, "Phil needs me to fly to Denver tomorrow, but I'll need to go home and pack first. My bags are in the car. We leave in an hour."

Without another word, he slams his way out of the hotel room.

The door's shivering against the jam before I can point out the hard truth I've just learned. Jake thought about Alex's feelings. He thought about his own feelings. He even thought about his running groups' feelings.

But not once did he mention my feelings.

Not once did he think about me. His wife of twenty years.

But why would he? I can't remember the last time anyone put my feelings first. Not even me. I've lost that too. I've lost so much of myself.

I shove the last of my belongings into my suitcase and finally remember why I'd gone into the other room. Nearly growling, I drag my feet to the living area, snatch my skirt and sweatshirt off the floor, and head back to the bed. With a flip of fabric, I smooth my skirt flat, fold it, and put it inside my suitcase.

When I shake out my sweatshirt, a piece of pale-green paper slips out of the pocket. My eyes follow it as it flutters to the ground. Pam's words, written in red ink, stare up at me.

You have to lose something first, before you can find it.

I pick up the paper, gently fold it, and slide it into my pants pocket. Losing something is the easy part, I've proven that. And I'm sure I can find a lost shoe,

39

or a missing set of car keys, or the bracelet I misplaced last week. But how does a person pinpoint their reason for living?

How exactly am I supposed to find out who I am after I've lived more than half my life?

THREE

THE RIDE HOME WILL never end.

It's my own personal and eternal hell. I'd forgotten we'd come to this employee's retreat with the Jenkins. Kacie and Mark. They sit in the backseat of our car as Jake drives us all home.

Will this weekend never be over? Will I have to hold this smile on my face forever?

After two hours of Kacie's prattle, I can no longer feel my cheeks. Either set. My face is numb from my forced smile, and my backside hasn't moved since we started this road trip. I need to adjust in my seat. I need to relax my face. I need narcotics, for me or for Kacie. At this point I'm willing to drug us both.

"So, Bethany." Kacie says my name so brightly, I almost feel guilty about my internal groan. It's not her fault my life's crumbling. It's not her fault my husband's an ass.

I crane my neck so I can see her face. "Yes?" I add a cheerful blink to my overly happy smile.

"The boys are off at college, right? So, what are you going to do now? Any plans?" Her eyebrows lift and her face lights up, as if she's just asked me the most exciting question in the world. She sits forward, wide eyed and expectant, awaiting my answer.

The only problem is—I don't have an answer. I don't even have an idea for an answer.

"Still trying to figure that one out." I tap the side of my forehead with one finger. "Working on it."

Taking the strain in my voice as a cue, Jake steers the conversation away from any topics involving me, which allows me to tune out for a moment. I'm both grateful and pissed off that he knows it's what I need right now. How can he be so thoughtful one minute and so completely clueless the next?

After my sleepless night, I allow myself to close my eyes for just a second . . .

HANDS CLASP THE UNDERSIDE of my legs and grab at my back. I scream and lash out. Stop! Let go of me. I open my eyes.

Jake is lifting me out of the car. We're home.

"Sheesh, B. Nice freak out." He laughs.

"Put me down." He does. "And don't call me B."

"You love it when I call you B."

"Yeah. I did love it. But that was before." I turn my back to him and walk into the house, grabbing my bags on the way. No one's here. There's no need to pretend anymore.

We order in for dinner. He watches TV downstairs in the family room as he eats. I stay in the bedroom and eat directly out of the take-out tray. When it gets late enough, I pull on my ugliest, long-sleeved cotton nightgown. It fits me like a circus tent, and has a splotchy gray and pink pattern that could pass for clown vomit. It's a strategic wardrobe choice. In case Jake decides to wander up here, I want to make it clear—he's not getting any.

But he doesn't wander up. He sleeps on the couch again, which is fine by me.

The next morning, light creeps into my windows, and my eyes wake up with the sun. The rest of me is much more reluctant.

The sound of Jake's car driving away floats in with the morning breeze. He didn't even come into the bedroom before he left for his work trip this morning. Phil had asked Jake to "get progress back on track" on their new construction project. In the past, I would've gotten up, helped Jake pack his bag, and then given him a kiss that would have his toes curling all week.

But not today.

Today he left without saying goodbye, and I didn't even get out of bed.

He'll be gone for two weeks, and he walked out the door without so much as a peck on the cheek. Maybe he's worried I'll spit in his face again.

He should be worried.

We haven't spoken about his breakfast date or his *friend* or his inability to give her up since we've been home. I can't listen to his justifications any longer. Either he wants to be with me, or he has to have her.

Either.

Or.

Choose one.

No other options exist.

And everyone else must see them carrying on too. It's such a small town, the owner of the grocery store knows when it's my time of the month. And Alex lives just down our street. I'm sure everyone in the neighborhood has seen them together as well. It's ridiculous. He can't have his scantily-clad, sweet-bit-of-something-on-the-side, and his wife too. No matter how much he wants the best of all worlds.

I pull the covers over my head and try to block out the rising light, but instead, the blankets hold in the memories. One morning last week, I grabbed Jake's hand as he was climbing out of bed, threw the covers over the both of us, and said, "Let's stay in bed all day."

He'd kissed me and told me I was beautiful. Snuggled with me for a few minutes, then he hugged me tight and rolled away. To go on a run.

With Alex.

And now I understand why.

"Let's stay in bed all day today, okay B?" I say out loud to myself.

"Okay," I answer back. "I don't like running anyway."

Then, piece by piece, my heart breaks apart and the sobbing begins.

I can't catch my breath. One sob starts before another ends. My eyes burn, and more tears come. I didn't know a single person could cry so many tears.

Harsh breaths and even harsher sobs rub my throat raw. It's as if I've swallowed razor blades. Although I don't know why anyone would swallow razor blades. If they want to feel true pain, all they have to do is devote their life to someone for more than twenty years, and then have him say he misses another woman. A lot. Have her feed him at breakfast while holding hands and sharing whispers as they say I love you to each other.

Moisture trickles out my nose, and I try to sniff it away. But more follows. I turn to the bedside table. My tissue box is empty. "Dammit!" I yell at the empty box, and throw it across the room. The extra tissues are downstairs.

I trip out of bed, slump down the hallway, and punish the stairs with my stomping feet.

Grabbing a fresh package of tissues and a box of old-fashioned donuts, I bring them both back to the bedroom with me. Still wearing my ugly, circus-tent night gown, I glance in the wall mirror as I pass. A knotted mess of strawberry-blonde hair falls sideways over my left ear. My messy bun has become a crazy nest of hair even the most desperate of birds would never call home. But I don't try to fix it. I don't care. I hold tissues in one hand, and donuts in the other, as I sink back onto the mattress.

I'm not my normal prize-winning self today.

But why does it matter? Even when I am my prize-winning self, he still misses another woman. Still eats her strawberries. And they go running together, with her perky boobs bouncing along with every step.

And then he tells *me* he needs to be there for *her*.

For *her*!

"Why aren't you there for me!" I scream my complaint to the vaulted ceiling above the bed, and throw a half-eaten donut across the room. It hits the perfectly-painted taupe walls in an impressive explosion of glazed-pastry goodness. I enjoy it so much—I throw another. "Stupid!" And another. "Selfish!" And another. "Fraggard!" I keep throwing donuts and screaming, until I'm out of ammo and have to go search for something else to eat.

There's nothing in the cupboard. Nothing with high calories and no nutrition and not a single bottle of liquor. Damn my healthy eating habits. Why bother with a slim waist when husbands have *friends* like Alex?

I wrench the cupboard door open, pull out a pile of ingredients, and mix up a quick batch of double-fudge brownies. As they cook, I watch the timer tick down. For thirty minutes, I do nothing but stand in front of the oven and watch brownies bake and rise. When the timer dings, into the freezer they go to cool, then the entire pan comes with me back to the bedroom.

Since I believe in giving a hundred and ten percent to everything I do, I throw myself into wallowing with every ounce of my being. This is wallowing to the nth degree. If they gave an Academy Award for wallowing, there'd be a tiny golden man in my bedroom right now. And he'd probably be missing another woman. A lot.

The brownies taste delicious. I eat them straight from the pan with my hands. Starting right in the middle. Who knew brownies for breakfast would be so satisfying?

I feast on brownies and stare out the window, watching the curtains lift and dance on the breeze as I pray to go numb. The open window lets in the sounds of the neighborhood, and I can hear Mrs. Platt next door, tending to her garden. She's talking to her flowers this morning, or her grass, or trees. She's always talking to something in her yard. Swears it helps them grow. It must work. Her grass is the greenest on the block. Her flowers, the biggest and the brightest. But the state of her yard hardly makes talking to plants seem any less crazy to me.

"But what do I know about crazy?" I ask the empty room. "I'm not crazy." I yell. "I'm sad. There's a difference!"

Mrs. Platt goes silent, and I wonder if I've scared her flowers out of their pots. I hope not, even if she is constantly criticizing my yard and pointing out my poor gardening abilities.

"I like Mrs. Platt. I like her flowers. I'd miss them if they were gone." I sniff away another flood of tears, and rip a handful of brownies out of the pan. "I'd miss them . . . a lot." Another wave of sobbing hits, a tsunami level of tears. I try to breathe while I cry, and I sound like a bird who's forgotten how to sing. Maybe a songless bird would stop to nest in my crazy hair.

Three hours pass, and I stay in bed, staring at the walls. Doing nothing. Crying quietly. Eating brownies occasionally. But mostly I just lie still and try not to feel.

I fail at that too.

It's as if my happy life has been yanked out from underneath me, and I'm falling. And I'll keep falling forever. I'll never land. I'll never feel my feet underneath me again.

Falling.

Falling.

Falling.

Afternoon comes and goes. My clown-puke pajamas have brownie stains on them, and I'm certain I have chocolate coating my teeth. I lift the hem of my nightgown and wipe my mouth.

Yup. Chocolate. All along my lips.

But who cares? No one is here to see me.

I should call Lettie. She'd want to help me out of this. Best friends always come to the rescue. But I'm just too miserable and so embarrassed. My husband's in a relationship with another woman. I'm a cliché. How did I become a cliché?

I blow my nose as loud as I can and toss the used tissue on the ground. It's become a game of sorts. The cover-the-rug-in-tissues game. I lie on my stomach and peek over the bed. I'm winning. I'm the grand champion of this event.

With a pillow sandwiched between my chin and my knees, I curl into a ball. "How come he doesn't feel lucky to have me?" I ask the pillow.

The pillow remains silent. I follow its example and stop talking.

When I get tired of the silence, I turn on a movie, scrolling through the options until I find the perfect cinematic masterpiece to fit my mood.

He's Just Not That into You.

Truer words were never spoken.

The realistic love stories play out before me. "Ben, you snake in the grass," I snap. "With your sexy swimming buddy. I wonder how many times you told your wife she was just a friend." I talk to the screen like the actors can hear me.

I watch as good-ole Ben tells lie after lie to his movie wife. "Yup. You lied. Of course you did. It's what you all do." I throw a pillow at the screen. "And we believe you. Because we're idiots. And we want it to be true."

The touching climax of the movie begins. The dark-haired actor leans toward the smiling actress in the slinky black dress. Then they kiss. They hug. They live happily ever after.

"Check his phone," I yell at the TV. "He's probably texting someone else. Because he misses her." I lean forward, sharing a secret that's not a secret to me anymore. "Do you know how much he misses her?" My voice fades to a whisper as the tears begin again. "A lot. That's how much." Moisture covers my face, and six more tissues join their friends on the floor.

I'm a mess. Drunk on depression. Wasted under the influence of a broken heart. Slumped against chocolate-stained pillows in my ugliest nightgown. If only Jake could see me now.

The movie credits end, and I flop to the side.

And there I stay.

Hair a tangled mess. Brownie smush on my face and hands. My heart slowly filling with tears. Beat by beat. Sob by sob.

Raw emotion pours from me. I'm sore in ways I never knew could hurt. My eyes burn, and soft lids bring soothing relief as I let them close—not caring when they open again.

Who would miss me anyway? Jake has Alex, and my boys have each other. Who else really needs me in this world?

I'm alone.

Sad and alone.

Blessedly, I start to relax, finally allowing myself to collapse into the arms of sleep.

And sleeping stops my tears.

FOUR

MRS. PLATT'S LAWNMOWER WAKES ME.

I slam upright, fling my eyes open, and immediately regret it. A soft pounding starts, small at first, then grows to violent levels in my head. It feels like someone stuffed tiny bits of sand under my eyelids during the night, and my stomach threatens to send up an unwanted encore of my brownie binge. My wallowing hangover is in full swing.

With a sigh, I sit on the edge of the bed and slap my hand along my nightstand until I find my phone. A quick tap shows me the time. It's 7:12. Mrs. Platt always was an early mower. *"Best to do it before it gets too hot, dear."*

When the phone registers back to the home screen, I see a notification on my message app pops up. Jake has sent me a text.

> *Jake:* Hey Babe. Is your phone working? I tried to call a few times. Hope you're not still upset. Maybe text or call so I know things are okay.

Except things are not okay. But even as I acknowledge this truth, a small, guilty voice whispers in my head. Maybe it's not that big of a deal. If Jake thinks things are okay, maybe I'm overacting. Maybe I'm the one in the wrong here.

Guilt and second guesses gnaw at my mind, old habits nudging me to try and work things out with my husband before things go too far. All the instincts I've gained in the years of my marriage tell me to forget about it and ignore my pain.

But I can't do it.

I can't be okay.

I'm not okay.

He hurt me. And that matters. At the very least, he needs to acknowledge my pain. Jake wants to act like it's no big deal, like he's done nothing wrong. But the fact remains. He broke my trust. He told another woman he loves her.

And that will never be okay with me.

I ignore Jake's text, open my favorites list in my contacts, and see my mother's tiny picture at the top. This feels like something a daughter would want to share with her mother. Eventually, she'll have to know. But to be honest, she loves Jake so much, it wouldn't surprise me if she took his side. And I'm not ready for that.

I call Lettie instead. Since my life is falling apart, and someone needs to know, it might as well be my best friend.

The phone rings six times before her familiar voice reminds me she's out of town for the holiday weekend, and she'll be back tomorrow.

An overly-loud beep startles me into speaking.

"Hey Lettie. Wish you were here..." I try to leave a message, but can't even form a complete sentence before I start to cry. *Wish you were here with me.* Jake's words slam into me yet again. I hit end on my phone and finish my cry rather than my message.

Fifteen minutes later, I've settled down enough to call her back. I grab my phone again, and the date flashes up at me.

September 3rd. Labor Day Weekend. One of the overlooked holidays. Jake misses it often, but the boys and I always celebrate with a barbecue. We usually have a full house. This year, Lettie's family is on vacation, my boys chose an incredibly inconvenient time to start college, and Jake's an ass.

I'm all alone.

The lawnmower cuts out and a few minutes later there's a pounding at the front door, and I hear Mrs. Platt's muffled voice. "Bethany. We need to talk about your grass. When your yard looks bad, it makes the whole neighborhood look bad. The patch of grass under your trees out back is completely dead. If you're in there, come out and get some fertilizer from me."

I don't get up to go talk to her.

I lie back on my bed and count the blades of the ceiling fan as they spin above me. One. Two. Three. Four. Five. I try to follow each individual blade with my eyes as they travel around the full circle, keeping one blade steady in my view as the rest blur around it.

The damaged one is the easiest to track visually. Jake cracked it with the extendable duster last year.

Jake.

The simple thought of his name causes bile to rise up my throat and my emotions to slam into overdrive. Will I never get over this?

I stare at the ceiling fan and banish all images of Jake from my mind. I don't think of Alex. I don't think of texting. I don't think of anything. Soon my eyes dry out from following fan blades, and I close them for just a minute.

A GENTLE SHAKING AND a soft voice wake me. The afternoon sun shines bright through my open curtains, and I squint at the face before me. Dark eyes framed by dark, straight-cut bangs.

Lettie.

"You came!" I breathe out as I throw my arms around her neck in a fierce hug.

Lettie gasps and coughs. "Oh, for the love of breathable air," she says. "You stink, sweetie."

I turn my head and sniff. Words can't even begin to describe the odors drifting from my open mouth and unshowered body. I look up at Lettie, and my lips droop. "I do stink."

"Well, there's an easy fix for it. Let's get you cleaned up."

Lettie pulls me to my feet, and I'm once again reminded of how tall she is. I feel small in every way right now. With her hands on my shoulders, she easily guides me toward my master bathroom.

I pass by the vanity mirror and come to a full stop. My hair resembles the before picture in a shampoo commercial. Skin, once healthy and freckled, is now sallow and pale. And my eyes are almost unrecognizable, red rimmed and swollen with dried tear tracks still visible on my cheeks.

I'm Zombie-Beth come to life. Tears spill over again as I realize my sorry state. Lettie looks at me in the mirror.

"Hey, come on now." She squeezes my shoulder. "Whatever it is, it'll be okay. Showers fix everything but world hunger and cheating husbands."

My shoulders begin to shake as more tears come. Lettie pulls me in close and pats me on the back. Over her shoulder, I stare at my sad eyes in the mirror and promise myself I'll never let it get this bad again.

Lettie turns the water to the correct temperature and smiles at me. "Shower first. Then you'll tell me everything. Okay?"

I nod once, and she kisses my cheek on her way out the door. The clown-puke nightgown is off my body and in the trash can seconds later. I never want to see it again. Never want to be reminded of this day.

The warm water brings instant relief. I stand under the spray, letting the shower wash away the mess I've become, letting it drown out my negative thoughts and heartaches. Water is healing. Water is cleansing. Water will kill this thing eating me from the inside out.

This shower is the first step. A step in the right direction. Everything's better without body odor.

An hour later, I dry myself off and dress in my comfiest yoga pants and sweatshirt. I pull my hair into a tidy bun any bird would be proud to call home and leave the bathroom in search of Lettie.

Following the trail of well-packed garbage bags, I find her in the living room.

She smiles. "Hey you. It took me three garbage bags and the better part of an hour before I could see the rug on the wood floor in your bedroom. Ready to tell me why you single handedly tried to wipe out the entire tissue population in the state of Montana?"

I try to explain, but emotion chokes off my words.

Lettie's at my side in an instant. "Take a deep breath."

I do.

"We don't have to talk about it now," she says. "I'll keep cleaning. And you can take care of the laundry. I draw the line at touching your delicates."

"Thanks." I manage a small smile and take another breath.

Lettie turns on the vacuum, and I tackle my still-full suitcase. As I unpack, I toss clothes into the hamper, I empty pockets and find a few coins, a five-dollar bill, and a parking receipt. In my pants pocket there's a slip of pale-green paper with deep crimson writing.

No charge for the tea.
Just remember . . .
You have to lose something first,
before you can find it.

Pam's voice comes to life in her words and the taste of lemon fills my mouth; the smell of bacon and maple syrup stirs in the air. I leave the rest of the laundry. Half in the hamper, half in the suitcase—forgotten. Her written words stir something in my mind. I'm tired of wallowing. I'm tired of my sad, non-existent life.

I grab a roll of scotch tape out of my desk drawer and in three strides I'm in front of my dresser. With a small piece of clear tape, I fasten the note to the mirror above it.

You have to lose something first, before you can find it.

I wander to the window thinking of all I've lost. Lists form and grow in my mind as sunlight begins to fade. I'm still staring out the window when Lettie finishes cleaning. She touches my arm.

"So . . . do you want to talk?" Lettie asks. "I haven't ever seen you like this. I thought you'd be happy after your weekend away. You've been looking forward to it for months."

And just like that, I snap back in time. Alex's face blurs in my mind as my husband's voice repeats. *I miss you. A lot. I love you.* Memories pour over me and my emotions boil and burn inside me. I turn away, but Lettie still notices.

"Hey, what is going on?" With one hand she turns my face toward her. "Okay, that's it. I need to know everything." She disappears into my closet and tosses my favorite pair of red-leather shoes onto the bed. While I put them on, she sends a quick text. "We're good to go. Scarlett is making food for her little brothers, so we're headed to dinner. It's time for a girl's night out!"

I TELL LETTIE EVERYTHING as we munch on chips and salsa at our favorite Mexican restaurant. The story begins with the words *I miss you a lot,* and includes all the details, from the hurtful things Jake said, to the hours spent in clown-puke pajamas.

"And that's it. You're officially caught up on my pathetic life. Here look . . . I even took a picture of them at breakfast." I pull out my phone, cue up the photo, and pass it to Lettie.

As she stares at the screen, Lettie raises both of her perfectly-maintained eyebrows, and pulls her lips into a thin line. "I hope you can love your best friend from prison because I'm about to become a murderer. Seriously, how can he hurt my friend that way? If Jake can't see how amazing you are, he doesn't deserve you."

"And that's why I love you." I grab hand sanitizer, and apply it liberally just as they set another basket of chips and salsa in front of me. I carefully take the time to wipe down the outside of the basket with sanitary wipes, and then do the same with my cup. Germs in full daylight will always scare me exponentially more than any horror flick after dark. I toss the wipes into the growing garbage pile and slump back in my seat. "Everything's just so messed up right now. It's been a long time since I've felt like me. Maybe that's why he needs another woman in his life."

"Hey!" Lettie snaps. "No! You do not get to make excuses for him. Even on your worst day, you're a frickin' rock star. Honestly. I'd dance naked under the full moon and promise my firstborn child to the forest sprites if there was even a chance that I could be as amazing as you are." She grabs my hand. "Honestly, B, you should never be made to feel like anyone's second choice. Ever."

I finally find a smile. "You're the best, best-friend in the world. You know?"

"Of course I am." She squeezes my hand once before she lets go. "Which is why you should have called me sooner."

"I couldn't. I was soooo not in a good place. And I didn't want to ruin your holiday."

"I miss you. A lot. And I love you. He really texted that to her?"

I drink my Diet Coke and nod. "He really did. And so many other things."

"Unbelievable." She shakes her head, making her dangly earrings sparkle in the lights. "Well, I can tell you how I think we should solve this problem, but it involves a pair of pliers and a really sharp knife. And maybe relocating to Morocco."

I manage to give her a ridiculous look before I start to laugh.

"It's a no-go, then?" Lettie shrugs. "Okay, but just so you know, the offer stands."

Every minute I spend with my friend, my worries begin to fall away and hope stretches up inside me. By the time we finish our meal and pay the bill, I can feel a sliver of my old self waking up.

Which just shows me how lost I've been.

When Lettie drops me off, she reads me a text from her daughter.

> *Scarlett:* Tell Aunt B she's my favorite and if she's having a bad
> day tomorrow, she can borrow my red sweater.

I send Scarlett a text letting her know she's the sweetest girl on earth, and promise to call Lettie tomorrow. The quiet of my empty house comforts me as I make my way to my bedroom.

First stop is my closet. As I slide out of my going-out clothes, and slip into my comfiest pair of yoga pants, Jake's ringtone sounds from my purse. I grab the phone, one finger poised over the green answer button.

I should just get it over with, right? Rip the bandage off and all that. Putting it off is only going to make it harder to talk to him.

But even as I try to convince myself to answer, my finger presses the ignore button.

I'm still not ready.

It's obvious Jake has moved past this like it's nothing, but I'm still struggling to visualize a better tomorrow. Maybe one where twenty-six-year-olds get black eyes from their bouncing boobs. The thought makes me smile, and for the first time I don't have to wonder what life will be like in the morning. For the first time, I think I just might be able to find a way to make my life better.

To make my life—mine.

FIVE

SUNLIGHT SLIDES THROUGH MY bedroom's open window and a soft wind skims my cheeks. Mrs. Platt's voice drifts in as she greets her flowers, and the curtains billow and twirl in the breeze. The beautiful day draws something out of me, and I get the craziest idea I've ever had.

I'm going to go on a run.

Apparently running is a great stress reliever. Especially if you have a special running buddy. Just ask my husband.

I've never been much of a runner, but I need to try something. Anything to get my life back on track.I need to be done wallowing.

So today, I'm going to be my own running buddy.

With a pair of old tennis shoes on my feet, and dark sunglasses to cover my puffy, naked eyes, I head out the front door. On the porch, the late-morning sun hits me full force and sweat trickles down my cleavage before I've even reached the end of the driveway.

Black lace scratches at my skin, and I tug at my bra. What was I thinking? I'm not a runner. When I exercise, I prefer to do it where no one else can see me. Usually, it's YouTube yoga or aerobics in my living room, where I can get fit without becoming the next item on the neighborhood watch list.

I stop before I even get started—glance to the left—glance to the right—pull at my bra again and decide to make another change.

Heading back inside my house, I walk directly to my closet. It takes some time to dig through my stacks of yoga pants and rayon blend T-shirts to find what I'm looking for. My indecently tight spandex shorts. The ones I wore for the six whole weeks I did cycling last year.

It takes even more time to root around in my lingerie drawer to find the single sports bra I own. It's bright coral orange, and for some reason that makes me happy.

I peel off my yoga pants and slip out of my lace panties. I'm going commando today. The shorts are as tight as I remember, and they help me suck in all the extra folds that come with age. Wearing these shorts, I look slimmer and more toned in an instant.

My shirt comes off next, and again I discard a scrap of lace as I unlatch my conventional bra. I wrestle myself into the padded sports bra and pull it down over the ladies, then turn and look in the mirror.

Wow.

These things really work. My breasts haven't looked this perky in ten years. I turn to one side and then the other. Ogling myself like I've never seen a woman before. And I haven't. Not this woman anyway. Not in a long, long time.

Before I chicken out, I slide both feet back into my tennis shoes and head for the front door. Here goes nothing.

I step out onto the porch more naked than I've been in public since the day of my birth. I'm more of a wear-a-cover-up-over-my-one-piece-bathing-suit kind of girl. Both arms wrap around my bare midsection as I walk to the edge of the driveway. I look down the street, one way and then the other, and put my right foot on the line where my driveway touches asphalt. After a single deep breath, I lift my arms into a ready position—and run.

My feet pound against the pavement in a steady methodical beat. *Wham wham wham wham.* I slam my worries into the street under the soles of my worn tennis-shoes. Air rushes into my lungs, sending tingles throughout my body. The sun slides over my face, warming me from the outside in.

And the wind!

The soft brush of wind against my bare skin is unlike any sensation I've ever felt before. It curls around my stomach, my back, my shoulders, caressing me like a glorious whispered secret come to life. With the silky touch of cool air on my body, I lift my head high and breathe in life. I'm stronger than I thought.

And I feel sexy.

Even if I don't fully trust the feeling yet, I pretend I do.

I drink it in. I run until my legs start to tremble, until my feet hurt, and my muscles itch.

After a while, I stop to catch my breath. I fight off the need to collapse to the ground and put a hand on each knee to steady myself.

Five minutes later, my feet are pounding the pavement once again, slamming my problems into the ground as I head back the way I came.

My bright coral top and tighter-than-necessary shorts attract stares like a magnet. I am the magnet and every straight, red-blooded man in the area is pulled toward me. They honk, they wave, they stare and smile.

"Looking good, Bethany!" a male voice calls as I turn the corner.

What? I turn my head, but see only taillights. Who was that? I'm not used to getting catcalled on my own street. My skin flushes, and I fight the urge to cover up as I pick up my pace and head home.

I wonder what Jake would think of some random guy telling me I look good? I wonder if he'd even notice.

Hopefully the neighbors will get used to me running, and learn to ignore me. Because this is definitely something I'm going to do again. This is something I'll do every day. Just to feel the wind against my bare skin.

To free myself.

When I reach my house, my shaky legs want to collapse, but I keep walking, slowly now, pushing away the weakness in my muscles, pacing in front of my thirsty yard. When I wander closer to Mrs. Platt's house, I hear her singing to her Irises.

"Drink up my darlings, drink up."

Her made-up melody could start someone drinking for sure, even this early in the day.

"Hello, Mrs. Platt," I say as I cross over to her front lawn. Still trying to get my breathing back to normal levels. "Your yard looks gorgeous as always." I stop in front of her perfectly manicured grass marveling at the healthy green sod. "You have a gift."

Mrs. Platt places her watering can beside her precious flower garden and pulls her fingers free of her striped gloves. "It just takes time. You should know better than anyone . . . some things just get better with age." She winks at me, and I laugh.

"Yeah. Well, I'm definitely feeling my age today." Already my muscles are rebelling, stiffening up. The soreness will set in soon.

"Well, you surely don't look it." Mrs. Platt takes my hand in hers. "So—maybe you could spend a little more time tending to other things. Things like that back yard of yours."

Her critical words clash with her gentle touch. I pull my shoulders back and lift my chin, preparing for the battle to come. Of all the days Mrs. Platt decides to criticize my dying lawn.

"I don't mean to be rude, sweetie." She gives my fingers a little squeeze, and I yank them away from her. The smile falls off her face. "There's no need to get huffy. It's just that I peeked over our shared fence the other morning, and there are some definite yellow spots forming in your backyard. You've got to stop that in its tracks before it spreads. It only gets worse if you neglect it."

I force my smile to stay on my face. "I better go fix it now then, since it's such an emergency." In one quick motion, I turn and walk toward my front door.

"They say the grass is always greener on the other side of the fence," she calls after me as I walk away. "But in my case, it's just not true."

"Yes, well, they also say women get meaner as they get older," I call over my shoulder.

Mrs. Platt places one hand over her heart. Sounds of shock and grumbled mumbling follow behind me as I enter my house. With a quick flick of my wrist, I slam my front door and cross directly through the kitchen and into the family room. I stand at the French doors overlooking my back yard and glare at my grass. Sure enough, Mrs. Platt's right. Yellow spots seep up through the green, forming a four-foot-wide band of dead grass between my willow trees.

I stare at the dying turf and can't help but think of my life. Or lack thereof. I haven't been paying much attention to either of late. My grass or my life. The yellowing lawn has just become another reminder of my jaundiced existence. A mascot for my absent life.

"Bad timing, grass." My frown reflects back at me in the glass of the French doors.

Of the two, getting my life together should be job one, but the overwhelming task threatens to ruin all the progress I made with my run. So, I decide to do something about the damn grass.

Today.

"You want green grass, Mrs. Platt. You got it." I turn away from my sad-looking yard and head out to my garage. First stop, the hardware store.

"HELLO, BETHANY, CAN I help you find anything?" Todd asks.

"Yes! Todd, thank you. I can handle the smaller stuff. But I do need three two-by-fours cut to four-foot lengths. Could you do that for me, and bring it to my rig? The back's open."

"Sure thing. I'll take care of it."

"Thank you." I weave through the aisles, pushing my squeaky-wheeled cart along the smooth floors until I reach the section I'm looking for. Cans of spray paint line the shelf in front of me, and I locate the brightest green I can find.

I grab two cans, shaking them as I picture a green sheen covering my yellow grass—an instant-fix. Maybe not the one Mrs. Platt would choose, but one I'm excited to try. In a few hours, I'll have my lawn looking better than it has in months.

Too bad my life can't be fixed as easily. A few cans of spray paint, a steady hand, and voila—a shiny new life. That would be nice. Too bad there are some problems a smooth coat of paint won't fix.

An image comes to my mind, and a slow smile lifts the corners of my mouth. But what if it could? What if I can figure out a way to paint a new life for myself?

I drop the two cans of green into the basket and fill my cart with paint of every color. Two bundles of rope, a roll of black plastic, a box-cutter knife, a rubber mallet, and dozens of cans of spray paint later, I'm ready to check out.

At the store counter, Arthur himself greets me.

"Well, hello Bethany. No Jake today? Where's he off to now?"

"In Denver. Overseeing construction on a new project."

"Looks like you've got quite the project going yourself."

"Yup. Just starting today."

"Should I put all this on Jake's account?"

"That's a great idea. And don't forget the two-by-fours. Three of them." The cash register rings out the completed transactions, and I sign the receipt.

"We're open until five-thirty now. In case you need something else," Arthur says.

"Good to know. Thank you." I try to muscle a half-dozen large bags into each hand, and shove the roll of plastic under one arm. Todd comes up behind me and takes the plastic and several of the bags.

"Here, let me help." He follows me to my SUV. "What are you doing with all this stuff anyway?"

"I'm going to do something I should've done years ago." I drop the bags into the back of my SUV next to the neatly stacked wood, slam the door shut, and smile. "I'm going to paint the grass."

SIX

I T TAKES TWICE AS long as expected to wrangle all the supplies through the side gate leading to our not-so-well-tended backyard. The wispy branches of our Weeping Willow trees wave hello as I enter the garden area. Our manicured yard, well-kept and gorgeous when we bought the house, has been neglected over the years, but the bones of beauty still live here.

And I'm about to give it a facelift.

I stare at the haphazard pile of wood, plastic, and paint laid out on the grass before me, and again think of my life. What should I build? What should I become?

But first, where to start? Over the past couple weeks since they moved out, I've missed my two boys for various reason. I find myself missing them again today, though not for any sentimental reasons. Today, I need some muscle.

"Too bad, B," I say aloud. "This is all you."

I head to the shed to get our deluxe staple gun, and remember the day I'd bought if for Jake. He accidently stapled his sweatshirt to the roof of this very shed. The bright yellow stapler brings back the memory of Jake yelling for help. His new stapler had started to slide off the roof, but with one arm stapled behind him, he couldn't reach it. I came running from the house and had to climb up next to him in order to save his stapler and free him from the tar paper. Afterward, I told him the princess rescued the knight that day, and he laughed and said, "Then how about a kiss to reward your bravery." And we made out like teenagers, right on top of the roof.

Warmth rises up inside me, and I push it away.

He smiled the same smile at Alex while they were eating breakfast together.

I grab the stapler, the cordless power drill and some screws, and head to my work station.

I'm done thinking about Jake.

With the help of a few cuss words and a mound of patience, I screw the boards together at the corners, creating a four-foot wooden frame. When I finish, I lay it flat on the ground to test the size.

"Yup." I glance at the shared fence separating my yard from the neighbor's. "Mrs. Platt will definitely notice that." I smile. It's perfect.

The inside of the square remains empty, like a picture frame lacking a photo. I staple the plastic around the outside edge of the wood until a smooth black flap surrounds the frame.

"That should work." I step back to look at my progress. "Main stencil complete. Spray shield added." I glance around. "Now where to put it."

With a quick inspection of the yard, I look for the most prominent dead spot and drag the four-foot square between the two largest willow trees. Positioning the frame over the granddaddy of all yellow spots, I lift and slide and finally set it in place. The work makes me feel strong and capable, and when I finish, my paint template is as steady as a boat in dry dock.

Now for the fun part.

With the kitchen shears, I cut rope into different lengths. Two feet. Three feet. One foot. Four inches. All different sizes. They fall at my feet. Little rope noodles, curling up at the ends.

With the careful precision of a mosaic artist, I arrange them inside the square. Some I lay out flat. Some I wind into a spiral pattern. Some I fold at angles. I twist and bend and scrunch the rope in every way possible, and place them at random on the square of grass. When I finish, this four-foot section of ground looks like a high-end modern art piece New York might be calling for any minute.

I pick up my chosen can and shake and shake and shake. Once it's well mixed, I don a pale-blue face mask and begin to spray.

Bright neon paint covers the grass. The greenest green in all the world.

A light spray of the four-foot square won't harm the grass, but it certainly makes it look more interesting as I cover the dead spots with an artistic flare. With each spritz from the can, my grass grows greener and greener.

When the final inch of the square is covered, I step back and laugh. One thing's for sure, my grass has never been greener. No grass, anywhere in the world, is greener than mine at this moment.

With the aid of the soft breeze, it will only take a few minutes to dry. I settle to the ground to wait, the non-painted grass tickling my legs as I sit.

The smell of spray paint usually reminds me of school projects, mostly from Robert's Physics class. But today it brings to mind the first apartment Jake and I lived in as a married couple, which had a small balcony full of rusty wrought iron furniture. It was an eyesore, complete with a wobbly railing that enclosed the space. I hated it and always kept the drapes closed. We never set foot out there.

Until Jake surprised me with dinner on the balcony for our first anniversary. Earlier in the day, he had painted the railing and all the furniture a shiny, glossy black. Very classic. Very well covered. And very wet when we sat down to eat.

We ruined our best dress clothes at dinner, and the memory still brings a smile to my face. Out of tradition, on the night of our anniversary, we've worn our paint-stained clothing out to a restaurant every year.

Until this year.

What happened to my Jake?

Emotion pricks the back of my eyes.

Nope. Not today.

I blink away all thoughts of tears.

There's no room in my life for crying just now. I'm painting the grass.

The next step is a delicate one. Jake would roll his eyes and tell me I've lost my mind. I hold an empty brown-paper sack in one hand and a pair of needle nose pliers in the other. It's time to go rope picking.

I use the pliers to grip each individual piece of rope and pull it free from my painted square. Then, I lift the wooden template away from the grass. Tilting it up at an awkward angle, I half-drag, half-carry it over to prop it up inside the shed.

The outdoor lights we usually save for parties and other special occasions, sit on a shelf next to the paint. Before I can over think it, I grab the lights and secure one end to the tree by my square. I drape them just so, until they stretch from tree to tree to tree, and I'm nearly sixty feet away on the other side of the lawn.

With a simple extension cord, I'm able to get the power I need from the electrical box in the far corner of the yard. As evening falls, I plug in the lights and brighten the night around me.

Highlighting the greenest grass on the street.

Misshapen lines mark the florescent green. Some twist and curl. Some form straight rods or odd angles. There is no pattern. No consistency. No design or premade form. And no warning as to when an unexpected dark spot will come up.

Just like in life.

I focus on the green. The neon square sparkles on my dead grass, catching the light and shining like fresh growth. A bright bit of newness, peeking out from my yellow, dying yard.

It makes me think of life. New life. Maybe even one for me.

I spent more than twenty years, serving the men I love most. I don't regret it. I'm proud of my work as a mother and a wife. My husband wouldn't be where he is today without me. It's a fact, whether he realizes it or not. My boys are a testament to my sacrifice. They are amazing young men who make me proud every day.

But now, as I look over the greenest grass on earth, I see nothing but a clean slate. A fresh green chalkboard waiting for me to write my story. And an entire yard of blank canvas, waiting for me to paint my new world.

I take my time cleaning up, and then organize the spray paint cans on the lowest shelf in the shed. Fourteen colors in all. Two cans of each. Mrs. Platt is right.

I'm going to make my grass whatever damn color I want it to be.

It's time for me to figure out how to live my life for me again.

I'll write a new chapter every day—and illustrate it in grass.

SEVEN

I'M THE FIRST CUSTOMER of the day at the small running store on Main Street. I've never been inside *Sole Mates* before, but now I load my basket with everything a running enthusiast might need. Bright-colored sports bras, tight running shorts, an arm strap for my phone, and a shiny new pair of silver running shoes—with neon orange laces.

As soon as I get home, I struggle into a bright-purple bra, slide into some smooth spandex shorts, and tie-on my new shoes. I'm ready to head out the door in just over five minutes. My phone, secured to my bicep, blares my favorite music aloud for all to hear.

It's a bit cool this morning, and goosebumps rise along my skin as I stretch my sore muscles on the front porch. Without the hesitation from the day before, I push out onto the road.

In six strides, I find my rhythm. A steady pulse of feet hitting pavement matches the beat of my music. The cool morning breeze grazes my back, as soothing as a healer's touch. I breathe in the day, and the clear air settles my mind. This is even better than gorging on brownies. With adrenaline drugging my senses, I'm happier this morning than I have been in months.

Dopamine is my new friend. A friend who won't get in the middle of my marriage.

Though I try to turn away from the small white house on the corner, my eyes drift to the bits of green growing over the mound of dirt in her front yard. Looks like Alex finally got around to planting grass. Depending on the route I take, Alex's house falls along my running path. I glare at her house as I run by.

"Hey Alex. Enjoy flirting with my husband."

My speed picks up, and I run along the park at the edge of the subdivision. Tree branches sway as I pass, and I listen to the leaves rustle in the morning breeze. Today I have no problem understanding what they say to me.

I'm strong. I'm worthy. I matter.

The words become a chant in my head. A chant that harmonizes with the rhythm of my feet. I'm strong. I'm worthy. I matter. If I repeat the words often enough, maybe I'll believe them. I'm strong. I'm worthy. I matter.

By the time I reach home, I've run just over a mile, and I'm high on endorphins and fresh air. I wave hello to Mrs. Platt as she sings to her hydrangea bushes.

She stops her garden lullaby when she notices me and cups one hand to the side of her mouth. "We need to talk about your yard. Did I see paint on your grass?"

"Can't talk now, Mrs. Platt." I bend down to grab the newspaper off my porch. "I'm late." I head inside to shower, not waiting to hear what else she has to say about my painted grass. I set the paper on the desk in the office as I walk to my bathroom, smiling as I imagine Mrs. Platt's conversation with her flowers this morning. Lots of grumbling about my unique gardening choices, I'm sure. And she'll have plenty more to grumble about in the future.

I'm just getting started.

The shower's warmth clears my head and it takes only a few minutes to rinse away the sweat and street grime. My feet touch smooth tile as I step out of the shower and the words from my run stay with me as I get ready for the day.

I'm strong. I'm worthy. I matter.

My voice. My ideas. My life. It all matters.

It's such a novel concept, I say it aloud. "I matter." The words take root inside me, and a whisper of a thought forms in my mind.

I have ideas, and they need to be written down and remembered.

The smell of peppermint body lotion lingers as I pull on gray yoga pants and an olive-green top. I slide my feet into my oldest pair of flipflops and head to my office.

On the middle shelf, pressed between a crime novel and a romance, is a thin leather-bound notebook. The one my mother bought me in Florence ten years ago. The same one I tried to fill with all my hopes and dreams after the boys left home.

I pull it from the shelf and run my hands across the bright leather. Ornate carvings decorate the cover and the binding crackles in the silence of the room as I open it to the first page. It's still blank. I've never had anything worth mentioning on its handmade pages.

Until today.

I'm going to use this notebook, to find me.

I rest a deep-purple pen against my lips, pondering exactly what I want to say. What is it I want? How do I even start?

A slow smile climbs onto my face. It's so simple. But it's the perfect way to begin my journey. I put pen to paper and write.

> To paint the grass today, I will . . .
> Remember what I love.

The person I used to be, the things I loved before, should all be a part of who I am today. Our past experiences help to shape who we become. So why have I forgotten everything about my pre-marriage self?

I close the book and start to brainstorm. How did I spend my days before I became a wife and mother? What did I do just for me?

Tapping a pen on the notebook, I try to come up with ideas of what pre-marriage Bethany liked to do. The newspaper on the corner of the desk makes me think of writing. I was on the school paper in Jr High. I grab the paper and unroll it.

Newspaper ink covers my fingertips, and I cough. There's a reason I didn't take journalism in high school. I hate the smell of printer's ink, and writing has never been my true passion.

I skim the front page, hoping to find something . . . anything. Ads for business school. Nope. Dog walker wanted. Absolutely not. Lawn care. I laugh out loud at that one. And then I see it. An ad on the bottom corner of the front page.

Actress needed.

I used to love acting. In high school I developed my love of musical theater. I performed in every school play and musical put on for all four years. In college I took part in at least one theatrical production a semester. Just to keep my sanity.

In fact, Jake and I met after one such performance.

During my junior year at university, I had played Juliet in a modern interpretation of Shakespeare's classic.

After the performance, Jake had followed me to the after party. This sexy, dark-haired man with the most chiseled jaw I'd ever seen on a human being, stalked me at the party for forty minutes before he finally approached. He leaned against the wall next to me, making the most of his tall, muscular frame.

"Hello," I said.

"Hello back," he said.

73

"Ah. So, you do speak."

Then we stood in awkward silence for a few heartbeats.

"Did you—"

"Are you—"

We spoke at the same time and then started laughing together.

"You first," I said.

Jake nodded and swallowed hard. "Are you dating the guy who played Romeo? 'Cause that was some kiss."

A smile stretched across my face, but I didn't say anything. It was the first time I'd kissed anyone onstage. Apparently, I was very convincing.

"I mean, just tell me if you guys are a thing, and I'll back off. But man..." He looked me in the eye. "If you're not, I'd sure like to take you out sometime. Tomorrow, maybe? Or whenever. Or, you know, now."

I laughed at his enthusiasm. "Charlie and I aren't dating. That was just a stage kiss. I'm not dating anyone." I lean toward him. "It's been a while since I've had a real kiss."

When I leaned back, Jake had the most glorious smile on his face and a heated look in his gorgeous eyes. He audibly swallowed. "Wow."

The next day he took me out on our first date, and later that week he experienced a real kiss. And he's been experiencing it daily for twenty years. I haven't kissed another man in all that time. I've never even wanted to. It's always been Jake.

Or so I thought.

I shake my head clear of the memories and read the rest of the article.

Actress Needed:

Role of Lilli/Katherine available in a production of Kiss Me Kate beginning September 25th. Email to set up audition time.

I open the notebook's cover once again and beneath my initial goal, I write:

Audition for musical.

I check the dates again.

Three weeks.

I could pull this off in three weeks. I played the part of Katherine in college. Surely that will give me an advantage. Before I can change my mind, I send off a quick email asking for an audition time.

An hour later, I'm breathless as I read the director's reply.

I would be available for an audition as early as this afternoon. Our lead actress broke her leg, and we need to fill the part ASAP.

After a thirty-second squeal of delight, I immediately respond and set up an audition for three o'clock this afternoon. They must really be desperate, or the universe knows I need a miracle in my life right now. My heart bursts with gratitude. Miracle or desperation, the reason doesn't matter to me.

But now I'm on a time crunch. I have five hours. Five hours to perfect an audition piece. Let's hope I can knock twenty-years of rust off with one good whack. I quickly print a portion of the script he emails me and call for reinforcements. I'm going to need all the help I can get.

Twenty minutes later, there's a knock at the door. Before I can answer it, it opens and Lettie walks into the room.

"You're looking much better. Did you find where Jake keeps the good booze? Come on, give up his hiding place." She wags her eyebrows at me, and I roll my eyes back at her.

Her six-foot frame and boisterous personality fill the room, and I'm extremely grateful she showed up—again. I stand up and pull her into a tight hug. "Thank you for coming. Were you busy?"

"Nope. It's my day off," Lettie says. "Eric took the boys fishing like the good husband he is, and Scarlett's with her dad this week, which frees me up to help you. So, what're we doing?"

Without explanation, I hand her a stack of papers. "How are you at reading lines?"

She snatches the papers out of my hand. "I'm practically an expert." With a smile, she begins to read aloud.

FOUR HOURS LATER, I've adequately memorized my audition piece. I decide to read the scene where Lilli finds out her ex-husband didn't send flowers to her as she had originally believed. It's a wonderful bit of writing by Bella and Samuel Spewack, and *bonus,* it's my favorite scene.

The reading portion of the audition should be a breeze, but the musical portion is another story. I haven't performed for anyone but my shampoo bottles in years, so I choose a song I can really relate to at this moment in my life.

I Hate Men.

Even if the notes aren't exactly right, my emotion behind the piece will be spot on.

Lettie and I rehearse together until we have to leave for the audition. It takes twenty-five minutes to reach the Ellen Theater in Bozeman, and Lettie insists on driving me.

"As if I'm going to let you get up onstage without proper moral support," she says. "I'll be cheering you on from the friends and family section. Always."

The minute we step into the theater, I'm transported back twenty years. The smells, the buzz of the lights, the bright colored sets—it all speaks to a time when my life made sense. A time when my life was mine.

"Bethany Taylor?" the director asks.

"Yes. I'm Bethany."

A man with a dark scruffy beard and glasses comes toward me.

"Kyle Woods. Director." He shakes my hand and then motions toward the stage. "We'll start whenever you're ready."

My phone rings, and I yank it out of my pocket. "Sorry." I fumble with the phone. It's Jake calling. Of course, he always has such great timing. Thankfully, I don't have to think of an excuse not to answer today. With a tap of the screen, the ringing stops. I clear my throat. "Sorry about that. Forgot to put it on silent."

"Not a problem." Kyle smiles.

As I make my way up onstage, my hands start to shake. Dammit, Jake. Why did you have to call at this exact moment? Thoughts of Jake equal thoughts of failure in my mind, and now is not a good time for me to be thinking about failing.

The director takes his seat, and the very real possibility of falling flat on my face creeps its way into the spot where panic hides inside me. My heart speeds up, thumping faster and faster, until it resembles a drumroll. A drumroll paired with sweaty palms, never a good combination. As I step to stage center, I'm envisioning drumsticks flying out of hands and bodies tripping off the stage. Not the ideal thought to have in my mind as I begin my adult debut.

Lights above the stage turn on, blinding me. I hold up one hand as a shield and blink several times until I get used to the brightness of the stage once again.

I swallow down my overactive nerves, take a deep breath, and open my mouth. Nothing comes out. Fear seizes-up the memorized words, and I clear my throat, holding up one finger to communicate my delay.

"Take your time," Director Kyle says. He shakes his playbook. "I'll read Fred's lines, and you can read Lilli's."

I nod and smile, trying to ignore the doubts surging through me. What am I doing? As if I could walk onto a stage after a twenty-year hiatus and think I could just jump right back into it. I close my eyes and take in a deep breath. The smell of old wood and new paint binds me to the moment.

New paint.

A fresh, green canvas of grass.

I'm painting my new life. And this is the moment where I decide whether or not I succeed or fail. It's up to me.

I open my eyes and search for Lettie.

There . . . in the third row . . . just behind the director. She gives me jazz hands and a smile, and I instantly relax. How can I not succeed with a woman like Lettie supporting me?

I step forward and begin my audition scene.

My voice is strong and flirty, angry and emotional, everything it needs to be to portray the character. I skip one line of the scene but recover just fine and manage not to rush as I finish my reading.

The accompanist joins me on the stage and begins to play my selected musical piece. The reality of the moment hits me. I'm about to sing in public for the first time in over twenty years, and it's for an audition in front of a director. I fight the rapid wings of nervousness fluttering deep inside and swallow hard before I miss my entrance. I open my mouth and sing the words describing all the deepest feelings of my heart.

"I hate men!" I toss my hair over one shoulder and wink at the director. My voice carries the sass of a jaded woman. I flirt with the empty audience as I sing about refusing to marry a man and compare him to Lassie. All the hurt, all the raw emotion ruling my life for the last few days, adds strength to my voice. I'm having a wickedly good time. The words make me smile and give me even more confidence.

Lettie laughs out loud, and my voice rises clear and strong in the nearly empty theater. I'm having so much fun. The stage. The song. The character. It's everything I remember and more. I'm falling in love all over again.

As I move across the stage, sounds are stronger, lights are brighter, emotions are higher. Life is better from the stage. I can't believe I cut this out of my life for so long.

When I finish the final note, I lift my chin high and allow the awed silence in the room to fill me with hope.

After exactly three heartbeats, Lettie bursts from her chair, applauding wildly. I'm smiling and laughing and loving life as I walk to the edge of the stage and take a small bow.

The director stands and leans forward, placing both hands on the chair in front of him. He doesn't even try to contain his glee as he looks up at me. "Very well done. That was incredible. I do believe you have just saved our collective asses."

Lettie hoots and hollers and waves her arms in the air like we're at a sporting event.

"So, I got the part?" I step to the very edge of the stage. Old wood creaks beneath my feet as I await his answer.

The director walks around the theater chairs toward me. "Yes, Ms. Taylor, you definitely got the part."

"Please, call me Bethany." I smile at him and take a breath, inhaling the scent of hot lights and mothballed costumes. This memory will be forever marked by the smell of this old theater, and I couldn't be happier.

"Well, Bethany. Do you have time for me to give you the grand tour? We'll restart rehearsals tomorrow morning at nine."

As he shows me around the stage and set, I catch a small thrill of excitement humming through my blood. It's incredible. Like I've been brought back to life after years of cold-storage hibernation. I can feel it.

Passion stretches up inside me, coming awake at long last. And I can't stop smiling.

We finish the tour, and I stand on the edge of the stage looking out at the invisible audience. It's not the answer to all of my problems. I still have a long way to go before I find what I've lost. But for the first time in a long while, I can taste my dreams fresh on my lips. And I can't wait to get up tomorrow morning and do something I *want* to do.

It's a great start.

EIGHT

I'M STILL FLOATING AS Lettie drives me home. My face aches from smiling, and all I want to do is read my script. To memorize all the beautiful words. I can't wait to feel the stage lights on my skin again. To smell the musty-wooden stage and the freshly-painted set. My mind is incapable of thinking about anything else.

Until Lettie asks me how I managed to perk myself up so much over the course a single day.

"I went running."

"No way. You hate to run."

I nod. "I used to hate to run. But that was the old me. Bethany 2.0 is giving it a try. And it hasn't killed me yet, so I'll keep at it."

"Seriously. All this energy, and the idea to try out for a play, it all came from running?"

"Oh, and I painted the grass in the backyard."

"You what? How?"

I hold up my finger like I'm spritzing a paint can. "Spray paint. I made a stencil and sprayed a square of grass green."

"You did not! I can't believe you took spray paint to your fancy-ass landscaping."

"Uh. You mean my neglected fancy-ass landscaping. The grass was dying."

"Ever heard of fertilizer?"

I laugh out loud.

"So, when can I see it?" Lettie asks. "You have to show me."

"I'll do better than show you. I'll let you paint."

Lettie has never driven so fast in her life.

"WELL." LETTIE NODS AS she stands in front of my painted square. "I'll give you one thing. That is definitely the greenest grass I've ever seen. There is no grass greener anywhere on any side of any fence."

"I know. Isn't it fantastic?" I grab her hand and pull her to the shed. "And I have all the tools to keep the madness going."

Together we drag the square into the yard and lay it down on the grass next to the lime-green square. "You can paint it anyway you like. Solid color. Stripes. Pattern. It's all you, baby!"

Lettie leans over the square and starts to paint. She moves her arms just so, and the paint obeys her command. It's a much more artistic approach than mine. A wavy curtain stretches across the top, and two rich side panels form under her expert fingertips. She has painted my stage. The one I performed on just a few hours ago.

She switches paint cans to add shading. After a few more swipes, the natural waves in the curtains are visible and a dark shadow of a stage lies beneath them. "What do you think?" Lettie asks as she finishes the last touch up.

"It's perfect." When she stands, I wrap one arm around her. "I love it."

A gasp sounds from the neighbor's yard. From her position on top of her stool, Mrs. Platt's disapproving stare is clearly visible above the fence. It's as if she just caught us parading around naked in the backyard. Shocked dismay shows in every line of her face. "I . . . I can't even . . ." she sputters before she steps down and stomps off toward her house.

Lettie and I wipe paint from our fingers and laugh.

While the paint dries, I grab a few supplies from the house and soon we're lounging in lawn chairs, with drinks in hand, facing two painted squares of grass.

"This is the best idea ever." Lettie sips her flavored lemonade and then lifts it toward me. "A toast to your brilliance. Seriously, landscape architects should have thought about this painted grass look ages ago. It's amazing."

"I think so." I take a long sip through my straw. "I'm making changes, Lettie. Amazing changes."

"Good for you. You deserve to be happy." She clinks my glass again.

And I let out a contented sigh.

Lettie's phone buzzes, and she reads a text. "Damn. I lost track of time. It's almost eight."

"Yeah, so?"

"I gotta go." She stands up and hands me her glass. "I'm supposed to have dinner for the boys and Eric when they get back from fishing."

"No worries." I stand and put my hand on her arm when she starts to fold her chair. "It's fine. Just go. I'll call their favorite pizza into that place they love on Freemont. It's on your way. All you'll have to do is pick it up."

Lettie kisses my cheek. "You are literally the best. Eric said they'd be home by 8:30."

"Perfect. The pizza will still be hot."

As Lettie rushes off, I pull out my phone to order. I'd step in front of a bus to save Lettie from harm or heartache. Paying for a pizza is a small token in comparison. But today, it's what she needs.

The quiet night surrounds me as I fold the chairs and carry them to the shed. Mrs. Platt must have stopped her fuming and finally turned in. Most nights it's lights-out inside her house before nine. I'd go to bed that early too if I woke up at the ungodly hour she does every day. My eyes don't open before the sun comes up. Not since I had toddlers who forced them open at all hours of the night.

The phone buzzes in my hand. It's Jake calling.

It would be so easy to answer and fall back into our relationship. I'm not really one to ignore my husband. In the twenty years of our marriage, his needs have always been my priority. Until he chose someone else over me.

I press ignore.

Two minutes later, it buzzes a second time as I'm walking toward the house.

Jake again.

"He's persistent. I'll give him that." But I still don't answer.

I'm not ready to talk. I can't even think his name without wanting to take an ax to everything he's ever bought me. He just—what he did can't be undone with a phone call. Wounds take time to heal. Time and margaritas. Lots of margaritas.

A message pops up on my screen. A voicemail from Jake. I tap the triangle on the left side of the screen and listen.

"Are you ever going to pick up? I gave you some space for a few days, but . . . you're ignoring my texts, and this is the second time I've called in five minutes... sigh ... Just please talk to me. Come on, B. I need you to talk to me. How are we going to work through this if you won't even pick up the damn phone? . . . Look, I just need to know if you'll be home when I get back from my trip. Two weeks away is a long time, and I might be jumping the gun, but my wife won't answer my phone calls. What's the take-away here? Tomorrow I'm in meetings all day, but I'll call the day after. Pick up, okay?"

Guilt sears through me at the obvious desperation in his voice. Avoiding my husband might become a habit for me. Or maybe I should just answer the phone and get it over with. Am I the one who needs to give in here? Is it so wrong for me to not want him to be in love with someone else?

That's not exactly something I can overlook.

"Why do you need her so badly?" I say to my silent phone. "Why am I not enough?"

I delete the message and settle onto the couch to soothe my sadness with my script.

MY ALARM GOES OFF at seven Wednesday morning, and I squint at my phone. "Seriously? Already?" Soft morning sun seeps through my curtains as the truth flashes up at me. It's morning. Time to get up.

With one arm, I flop the blankets off me and stumble out of bed. I haven't been up this early in a while. And I can't believe I set my alarm clock so I could go running. Who am I?

I smile at the thought. I'm the lead in a play, that's who I am.

It's a bit of a fight to slide my bright-pink sports bra over my head, but I finally get it settled overtop the ladies and quickly slip into my shorts and shoes, then head out the door. I have exactly two hours to run and shower and be at the theater. Here goes nothing.

The soft morning breeze wakes me further, and my skin pebbles up in reaction to the touch of wind against my ribcage. I will never get used to the contact of the air on my bare skin. It makes me feel alive. It makes me feel sexy. It makes me feel. And that's what I need right now.

When I get back from my run, Mrs. Platt's waiting.

"Bethany." She points toward my backyard. "We need to talk about your grass again."

I slap on my trademarked smile. "Good morning to you too."

"Don't good morning me. I looked over the back fence again this morning, and do you know what I saw on your lawn?"

"Paint?"

"Well," she sputters. "Yes, spray paint." Surprise deepens the natural creases of her face.

"I forgot to thank you, Mrs. Platt."

"Thank me?"

"Yes. I took your advice, and I'm making my grass just the way I want it."

"But . . . but . . ." Her face asks the questions she doesn't dare voice. Several probably have the word crazy in them. But she wisely stops herself and straightens her shoulders. "I'm not sure painting the grass is legal in this neighborhood. I'll have to check with the HOA board."

"You do whatever you have to do," I say. "I'm running a bit short on time this morning, so we'll have to talk about it later. Have a good day."

My longer than normal run and my conversation with Mrs. Platt puts me in a bind for time, so my shower becomes a crazy whirlwind of body washes and face scrubs. I hope I rinsed the conditioner out of my hair, but I don't have time to worry now.

It's been so many years since I've been to a play rehearsal, I have no idea what to wear. I drop six outfits on the floor and deem all of them unworthy before settling on a simple pair of black yoga pants topped with a bright red and white striped shirt.

Without a second to spare, I grab my script, a bag of mini muffins to go, and my purse. I recite lines on the way, and the thirty-minute drive speeds by. My knees actually shake as I step out of the car, and I wobble like a drunk flamingo all the way across the parking lot.

When I yank the front door wide, the smells of the theater hit me. And I stop and breathe it in. It's like a shot of Valium for my soul, and I'm instantly calmed. With each deep breath I take, my worries drift away. I stand in the entryway with my eyes closed, doing nothing but inhaling and exhaling until someone clears their throat.

My eyes flash open.

The entire cast stares at me from the stage.

"Don't mind me." I give a nervous smile.

A smattering of laughter follows, and the cast and crew get back to work.

As I approach the stage, a tall, well-built man steps forward, crouches down, and offers me his hand to shake. "That's some impressive meditative breathing there. Where'd you learn it?"

"Raising my twin boys." I tilt my head back to look up at him and shake his offered hand. "I got in a lot of practice."

He laughs. "I'm Cole Kimber." His deep baritone voice matches the rich brown hues of his skin, and his short-cropped, curly hair hints at his African heritage. But his eyes, his ice-blue eyes, come from a whole other place. He's stunning.

"Nice to meet you, Cole. Who do you play opposite of?"

He laughs again. "You. Actually." He grabs both my hands and pulls me up onstage. "I play Fred." His smile is now nearly level with mine. "And I'm really looking forward to getting to know our new leading lady."

I swallow hard and blink three times. I have to act opposite him? How? My heart jumps and stutters into my rib cage. He's so gorgeous, so confident, and I can't even hold my husband's interest. I fight to keep my shoulders from drooping. Well, at least no one will be looking at me while we're onstage together, not when they have him to stare at. I try to laugh, but it comes across as a raspy, cough-like sound. "I'm looking forward to it too," I lie.

His smile widens, showing off brilliant white teeth. "Let me introduce you." He motions me toward center stage. "Listen up, everyone. Our new Lilli is here."

The commotion on set stops at once. With one hand, Cole holds my arm high in the air and gives a small bow in my direction. "Meet Bethany Taylor. She's going to bring down the house on opening night."

I snatch my hand away from his. "Ha ha." Shaking my head, I turn to memorize every face in the room. People begin to shout names toward me, and I try to match the faces with their names as quickly as I can.

A pale blonde woman raises her hand. "Hey there, I'm Heather Jenkins. I play Lois."

"Brian Kleeger." A thin man with a receding hairline flips a baseball cap on his head. "I play Bill."

"We're Lippy and Slug." Two huge men with bald heads motion to each other.

"Yes, you are," I laugh.

One by one, each person introduces themselves. There are as many stage crew members as actors, and it will be a miracle if I can remember everyone.

Cole seems to sense my panic. "Don't worry," he says. "No one expects you to know their names on day one. Except for me, of course. I'm not sharing a kissing scene with someone who can't even call me by my first name."

"I think I've got it down. Clint, right?" I wink at him.

He laughs at the intended slip-up. "Good to know. I'm learning a lot about you, Ms. Taylor."

Kyle Woods, the director, scurries onto the stage wearing a leather newsboy cap and thick glasses. "All right, everyone. It's nine o'clock. Time to start. We only have three weeks, and more work to do than we'll ever get through, so . . ." He turns to me. "Ah, Bethany. Glad you're here. Did they make you feel welcome?"

"Yes, they did."

"Perfect. Looks like everyone's here except . . ." He pauses, looking around as if he's lost something. "Where's Piper? Has anyone seen Piper?"

"Down here, Kyle. Only why I need to be here isn't super clear."

We all turn at once.

A gorgeous red-haired woman waves at us from the front row of the theater. Her leg is casted from ankle to hip, and she glares as she says, "It's a bit harder for me to make my way up onstage now. So I think I'll have to help our new leading lady from here."

"Fine. Fine. Whatever works." Kyle waves off her complaints as he pulls me around to introduce us. "Bethany Taylor, meet Piper Gibson, our previous Lilli, until she took our advice to heart and literally did break a leg." He motions to the lone woman in the audience. "Piper, meet Bethany."

"Nice to meet you," I say.

"I'm sure it is," she snips.

I expect Piper to be upset over her broken leg, but the anger she throws my way feels like a physical thing.

"This play was supposed to be my big break. I was supposed to steal the show. So just do me one favor, okay?" she says.

"Of course, anything." I'm a people-pleaser by trade, and I'd be willing to do a lot to keep her from glaring at me again.

"Don't suck," she says. "I haven't been working ten hours a day for the last six weeks to have this play flop on opening night because of you."

Her words hit me like a bucket of liquid nitrogen to the face. Harsh and cold. My emotions freeze over in an instant. More than a few seconds pass before I'm able to break out of my shock and take a deep calming breath.

In and out.

"I think I can manage that," I snip and turn away from her.

"All right, then," Director Woods shouts. "It's time. Let's take it from the top."

My breathing speeds up once again. I'm doing this. I'm really doing this.

Cole comes up behind me. "Don't worry about Piper, she's grouchy with everyone."

"Really? Because it seemed pretty well-directed at me."

"Why do you think her understudy moved away so suddenly?" Cole swipes one finger across his throat, and I burst out laughing.

"Bethany," Kyle yells to get my attention.

"Yes. Sorry." I jab Cole in the ribs with my elbow.

"You'll use the script until we can get you off-book. Hopefully by end of week."

"Got it." I take my position offstage, determined to charge in and make my dramatic entrance on time and in character.

"Right, okay then." The director yells instructions up to the light crew and the sound guys. "Now, actors find your places. Get set and ready. On my go." Kyle makes his way to the unofficial director's seat, the middle chair three rows back from the stage. He cups his hands around his mouth and yells the single word I've waited nearly twenty years to hear.

"Action!"

Music swells from the small orchestra, and a flurry of colors bursts to life as the cast begins to sing "Another Op'nin', Another Show." I stand backstage with book in hand, listening to the blend of voices and waiting for my entrance. The cast is like a well-oiled machine, with each person moving and pausing at just the right moments to create a beautiful world onstage.

I follow along with the lines in my playbook, and before I'm ready, it's time. Embodying the soul of a famous movie star, I don my haughtiest look, part the curtains, and take a step forward.

The actors flow around me onstage, and the thrill of the moment fills my chest with more emotion than it can hold. I trip a bit as I make my way to stage right but recover nicely. *Focus*, I tell myself and continue across the stage with head held high, just like Lilli would do. I peer at the actors around me as if they're all lucky to know me, and I grandly walk through the scene with playbook in hand.

Once I reach Cole's side, I lean toward him.

"Excuse me? Should I be here or can I go—"

"One minute, Miss Vanessi." Cole turns to another actor, interacting with them and ignoring me. He makes an impressive Fred, just the right amount of cockiness and charm.

The scene continues to develop around me. I carry my book and try my best to follow the rest of the cast for blocking cues. The others have gone through this opening hundreds of times, and it shows. I'm definitely not as polished as the rest, but what I lack in luster, I make up for in spirit.

I stomp one foot, demanding Cole look at me, which he does. "When you're done giving acting lessons—"

"I saw your last film, Miss Vanessi. You could have used a good instructor." He turns his attention to someone else once again.

With all that's been going on in my life, it's easy to channel outrage at a man who treats me with disregard in front of others. Embracing my character's rage, I step in front of him and poke him in the chest with one finger. "I would like a moment of your time."

Cole is all charm as he gives me a condescending smile. I straighten my shoulders, standing full height, and send him my most scalding look. Sparks fly between us, and I step closer, making it impossible for him to ignore me.

"Cut!" Director Kyle yells, and we all turn toward him. He begins to clap slowly, and others in the cast join in.

But it's Cole's smile that says it all.

First day back, and I'm in my element. Amazing how becoming someone else onstage can so easily help me feel like myself again.

NINE

I SIGH INTO THE PHONE. "You wouldn't believe it, Lettie. I killed it! I actually killed it. It was incredible. The director cried. Real tears."

"Cried good or cried bad? Were they happy tears or dammit-my-career-is-over tears? I'm mean, you could have been awful." Lettie laughs.

"Shut your mouth. I wasn't awful." I stretch out on the grass in my backyard and look up at the clouds. "It was amazing! I'm living my life again."

"Acting like someone else, of course."

"Of course," I agree. "Hey, you never told me, how did the boys like the pizza last night?"

"Loved it! They knew Auntie Bethany had ordered because she got the cinnamon knots for dessert. Apparently, their awful mother never orders them sweets."

"Well, Auntie Bethany will be buying lots more sweets for them because—I got a check today."

"What?"

"Yeah. Apparently, they give signing bonuses to actors at this theater. Can you believe it? I made money on my first day there."

"You deserve it. You'd already be a millionaire a thousand times over if wives got paid for their work. You'd be winning Tony awards for Best All-time Mom and an Emmy for Wife of the year." Lettie clucks her tongue. "I'm telling you. It's true."

"Yeah. Wife of the year. That's me. I'm so amazing, my husband needs an Alex." I roll my eyes even though she can't see me.

"Don't roll your eyes at me."

"How did you—"

"I have a teenage daughter, I can hear eye rolls," she snaps. "And it doesn't matter if you believe me or not. I'm telling you; you deserve this. The universe is finally setting things straight."

"Well, I'm happy to let it do its thing, then. It's about dang time."

A muffled crash sounds in the background followed by several yelling voices. "Well, that's my cue," Lettie says. "Better go see what the hellions are up to. Love you."

"Love you too. Good luck. Don't kill any of them."

"No promises."

I hang up and look at the check in my hands. Eight hundred dollars. I can't believe it! It's not anything close to Jake's monthly salary, but I can't bring myself to care. This came from me. From my talent. And I'm going to smile all the way to the bank.

I consider depositing it into our joint account, but almost immediately decide against it. I do believe I'll go out later today and get this check cashed.

Eight hundred dollars cash to be spent by me and only me. Any way I want to spend it. I've never had that option before. The thought makes me smile.

Such a life-changing moment needs to be documented.

Time to paint the grass.

I follow the path to the shed and pull out my supplies once again. This time, I choose a metallic gold spray paint. With the help of a piece of poster board and a ruler, I cut out a single shape, lay it over top the square, and paint. The shimmering gold spray covers the grass more quickly than the others, and it only takes a few sprays to completely coat the stencil.

The sound of spray paint attracts Mrs. Platt, and she peeks over the fence to shake her head at me.

I smile and wave.

When I finally pull the cardboard stencil away, a giant golden star shines up at me from a black border. It's perfect.

Today I felt like a star . . . again!

My phone buzzes inside my pocket, and I realize I forgot to take it off silent mode after rehearsal. Paint-covered fingers slide it free, and Jake's name and number flash up at me. I grit my teeth. He said he'd call tomorrow. It's a full day early. I thought I'd have more time to prepare myself to hear his voice, but it's going to happen sooner rather than later. Might as well be today. I can't ignore him forever.

Besides, I'm in such a good mood, nothing can ruin the day for me.

I tap the green circle on my phone screen.

"Hello."

"Bethany. Beth." He sighs. "Thank you for answering."

"I thought you weren't going to call until tomorrow."

"I was, but my meetings got done early and . . . I just," he pauses and I can feel him searching for the right words. "I just needed to hear your voice, B."

"My voice? I'm surprised it was my voice you wanted to hear."

"Seriously. Do you have to go there? We haven't spoken in days and you want to start in already?"

"We haven't spoken in days because of her."

"Fine," he snaps. "I won't talk to her or text her anymore. It's not worth all this drama. I'll cut her out of my life. Is that what you want?"

"What I want?" I shake my head. "You don't get it. No, that's not what I want. What I want is for you to never have fallen in love with another woman. What I want is for you to look at me and think—Wow, I can't believe I get to be married to her. And I want you to rush home from the office because you can't wait to be with me. I want you to tell other people *my* feelings come first, and *they'll* have to deal with it. I want the fairytale, okay? After twenty years, I deserve it."

"What are you talking about, B? You're important to me. You know that."

"Do I? Think back to our last conversation, and tell me you were letting me know how important I am. I haven't felt important to you in years. I have to parade around practically naked to get you to even notice me. You barely even glance away from your phone unless I'm taking my clothes off. Do you know how old and undesirable that makes me feel?"

"Come on. You know how sexy you are. Everyone with eyes can see how sexy you are."

"Yeah, well. You're the only man who gets to make me feel sexy, so it should say something to you that I haven't felt sexy in years. Until this week. This week I'm making some changes, and I'm finally feeling sexy again."

"Who's making you feel sexy? Is there another guy sniffing around you?"

"No, there isn't. Unlike you, I don't feel the need to find someone else. I have you. That's always been enough for me. I just wish you felt the same way."

Jake swears under his breath. "What do you want me to do?"

"You're going to have to figure it out on your own. I just hope you can do it before it's too late. I'd hate to feel like I wasted twenty years of my life. But it would be even worse for me to waste another year. Don't you think?"

"I don't think any of it has been a waste."

"Of course not. You've had someone who does your laundry and cooks and cleans for you, who puts on lingerie and keeps you happy in the bedroom, who supports you at work, and keeps your home running smoothly. Someone who takes care of the children *all the time*, but still takes the time to be on your arm at every company event. Of course, it hasn't been a waste for you. But when's the last time you did something just for me? Just to make me happy?"

"Well, you've had a roof over your head and money in the bank all these years. I've provided well for you."

"Yes, you have. But I want more in my life than a roof over head and money in the bank."

"I don't understand."

"I know you don't, but I have to go to bed now. I have early rehearsal."

"Rehearsal? What rehearsal? What are you talking about?"

"I'm talking about my new life. Goodbye, Jake."

The phone goes dark in my hand. I slip it into my back pocket and walk toward the house, dragging my toes in the grass as I go. With each step my confidence rises. At the French doors, I turn and look at my painted garden.

Three squares stand out against the grass in the dimming light of evening. I close my eyes and smile. The greenest grass on earth. A stage. A star. No matter what happens with Jake, I have a life to live. My life. I love the newness, the excitement. And I want more of it.

An idea for my next goal comes to mind.

When I enter the house, I walk to the bookshelf and grab my leather notebook. I smile as I read the first page, then turn to page two.

I begin it just like I did the day before, in deep purple ink.

> To paint the grass today, I will...
> Try something new.

Time to find my next adventure.

I've already been skydiving and snorkeling. What else could I try? I don't want to embarrass myself, or put my life in danger, and I'd like it to be something I'll enjoy. Something to make me feel good about life again.

A smile slips onto my face as I come up with the perfect idea. Beneath the previous line I write:

Sing karaoke in front of a live crowd.

I've sung classic songs while playing a part in musical productions, but that's totally different than singing a pop song, as myself, in front of a crowd at the local bar.

I slide my phone out of my pocket and text Lettie.

Me: Any plans for tomorrow night?

In less than ten seconds I get a reply.

Lettie: Nope. Have anything in mind?

My thumbs automatically start typing back.

Me: Dust off your party dress. We're going out on the town. Mama needs to sing.

One second later Lettie seals the deal with two small words.

Lettie: I'm in!

The butterflies in my stomach wrestle with my prickling nerves as I get ready for bed. I'm shaky and feeling slightly sick, but I'm not about to let that stop me.

I have a life to live.

TEN

MY NEW ROUTINE STARTS at seven o'clock. I go for a run, and then I'm off to play practice. I can hardly believe I have a routine. I can hardly believe it doesn't include grocery shopping, cleaning the house, cooking for kids, or appointment reminders for my husband.

Play practice Thursday morning starts off rough, but gets better as the day goes along. After the first day's success, the cast can't believe how well I'm embracing my shrewish character as day two begins.

If they only knew.

Everyone's happy with my performance, other than Piper. She has a dozen criticisms for me and yells at me ten times an hour. But still, I'm feeling absolute confidence until Kyle announces we'll start to work on the kissing scenes tomorrow.

"Bring your breath mints, Bethany." Cole smirks.

"I'll bring enough for both of us." I give him an exaggerated grin.

Thankfully my legs don't collapse until after he leaves the stage. With limbs trembling, I sit on the edge of the set's sofa and give myself a pep talk. I know how to kiss. That's not the problem. The fact that my lips haven't touched anyone's but Jake's in more than twenty years has me wondering if anything has changed in the kissing realm. Onstage or otherwise.

I'm not exactly a professional. But really, how hard can it be? Kissing's pretty basic.

Tomorrow, I tell myself. I'll worry about it tomorrow.

As I step outside, light, dewy rain hits my skin, and I close my eyes to breathe it in. It smells like fall, like cool days, old books, and leaves dropping from the sky. Autumn weather is my favorite, but it doesn't put me completely at ease.

I have a lot to accomplish before September ends.

My husband will be home in nine days, and I'm determined to figure out as much as I can about my new self before then. Just a few days to transform myself from a forgotten housewife into a confident woman. Play practice is already helping me remember all the old Bethany goodness. Maybe singing tonight will help unlock my forgotten self even more.

"Do what you love and love what you do," I say aloud as I open the car door.

I slide into the driver's seat and turn the key. It's already well past noon, and my stomach rumbles. Food. I need food. Food first, and then it's time to get my sexy on.

Guiding the car toward home, I sigh aloud. One of those things is going to be so much easier than the other. And I can make a sandwich in my sleep.

Three hours later, half the sandwich lies forgotten on a paper plate, and I'm still trying to pick out an outfit. The contents of my closet are strewn about my room. Shirts, pants, and skirts cover every piece of furniture surrounding me.

I have piles of prospective outfits not-so-neatly organized around the room. To the left there's the No-Way-In-Hell apparel, compiled of my most frumptastic clothing. Sitting on the chaise lounge next to me is a stack of my Maybe-If-I-Weren't-Over-Forty attire, consisting of the sexiest pieces in my closet. And then there's the array of Seriously-This-Is-What-I'm-Left-With, mundane articles that I'll most likely shuffle through to make something work. Every option sucks.

My eyes drift over to the Maybe-If-I-Weren't-Over-Forty pile, and my heart hits my chest hard enough to make even my thoughts sound breathy. I reach for the strappy dress on top, the one I bought for a summer wedding eight years ago and haven't worn since. It shows way too much cleavage, and its shimmery fabric will cling to every inch of my body. The eye-catching bright coral color will have every head swiveling my way. My hands itch to pull it over my head as I hold it up in front of me in the full-length mirror.

"I guess it can't hurt to try it on," I say to my reflection.

To wear this dress, I have to remove nearly all of my clothing. Only my white satin undies remain as I lift the slip of fabric over my head. Watery material slips over my skin as I pull the dress down over my body, adjusting the halter neck so it sits just so. I turn and look in the mirror.

My mouth drops open.

This dress is incredible. The deep-v neckline flatters my small chest-size, and the halter gives the ladies the exact amount of lift they need. The solid fabric liner stops midthigh, and a sheer overdress flows around me to kiss my knees. Peeking out from beneath the see-through layer, my legs stretch on forever. It's casual and dressy at the same time.

I add a pair of metallic bronze heels and some dangly earrings, and I'm ready to go when two knocks sound at the door. Lettie lets herself in just as I enter the living room.

"Holy mother of all that's holy. You look incredible." Lettie stares at me like I've become a supermodel overnight.

My loose hair drapes down my back in soft waves, and I brush it behind my shoulders. "I know it's been a while since I've dressed up, but," I laugh at her expression. "I didn't think it would be so shocking."

"Guys are going to drool over you tonight. Seriously," she points toward the kitchen. "Bring a towel for your own protection, or better yet for my protection. It's the best friend that always gets dripped on."

"Yeah, right. My best friend looks amazing. Black is a great color on you. With your dark hair, it's perfect."

Lettie comes forward and pulls me into a hug. "I can't believe this." When she steps back, she grabs one of my hands in hers and lifts it high. "Where has this Bethany been hiding?"

"Behind the three burly men in her house. But not anymore." I grab my purse and a light sweater and pull Lettie toward the door. "Tonight, we're going to be the hit of the town."

"You'll be a dead center hit for sure." Her classic half-smile follows her out the door. "I'll be more like the aftershock."

We laugh all the way to the karaoke bar. The Spotlight Bar is located beneath the fanciest restaurant in the area. It's pretty glitzy for our small town, complete with stage and lights and a full sound system. A huge spotlight showcases the local entertainers while they enjoy their five minutes of fame.

The wooden stairs creek as we make our way down to the side door entrance. When we step inside, the smell of fruity drinks and fried food hits me full force. Smiling servers carry circular trays heavy with appetizers and happy hour specials as they wind their way between tables.

"Bring on the calories. It's girls' night out!" Lettie shouts as we make our way to an empty table near the stage.

We get settled into our high-top chairs, and a server winds her way back to us.

"What can I get for you?" she asks.

I lean close to be heard over the music. "I'll have a virgin pina colada."

"Virgin?" Lettie asks.

"Yes." I nod. "Virgin. If I'm getting up onstage tonight, I don't want to sound like a drunk idiot. People will clap if I sing sober. They'll cover their ears if I sing drunk."

"Well, I'm not getting up onstage." She turns to the server. "I'll have a pina colada too. But I'm not a virgin, so I don't intend to drink like one."

The server laughs. "Got it. Two pina coladas coming right up."

In less than five minutes she's back with our drinks. I sip on the sweet coconut and pineapple drink, savoring the tropical flavors coating my tongue. We order fried zucchini, mozzarella sticks, and french fries topped with shredded pork and cheese. If they fried my purse and it was on the menu, we would've ordered it too.

As we wait for the food, I stare at the stage, and my breathing becomes an audible thing. I tap my fingernail on the table in a four-count rhythm and then answer the same beat back with a shoe tap on the chair leg. *One-two-three-four.* One-two-three-four. *One-two-three-four.*

"You all right there, Bethy-girl?"

I curl the tips of my fingers into the palms of my hands to stop the tapping. "Uh. Yeah. You bet. Unless . . ." I turn to face her. "Do you think this is a good idea? I mean. I never sing pop songs, unless I'm alone in the shower. And I've never done karaoke. What if I can't do it?" I put my face in my hands. "Maybe this was a bad idea."

Instead of answering my ramblings, Lettie pushes her chair away from the table and stands up. Without saying a word to me, she walks to the front of the room, speaks to the man fiddling with the microphone wires, and writes something on a piece of paper he hands her. She kisses both of his cheeks like she's from Europe, accepts a small silver microphone from him, and smiles all the way back to the table.

"What did you do?" I ask when she sits next to me again.

"You're up first." She holds the mic out to me.

"What?" I pull out a sanitizing wipe, and clean the microphone from tip to base, before I take it from her.

"You heard me." She takes a sip of her non-virgin drink before she continues. "I figure if you go first, the crowd won't have anyone to compare you to so it will be easier, right?"

"Yeah, but they'll still have ears."

"And eyes." She smiles. "And you look hot tonight. So . . . at the very least, you'll give them something pretty to look at while they cover their ears."

I laugh. "You're terrible."

"I'm not terrible. I'm right." She points at me. "And you feel better."

Oddly enough, I do feel better. Not confident exactly. But better.

Lettie makes a small coughing sound.

"You sure you can handle that drink?" I laugh, but Lettie's not paying attention to me. She's focused on something behind me. I turn to see what's gotten into her, and all the air rushes out of my body at once.

Approaching our table is a guy who would easily top the list of sexiest men alive in any year of any decade. His dark hair is perfectly styled and his dark skin shimmers under the lights. But it's his smile that keeps me from catching my breath. It's magic.

He's definitely not from around here.

"Hey," he says.

I keep staring. I think my mouth hangs open a little.

"Hey," Lettie says back.

He smiles at her, then looks at me and points to the microphone in my hand. "You singing tonight?"

I clear my throat and focus on my hands when I answer. "Yeah—I'm mean, yes. I'm gonna give it a try."

A strong hand covers mine, and my eyes trace along his fingers, then up his arm, and all the way to his warm brown eyes. My quickening heartbeat pulses through every nerve in my body.

"I'm looking forward to watching." His fingers curl around mine, and he lifts my hand toward his mouth. When he sees my wedding ring, he pauses, but then his lips press against the diamond, brushing against my skin at the same time. He leans in close, and his breath skims against my face when he speaks. "I hope he deserves you." And with a squeeze of my fingers, he's gone.

My lips slip open as I let out a shaky breath, then I force them closed with a swallow. My mouth is watering. Why is my mouth watering? "Is it hot in here?" I ask.

But Lettie doesn't answer. Her attention is centered on the backside of Mr. Sexiest Man Alive as he walks away.

"Holy hell, B. We've gotta go out together more often."

Girly giggles erupt from our table, and I raise my glass. "To us!"

Lettie clinks her glass with mine and says, "To finding Bethany again!" She waggles her eyebrows. "And to the woman who birthed that sweet-cherry-cola of a man!"

We both take a drink and watch him walk away. I smile. With one hand, I motion the server over. When she reaches our table, I lean toward her. "Two diet cherry colas please."

Lettie starts to laugh.

"What? I'm thirsty."

"Me too." Lettie grins. She nods to the man now standing at the back of the room. "In fact, I feel an addiction coming on."

We drink cherry colas until the clock reaches the top of the hour and the bar owner steps onto the stage.

"Welcome to Karaoke night at the Spotlight Bar." A cheer roars up from the crowd. "I'm Charlie, and I'll be your emcee. Who's ready for some brave singers?" More cheers. "We'll have some who make your ears bleed." Boos scatter among the cheers. "Some who have you clapping along to the beat." A few stray claps spatter around the room. "And some who will get your ass out of your chair and have you rushing the stage." Stomping and table slapping accompanies the cheers, and someone from the back yells, "Hell, yeah!"

Charlie laughs and holds up both hands to quiet them down. "Starting out the night will be a newcomer to our stage. Give it up for Bethany Taylor!"

My heart has a contest with my lungs to see which of them can move faster. My lungs win, and by the time I stand, I sound like I'm in a Lamaze class. Lettie grabs my hand.

"You got this. Relax. Have a little fun. And get these asses out of their chairs."

I nod once and start toward the stage, then turn back for just a second. "You'll be cheering for me?"

"I have my pompoms in my purse." She blows me a kiss and smiles.

Her smile calms me a bit as my shaky legs carry me the rest of the way to the stage. When I get close enough, the title of my chosen song flashes up at me from the karaoke machine.

Of course. Lettie took care of that too.

"You ready for this?" Charlie asks as he turns on my mic.

"I guess we'll find out." I push my lips into a smile as I step up onstage and turn to face the crowd. The cheers die down as my music starts, and I swallow once, then twice . . . and miss my entrance.

Great.

I hurry through the first three words and catch up to the music. My tongue is a little sluggish, even without any alcohol in me, and I fumble a bit during the first stanza. But when the chorus hits, I tune into all that has happened the past week and find my stride.

I sing about being invincible and unbreakable as I belt out the words to my favorite Carrie Underwood song.

The second verse flows from me like I've been doing this my entire life. As the crowd starts clapping and cheering to the music, I channel my inner

Underwood and feel myself dancing around the stage as I sing. I'm performing. Like it's my concert, and I'm the star.

I lose myself to the music during the second chorus, and it's absolutely transforming, a complete and natural high. My smile can't get any wider as my body floats along the stage, barely tethered to reality. Each word lifts me higher and higher, until I find Lettie in the crowd.

She sits at our table with her phone pressed to her ear, and she's crying.

Lettie never cries.

Never.

But she's crying now.

My voice drifts off, concentration gone, as worry takes over. "Sorry," I mumble into the microphone before I hand it back to Charlie. The crowd starts to boo. I ignore them and nod to Lettie. We communicate without words, and she exits the bar immediately. It takes ten minutes for me to pay our tab and follow. When I finally step into the cool evening air, Lettie's pacing near the corner.

Her crying has morphed into messy sobs.

"What is it?" I ask.

"Scarlett," she cries, throwing herself into my arms. "She's missing, B. She ran away from Steve's house. They have no idea where she went. He's been out looking for her." She pulls back, and the terror in her eyes leaks into her voice. "He said if he can't find her soon, he's going to go to the police station."

The fear emanating from Lettie makes the night colder in an instant, and I squeeze her tight, giving her someone to lean on. "We'll find her," I say, but she's already crying again. "Hey." I shake her shoulders gently. "Did you hear me? We'll find her. I promise. Do you remember when Scarlett got lost at the mall when she was four? Who found her?"

Lettie sniffs. "You did."

"That's right, and with your help, I'll find her again. You know her better than anyone else. We'll find her. We won't stop until we do."

Seconds later, we're in my car driving around to Scarlett's favorite places. She left her phone at her dad's house, which only makes Lettie worry more. Her daughter has no way to reach her, to reach anyone. But Lettie knows Scarlett, they're as close as any mother daughter duo I've ever known.

"We'll find her," I say again.

"I can't believe Steve let her out of his sight," Lettie snaps.

"What happened?" I ask.

"She stayed at his house this weekend. And . . ." Lettie turns to face me. "Did I tell you Steve got engaged last week?"

"No. Is Scarlett upset about it? Does she like his fiancé?"

"Scarlett's happy her dad's getting married again. It's a really good thing for him. But his soon-to-be-wife has a daughter just a few months older than Scarlett. And tonight, Steve told Scarlett their summer plans. They're going to Europe to celebrate the engagement. Steve, his new fiancé, and his step-daughter. Just the three of them." Lettie reaches over to grab one of my hands on the steering wheel. "Scarlett got upset because she's not invited. She lashed out and said some hurtful things. Steve left the room to let her calm down, and when he came back, she was gone."

"Only until we find her," I say again. I'll repeat it as many times as necessary, until Lettie starts to believe it.

For the next three hours, I drive and stop, and we search an area. I whisper words of comfort, and tell Lettie everything's going to be okay. I will lie or cheat or steal or do any number of illegal acts to make things right in her world again.

"What am I going to do?" Lettie asks after we've left the sixth location of the night. "What if we don't find her? Where is she? What if she's gone, B? What if I never see her again?"

At the panic in her voice, I pull the car to the side of the road. Job one is to calm her down. I turn toward her and place one hand on her arm. "Take a deep breath." She does. "And now another." I breathe with her. "Okay. Let's stop thinking the worst and start thinking about where we go next. Then we will drive there, and if we don't find her, then we'll go to the next spot, and the next spot, and the next. We will drive around all night until we find her. Understand?"

Lettie nods, and sniffs, and nods again.

"Think, Lettie," I whisper. "Where would she be? Not somewhere she hangs out with her friends. Not a place the two of you go now. Where did you guys spend time together as a family, when you were still married to Steve? Did Scarlett and Steve have a special place?"

Lettie closes her eyes, and a few minutes pass in silence.

"The dock." She opens her eyes, gesturing in circles with her hands. "We used to go fishing out on the dock at Clear Creek Lake. She spent hours there with her dad."

I start driving before she stops talking.

Ten minutes later, we pull up to Waterfront Park. The car rolls to a stop in the deserted lot, and we step out into the night. A single dock flows out toward the still lake. Moonlight shimmers on the surface and provides just enough light for us to see the water's edge. Two shadowy figures stand out against wood and water. One sits at the end of the dock, feet dangling over the edge. Head down and silent. A softly hummed melody drifts from the figure standing a few feet behind her.

"Scarlett!" Lettie squeezes my hand once and runs to her daughter.

The other woman on the dock stops humming and nods as Lettie rushes past. With slow movements, she gathers up her miniature dog and takes a few labored steps. She glances over her shoulder as mother and daughter reunite, and then makes her way toward me.

"They gonna be okay?" she asks in a raspy voice.

A few yards away, Lettie presses her daughter's head against her shoulder. "I hope so."

When I turn my attention to the woman, kind eyes look back at me. "You were watching out for her." It's a statement, not a question.

The woman nods and smiles.

"I'm Bethany." I extend my hand toward her.

"Edith," she says, giving my fingers a quick squeeze.

"Thank you, Edith. Thank you for staying until we could get to her."

"Of course." Her dog licks the side of her face, and I cringe a little, which makes Edith laugh. "Bailey and I were out for our walk when we saw that poor girl, crying her eyes out like she was, I just couldn't leave her. So, I stayed close and hummed her a song." She hums a few notes, and her rich tone warms up the night. "Bailey here laid her head in the girl's lap for more than an hour, and I just kept on humming."

"Did she say anything to you?"

Curly gray hair barely moves as she shakes her head. "Words weren't really necessary. Kindness is its own language. And she knew we were there for her."

Edith takes a slow step away from the dock. "I'm happy to hand her off to someone else, though. My humming was almost wore out, and my legs are shaky tired."

She wobbles, and I instinctively reach out and take her elbow.

"Can I drive you home?" I ask. "They're going to be a while, I'm sure."

Flashing a tooth-gapped smile, Edith shakes her head. "No need. I live right there." With one extended finger, she points at a house on the edge of the parking lot.

I laugh. "You sure have a great view."

"Been walking this waterfront every day for forty years."

"Not a bad place to walk," I say. We move together, slowly, across the parking lot. Me at her elbow. Bailey in her arms.

When we reach her front door, she makes a soft clucking sound. "Found lots of stray dogs and cats over the years." She looks toward the water's edge. "First time I ever found a stray girl, though. They don't make shelters for lost humans." Edith laughs quietly as she opens the door. "Wouldn't know what to do with a girl. I never had children. Glad you came along when you did."

"I'm glad you came along when you did too. Really glad. Thank you."

She nods once. "You have a good night and take care of that sweet girl."

"We will," I promise.

The door closes out the warmth from her small home, and I turn back toward the dock. I hesitate, slow to approach the mother/daughter reunion, not wanting to interrupt. When I step up onto the grass, I pause and look up at the stars, taking a moment to enjoy the beautiful night. I think back on all the times people have reached out to me without words, just to let me know they care.

Kindness really is its own language.

I drag my feet the rest of the way to the dock. One foot catches on the spot where soil meets wood, and a loud creek breaks the silence as I trip forward, steadying myself as I step onto the wooden planks. Lettie turns to look back at me while holding her daughter.

"Thank you." She mouths.

I allow my chin to drop to my chest and send a prayer to heaven, full of gratitude and relief and hope.

I DRIVE LETTIE AND Scarlett home and walk inside to help them buckle down for the night. The boys are still awake and worried about their sister, so I get them settled into bed. Lettie and Eric comfort Scarlett, letting her know how much she's loved and wanted. It's after two in the morning when I finally pull into my garage.

My feet find their own way inside my house. I'm functioning on autopilot as I hang up my jacket and purse. Before I settle myself into bed, I go in search of my notebook. Tonight took a turn toward the unexpected.

I find my notebook on the bookshelf and open it.

To paint the grass today, I will...
Try something new.

A great goal that didn't play out as I had planned.

Sing live karaoke in front of a crowd...

"Kind of," I sigh.
I uncap the pen and add another line to my notebook.

... until Lettie needed me.

Another goal accomplished, with a bonus lesson learned. Sometimes when you set out to do something, life has other plans. No amount of time singing onstage in front of a cheering crowd could ever be as fulfilling as the joy of Scarlett being held safely in her mother's arms.

And even when life turns in an unplanned direction, through all the detours and all the changes, with any luck it will end up somewhere even better than where it started.

In fact, I'm counting on it.

ELEVEN

"**D**AMN YOU, CHERRY COLAS," I mutter as I stub my toe on the bathroom door. The soft glow of a night light whispers over the darkness, illuminating the tiled room. Peeing in the dark is a dangerous habit, but one that can't be avoided for anyone who has given birth to twins.

Even though I'm up, sleep still burns my eyes. In less than five minutes, I'm headed back to my room, but there's really no use going back to bed. I'm awake. Awake, but still tired. An aggravating combination.

I stumble into the kitchen and fill the teapot with water. A nice strong cup of chai is the best way to start the morning. Maybe it will help wake me up.

Sleep was a fitful companion last night.

I couldn't stop thinking about Lettie. The scare Scarlett gave her probably took a year off her life. Thank goodness we found her as soon as we did, and we were lucky Edith found her first.

Edith's words jump into my mind: *Kindness is its own language.* In a single sentence, she taught me more about life than any of my professors at university. Imagine all the benefits humanity would gain if Edith's form of language was taught around the world.

Millions of people fluent in kindness.

What a wonderful world it would be.

"Kindness is its own language," I say aloud to the empty room, remembering Edith's soft voice.

The clock flashes five-thirty, and I sip my tea as I make my way to the office. My red journal lies open on my desk. No longer empty. Deep purple ink spells out my latest goals, and I grab my pen to add another.

> To paint the grass today, I will...
> Show kindness to a stranger

I think back on the server at the all-night diner all those nights ago. Pam—who brought me extra lemons and much needed kindness. Her advice hangs on my bedroom mirror. It started me down this path in the first place. Her kindness filled the emptiness inside me at my lowest moment. It's exactly what I needed.

I want to be someone else's Pam. Someone else's Edith. To pass kindness along and help them in some small way. I want to make someone feel a little better about their world, and brighten their life even if it's just for a few moments.

And why not today?

Beneath my new goal, I write:

> Help someone through a simple act of kindness.

I shut the notebook and smooth my fingers over the soft cover. Now I just have to be on the lookout for someone who might need a bit of a lift today. Should be easy enough. Almost everyone I know could benefit from a kind word or two.

Leaning my head against the office chair, I stare at the ceiling and my mind drifts. I'm sipping tea and enjoying the pre-dawn quiet, completely content—thinking of all the times people have helped me, or times I've helped someone else. Happy thoughts lift my contentment toward joy, until a memory of another kind act trickles in. I can't help but sigh.

It was our tenth anniversary dinner. Jake and I had gone out for steak and lobster, in our painted clothes. We noticed the young couple next to us, gazing at each other as if they were alone in the universe. He whispered something to her, and she leaned in close as if she wanted to share each breath.

"They're on their honeymoon," the server said, handing us our bill. "They just got married yesterday. Aren't they the cutest?"

"They look happy," I said, and my husband smiled.

"Do me a favor." Jake handed his card to the server. "Let me pay for their meal. A little anonymous wedding gift from a couple who've been happily married for ten years now."

But that was ten years ago. The boys were eight and going through their pirate/ninja phase. And Jake was a newbie at Phil's company.

Did he see me back then?

Or was he just playing the part of the perfect husband?

My contentment shatters. I need to move. To out run the memories. The gray darkness of early morning settles in around me as I make my way back to the bedroom to change. I don't turn on any lights, but I find myself humming as I move. I'm eager to start my day even if the sun isn't ready for me yet.

It takes two minutes to struggle into my sports bra and spandex shorts, and even less time to walk downstairs to the front porch. Hazy morning light filters up from behind the mountain as I step out onto the pavement to begin my run. It's much colder this early in the morning, and I find myself running faster to stay warm. I stretch my strides wide and pump my arms quick enough to chafe. Cold air raises chill-bumps along my skin. The push and pull of the movement stretches my muscles as I run. My feet pound on the pavement in time with my heartbeat, and every cell in my body trembles.

I feel alive.

After a mile and a half, I slow it down and start to walk back. My phone buzzes, and I pull it free from my arm band to read the incoming text. It's from Cole.

Cole: Don't forget the breath mints. See you in a few.

The kissing scene!

A fluttering bird of panic pecks a hole inside my chest and perches on my ribcage, making it hard to breathe. How could I have forgotten? Even with an interrupted karaoke night, Scarlett running away, and plans for random acts of kindness—how could the fact I have to kiss another man today slip out of my brain?

I shake my head, pick up the pace, and run the rest of the way home. The minute I step into my front yard, Mrs. Platt stops me. She's waiting on the front porch, guarding the door so I can't rush inside and avoid this conversation again.

"I've spoken with the HOA president," she says. "He said there's nothing in the homeowner's association contract that specifically prevents a person from spray painting their grass."

I smile.

"But," she continues, "since I filed a complaint, he'll have to come investigate."

"Of course he will."

She shakes her head. "I don't think he'll allow it."

"Why not? If it's in my fenced back yard, it shouldn't matter. It's not in the front where everyone can see it. And in two weeks, when I mow my lawn, it'll be gone." I spread my hands wide, gesturing toward her house. "It's not like I'm spray painting your prize-winning grass . . . unless . . ." I lift one eyebrow and look over to her yard as if I'm considering it.

She gasps and rushes toward her precious flowers.

"Have a good day, Mrs. Platt." I'm laughing as I walk inside.

I take a few minutes and call Lettie to check in with her. Scarlett is still sleeping, but she's agreed to have lunch with her father to work through the hurt feelings. And Lettie will be there to mediate, which is the best plan since the invention of all plans. I hang up with a little less weight on my shoulders and promise her I'll swing by later this afternoon.

After a long shower, I throw makeup on my face, pull my hair up, and watch ten YouTube videos on how to stage kiss. On screen, some young thing half my age tells me stage kissing is just another piece of blocking, just like walking to stage left or sitting on the edge of the sofa. Ha! Yeah right.

Another young YouTuber advises me to not get weird about it and just rely on the chemistry between the characters.

"Chemistry." I nod. "Okay. I can totally do that." Looking into the mirror, I pucker up my lips and send an air kiss to my reflection. "You got this." Sure I do.

When I climb into the car, I'm running fifteen minutes early. Just enough time for me to stop by the corner store. I turn the key and back out of the garage, hands still a little shaky in anticipation of what's to come.

My radio kicks on as soon as I reach my driveway. A song from my college years blares from the car speakers. It's Faith Hill singing "This Kiss." The words pull my high-strung nerves tight enough for all my doubts to walk across.

"You've got to be kidding me." I turn off the radio immediately.

With a push of a button, silence fills the car. I rest my head on the steering wheel for two breaths and give myself a pep-talk. "You can do this. It's like riding a bike." I leave the radio off and back out of the driveway.

I talk to myself all the while I drive to the store.

"Kiss another man. In front of a room full of people. No problem." I talk to myself while I buy two fresh packages of breath mints.

"You're amazing. Do you know who's amazing? You are." I'm still trying to convince myself as I pull into my parking spot at the theater.

The sun warms my face as I step out of the car, and I take a deep breath, adding one more, "You got this," for good measure before I rush inside.

Cole is lounging on the set couch when I walk onto the stage. Before he can mouth off with some smart comment, I toss him a package of mints.

"Keep it close." I point at him as I walk to the far side of the stage to get set for the day. I can feel Cole's eyes on me, so I pop a mint in my mouth just before I take my place offstage and get set for my first entrance.

The music starts for the opening number. "Another Op'nin', Another Show." Every rehearsal we start with the beginning number to get us warmed up, since everyone in the cast makes an appearance. Then we move on to whatever scenes we need to work on for the day's rehearsal.

Today we'll work on the kissing scene.

No biggie.

I paste a smile on my face and saunter out onto stage, every bit the big-screen star I'm supposed to be embodying. The brilliant woman playing my assistant, Hattie, sings the opening lines with incredible tone and power. Everyone works together. We're like the fingers of a single hand, cogs inside a perfectly-timed clock, pieces of one finely-tuned engine.

And as long as I have my play book in my hand, I don't detract from the other actors.

We make a strong showing together in the first scene and at the end of it, Kyle picks up his director's horn and shouts, "Nice work, everyone."

Just behind him, Piper props her broken leg onto a pillow-covered chair. Her glare says she doesn't agree with our esteemed director.

"Now, get set for Lilli and Fred's first kissing scene." Kyle looks at me. "You ready, Bethany?"

117

"Good to go," I lie.

Cole pops a mint into his mouth and winks at me.

As we take our places onstage, my limbs freeze up. My mind goes blank and all I can do is stare at Cole's lips. Breathing becomes my main focus, and I'm terribly good at it. So good, in fact, I start to hyperventilate.

"Okay, everyone," Kyle yells. "Are we all set?"

"Bethany," Piper calls toward the stage.

I focus on her face as if it's my lifeline. Maybe if she yells at me, it will give me something else to worry about besides kissing a stranger onstage.

"Hey!" She yells. "You look like you're about to puke. And if you do, poor Cole will have to kiss you anyway. So spare us all the dramatics and be a professional."

It works. I snap out of it.

I shake the stiffness out of my limbs and toss my hair behind my shoulders. Piper's right. Be professional, B!

Cole takes his place next to me on the stage and leans in to whisper in my ear. "Want to try a practice kiss? Just to get our lips warmed up. Couldn't hurt?"

Harnessing my inner Lilli, I say, "It could hurt if I slap you hard enough." Then I give him my sweetest smile and step next to him, ready to begin the scene.

Kyle yells, "Action!" and we're off.

The scene starts with Lilli and Fred in their dressing rooms remembering the good times when they were first married and doing shows together. They reminisce about one of their early appearances together and begin to sing a song in duet.

"Wunderbar," Cole sings.

"Wunderbar," I echo.

Together we waltz around the stage, turning and twirling on spot as we're blocked out to do. My voice doesn't shake, but my legs do, and several times,

Cole almost trips over me. But we make it to the final chord, and he dips me with an elaborate flourish. After a single heartbeat, he lifts me upright again and pulls me tight against his chest.

This is the moment.

The moment where Lilli shows Fred she still loves him.

Cole leans down, and I raise on tip toe. I twine my hands around his neck and sink my fingers into his hair, pulling his face to mine.

Our lips touch.

I'm shy at first. But then Cole leans into me ever so slightly, and his hand tightens on my lower back. My lips soften, and I press against him. Our lips slant across each other, exploring, getting to know one another better. I automatically start to judge his technique. Gentle lips, just the right amount of pressure, not sloppy at all, minimal awkwardness. No teeth bumping— this is very important.

Even as I critique him, my pulse increases. The kiss intensifies. My heart fights to break free of my ribcage as my nervousness gives way to confidence.

I'm doing it! I'm actually doing it!

And Cole doesn't seem repulsed at all. He's as into character as I am, and our lips never want to stop touching. I'm living this moment fully. There's nothing in the world but this section of stage and the feel of Lilli's lips on Fred's.

"Cut!" Kyle yells.

Cole starts to pull away, but I bring him closer and continue the kiss. He follows my lead. We're locked together, lip to lip, bodies close, completely in character, and I'm so thrilled it's going well I could stay here all day. Neither of us make a move to part.

"I said cut!" Kyle uses the bullhorn this time. "Someone get a bucket of water for our two leads."

His threat breaks through my haze, and I pull away, ending the kiss. Cole has to catch himself before he falls forward.

"Care to explain?" Kyle asks.

Cole motions to me.

"Uh . . . well." I pull out my mom-face, stern and serious. "I thought it was important to finish the scene. Since we were both there, in the moment."

Cole laughs. "Yeah, well, never let it be said Bethany Taylor ever stops halfway." Then he leans down and whispers in my ear. "That was very convincing."

"Thank you." I smile up at him. Unembarrassed. Unashamed. I did it. I successfully kissed another man. And I was very convincing.

I turn to Kyle and notice Piper sitting behind him.

"Try to make it a little less porn-starish next time," she yells at the stage.

Kyle clears his throat. "Yes. Well. It looked good from here. The chemistry was just right. Now take it from the top of the scene." He directs us back to our starting positions. "And this time, use the entire stage while you dance. I want to see movement from one side to the other."

We do as instructed, and soon we're in full swing again. This time as we dance, my legs and arms are fluid. Cole and I glide across the stage, using every inch of available space. When he dips me, I'm not nervous at all.

Our lips meet with barely contained passion, and I'm breathless as I say my final lines of the scene. We step apart and . . .

"Cut," Kyle yells and rushes up onto the stage. He pulls Cole and me into a tight hug, repeating the phrase, "Thank you, thank you, thank you," in rapid succession. When he pushes us back, pure happiness lights up his smile. "We're going to sell out on opening night!"

As he leaves the stage, we pick up the scene where we left off. He only interrupts us twice to correct misgiven lines and three times for mistakes in blocking. Overall, practice is amazing, and I can't help but smile when I think of my performance.

"Tomorrow we'll work on being more natural, and the scene will be even better," Cole says after walking me to my car. "Though I don't know how. You were incredible today."

"Thanks. So were you." I wave goodbye to him, open my car door, and collapse inside. The hot air steams my lungs as I breathe it in, and I can't turn the key fast enough. As soon as the air conditioning kicks on, I sigh. The September afternoon sun is too much for me. Fall temperatures tease with cool mornings and then release the scorching heat of a thousand suns by late afternoon. I'm already longing for the refreshing evening air, and it's barely three o'clock.

I grab my phone and dial Lettie's number before I even start to drive. "Hey you," I say after her recorded voice asks me to leave a message. "I kissed another man today, and it was awesome! Everyone watching said it looked completely natural and the chemistry felt just right. I'm stopping by the market to buy some celebratory salted caramel gelato and then I'll be headed your way. Tell the boys I'll bring popsicles. Love you. Be there soon."

It takes ten minutes to get to the market just off Main Street, and I'm in the door and raiding the freezer section three minutes later. With both items in hand, I head toward the forming line. Two people stand in front of me, and I glance around for any other open registers.

Nope.

Good thing patience is a virtue I've cultivated, pruned, and harvested over the course of my lifetime. While I wait, I wonder if bringing ice cream to Lettie could count as my act of kindness for the day. I shake my head. No. Of course it doesn't. I'm buying the gelato for me. Lettie will just be there to share my spoon.

A cart pulls up behind me in line, and I scoot forward to give them plenty of room. A child's cry sounds, and then another soon after. It's a duet of screaming babies. An anthem I remember well.

When I turn around, the scene transports me back in time—eighteen years. To the days I dragged my twin boys to the grocery store for emergency

121

purchases like milk, or diapers, or wine. The woman behind me has two crying boys, settled inside her cart in back-to-back car seats.

"Shhhhh," she coos, barely holding onto her smile through the forming tears. "It's okay." She tries to calm her boys. "Mama's getting you more food. I know you're hungry. We just have to buy it first, and then you can eat."

I glance at her cart. The corners are stuffed with cans of formula, boxes of rice cereal, and dozens of baby food containers. Bananas, sweet potatoes, pears, all pureed to smooth baby-ready goodness. A single bouquet of flowers tumbles in among the mix.

"You forgot the wine," I tell her, and she looks up at me, startled.

"What?" she says. Then she smiles and nods as she processes my joke. "Yeah. It's been a day. I could definitely use some." The son on the left sends out a wail loud enough to call in a humpback. The mama's lips turn down, and her shoulder's slump as she shakes her head in apology. "I'm so sorry. They're starving and tired. It's a bad combo."

"Don't worry about it." I send her my most genuine smile. "I know exactly what it's like. I have twin boys myself. In fact . . ." I set the gelato and popsicles down on the end of the conveyor belt and turn toward my fellow twin mom. "May I?"

She nods. "I'm willing to try anything."

I gently lift one car seat and turn it around. Then I do the same to the second one. The babies face each other now, and their chubby feet immediately tangle together. Identical feet touch identical feet, identical eyes twinkle and smile. The crying settles and stills.

The other shoppers in line take a collective breath.

"Amazing," the mother whispers.

"They like to see each other. To touch in some way. Separation anxiety is real for twins, especially when they're young. Being near the other helps. My boys are still happiest when they're together."

She reaches out and clasps my hand with her own, and warmth spills through my body at the gratitude displayed on her face. "Thank you," she whispers.

"You're welcome." I send her a soft smile. "Believe it or not, you'll miss these days. Not the crying, of course, but the times when they're little and at home. My twins are eighteen now. They moved out of the house a few weeks ago."

"Wow. You actually made it." She gives me the once over. "And you stayed sane through it all."

I laugh. "I've been meaning to get an 'I survived raising twin boys' T-shirt made. I think I've earned it."

"Miss," the cashier says. "Miss. I can help you right here."

I'm next in line, and even though my gelato runs the risk of melting, I step back. Leaving my frozen treats on the conveyor belt, I push the mother's cart forward.

"Here," I say, handing her items to the cashier. "You go first. The faster you get out of here, the faster you can get those babies home."

She sends me a watery smile. "Thank you so much."

I unload her cart as she steps around me. The cashier has her groceries bagged and put back in her cart in five minutes, and the woman reaches for her purse.

Before she can pull out her credit card, I realize this is my moment. My chance to do a small act of kindness for the day. I step up toward the small machine, just as the manager swipes a store card through the reader.

"You're our one hundredth customer today," he says. "This one's on us."

Tears form in the mother's eyes, and she wipes them away with one hand. "Thank you. That's so kind."

I paste on a smile and quickly buy my gelato, trying to fight away the feelings of failure rising up inside me. My good intention to show kindness thwarted by a grocery store giveaway.

The twin mom tucks a blanket around her little ones, and we walk out of the store together. We reach her car, and she tends to her babies. I unload the bags into the back of her van as she fastens the boys' car seats into their bases in the car.

When I walk around to her driver's-side door, she hesitates for just a moment and then pulls me into a hug. When she steps back, she looks at the ground. "Thank you. Thank you for helping me today."

"But I didn't do anything."

She puts one hand on my arm. "You showed me how to comfort my babies—"

I'm shaking my head before she can finish. "I turned their cars seats around. It was nothing."

"It gave me another tool to use when they're crying. And . . ." She motions to her van. "You took the time to help me load the groceries in my car. No one's ever done that for me before."

Happiness floods through me, spilling over into my smile. "Glad I could help." I nod to her back window. "Now go have a great afternoon with those boys. And give them an extra kiss today. They'll be gone before you know it."

"Somedays I wonder if I'll survive that long."

I'm laughing as she pulls her car door open. She sits down, then reaches across the seat to pull a single purple flower out of the bouquet she just bought and hands it to me. "Thank you. Really . . . even if you think it wasn't much . . . it was enough. It made a difference . . . to me."

I started out the day wanting to do a grand gesture, like buy someone groceries, or help rescue a lost child. It's strange to think anything so small could make a difference. But as I wave to the young mother while she drives away with her twins, her smile says it all.

TWELVE

THE GELATO IS PERFECTLY soft as I dish it into two shallow red bowls on Lettie's countertop. The boys attacked the popsicles like a swarm of locusts in a wheat field and headed outside with one flavor in each hand.

Lettie leans out the back door as they leave. "Don't set your popsicles in the grass. And if I find wrappers and sticks on the ground, I'll eat the rest of the bag all by myself." She slides the door shut and sighs. "Peace and quiet. Thanks, B."

"Glad I could help." I push her bowl across the counter and take a bite of my own. Sweet cream and soft caramel coat my tongue, and a small moan slips free.

"Is that moan for the ice cream, or are you remembering the kiss from this morning?"

"Shut up. The kiss was completely professional." I give her a gentle shove as she settles onto the stool next to me, grateful Piper isn't here to disagree. "And this isn't ice cream, it's gelato. Hence the moan."

"I'm surprised you didn't make Cole give you a health history before you let his lips anywhere near yours."

"What? Me?" I smile and give a small laugh. My friend knows me well.

"Maybe you're starting to get over your germaphobia."

Even as she makes the comment, I pull out a vial of hand sanitizer and apply it liberally to my hands and forearms. "Nope. Definitely not."

"I should have known." Lettie squints her eyes and stares at me. "Still, it must have been some kiss. You're beaming. Seriously. I can't remember the last time you've looked this happy."

"It's true." I sigh, trying to come up with the words to explain the riot of emotions inside me. "I did a really hard thing onstage today, and it made me feel free and—powerful. It was amazing. I'm not kidding. I think Kyle cried a little."

"Again?" Lettie laughs. "As long as Cole didn't cry, then I think you're good."

"Would you stop it?" I laugh as I pull her bowl away from her. "No more celebratory gelato for you."

"Come on. You know I'm proud of you."

I slide her bowl back toward her. "Proud enough to go to dinner with me later this week?"

Lettie stands as she clears off our bowls. "I wish I could, but unless you want to go somewhere with a play place, I doubt it's an option for me. Eric's working late every night this week."

"Well, at least we got to share some killer gelato together." I push away from the counter. "Have fun with the boys and Scarlett. How's she doing, anyway?"

"She's hanging in. She's agreed to see a family therapist with her dad. I'm sure I'll make a few appearances too, but I just hope it helps."

"Me too." I give her a quick hug. "Call if you need anything."

We walk out to my car, and as I open the door, Lettie surprises me with another hug.

"I can't wait to see you onstage opening night. You better get me a front row seat. As best friend of the leading lady, I demand a front row seat."

I sit down and situate myself behind the wheel. "I'll get you a front row seat for opening night and closing night and every night in between. Who do you think I'm going to look for in the audience if I forget a line and freeze up onstage?"

"Well, I promise to yell FIRE and clear the place out for you if you do. I'm always good for a distraction." She steps back as I close the door. "But seriously, Beth. Proud of you."

"I'm proud of me too." I start the car and nod to her. "See you when I see you."

She blows me a kiss.

Ten minutes later I wave to Mrs. Platt as I pull into my garage. Once inside the house, I tidy up my kitchen, fold a load of laundry, and settle in to read a book.

I flip to the first page and begin chapter one, allowing my eyes to scan the words. But the house is too quiet. The ticking clock on the mantle echoes through the room, and my eyebrows start to twitch in time with the beat. I've reread the same paragraph four times when I finally put my book aside and pick up the phone.

Since my boys moved out of the house, I've instilled the weekly phone call rule. Once a week I get to talk to two of my favorite people in the world. I press Ryan's picture on my phone and wait to see if he will pick up.

My older son answers the phone after three rings. "Hey, Mom. How's it going?"

"Pretty great. Thanks for asking."

"Here, hold on a sec. Let me do a conference call and link Rob in."

I hear a few buttons being pushed and a rustling sound in the background and then, "There, should be connected. You're on."

"Mom. You there?" an almost identical voice says.

"Hey, Robbie. You guys getting all settled in up there?"

"How could we not?" Ryan says. "You got us everything we could ever need."

"Well, that's what moms are for. That, and growing children."

"Gross, Mom," Robbie complains. "Seriously."

"Seriously? I'm joking. Moms should rule the world. We'd be amazing at it. It should be a job requirement for all world leaders. Speaking of which—how's work going?"

"Great. It's been a few weeks, so we're getting better shifts," Ryan says.

"Yeah. That's incredible!" My voice reflects my joy. I'm so happy for my boys. "Working at the gym on campus is a pretty sweet gig. You can stay in shape while you're getting paid."

"Best college job ever," Robbie says.

"Is Dad there?" Ryan asks.

I clear my throat. "Um, no. He's on a business trip."

"How long this time?" Robbie asks.

"Two weeks."

"Sorry you're alone." Ryan's tone shows his concern. "As soon as Dad gets home, how about we come down and we'll all go to that frozen custard place you love?"

"Yeah." I try to push excitement into my voice. "Sounds great. Can't wait to see you guys."

"As long as we can avoid the crud going around up here," Robbie adds.

"Are you guys sick?" I ask.

"No," Ryan sighs. "We're staying healthy so far, but everyone around here is coughing up a lung."

"Don't worry. We won't come home if we get it," Robbie says.

"What do you mean? Of course I want you to come home. Sick or not."

"But what about the germs?" Robbie asks.

"What about them?"

Ryan laughs. "Mom, you avoid germs like they're out to kill you, and sick people totally freak you out."

"They do not."

"You carry hand sanitizer in your purse and your car," Robbie says.

"So. Lots of people do."

"You wipe down tables at restaurants before we eat," Ryan says. "And you hate doctor's offices. You'd have to be on your death bed to go to a hospital."

"Not true. I went there to have you two, didn't I?"

"And you haven't been back since," Robbie adds.

"Thankfully, I haven't needed to." Nostalgic memories of bringing my boys home from the hospital fills me to bursting, and suddenly I want nothing more than to be with them. "Hey, how about we meet at our favorite BBQ joint tonight? It's about halfway, right? I'll buy."

"We'd love to, Mom. But we have to work tonight," Ryan says.

"Yeah. And after work we have the freshman social," Robbie adds.

"Okay... no worries. I forget, you're grown-ups now with lives of your own." I swallow down the loneliness and brighten my voice as much as I can. "Let's plan on getting together soon, though. We'll figure out something fun."

"Perfect," Robbie says.

"Awesome," Ryan says.

"It's a date. I'll put it on my calendar when you can work me into your schedule."

"Sounds great, Mom. We'll let you know when. Gotta head to the gym now. Our shift starts in fifteen minutes."

"Love you boys."

"Love you, Mom. Bye."

I tap end on the phone and close my eyes. Loneliness pours over me. I miss my boys. When I became a mother, no one mentioned how hard it would be to let my grown-up kids leave the house. No one thought to tell me how useless I'd feel when they no longer needed me.

That was a lesson I had to learn the hard way.

My eyes flutter open, and I push myself away from the sofa, determined to stay positive. Today, I conquered my fear of kissing someone onstage, and I'm amazed at how much it empowered me. I want more days like this. More days discovering myself. If getting over fears feels this good, sign me up.

SATURDAY'S REHEARSAL RAISES MY confidence to new levels, until I realize Jake has been gone for almost a week. In eight days, I'll have to face him again. I'm still not sure what I'll say to him the first time I see him. And how am I supposed to stay in the same house with him when I've dreamed about him falling off a cliff?

My spunky attitude and proud temperament last until the director calls for our lunch break. Lilli's character falls away from my shoulders like an unwanted shawl and with each step I take away from the stage, I sink deeper and deeper into my worries.

The wooden chair creaks beneath me as I settle into a backrow and open my notebook. I'm tapping the tip of my pen to my lip when Cole sits next to me.

"Diet or full sugar?" he holds out two sodas and drops a bag of chips in my lap.

I grab the can of diet. "Thanks."

"I'd like to say I came prepared, but these are from the vending machine in the lobby." He flips both feet up onto the seat in front of him and looks at my notebook. "What's this?"

"Oh, nothing, really." I close the cover before he can read anything. "It's just a few challenges I'm giving myself. A few things I want to do over the next couple weeks."

"Like what?"

"You know . . . challenges . . . goals . . . things I want to accomplish."

"Like go skydiving or climb Mt. Kilimanjaro?" He smiles, mocking me.

"No. Not skydiving. I've done it before."

Cole drops his bag of chips as he jerks upright. "You've been skydiving?"

I nod. "Yeah. Last year."

"Are you crazy? Why would you ever jump out of a perfectly good airplane? You could've broken your neck. Actually, physically, broken your neck." He shakes his head, as he picks up the chips. "I just . . . I can't . . ."

"You're serious." My mouth falls open, but I can't think of anything else to say.

He glares back at my shocked expression. "What?"

"I think I just found a chink in your armor." I poke him in the shoulder.

"I'm not..." He takes a long drink of his soda and looks toward the stage. "I'm not afraid of heights or anything, I just have this recurring nightmare of parachutes not opening. I could never do it."

I stop my teasing, the expression on his face communicating far too much truth. "It really scares you."

His gaze whips back to mine. "I'm not scared—just careful." He looks back at the stage, clears his throat, and quiets his voice. "And I don't do stupid things."

"Skydiving isn't stupid. Not if you go with someone who knows what they're doing." I nudge his shoulder. "It's liberating and exhilarating and just so...crazy fun."

"The crazy part I agree with."

"Seriously," I say. "You should try it. I bet you'll never have a parachuting nightmare ever again after you jump one time."

"Yeah. Not going to happen."

"Come on. I'll go with you. We can do it together."

He barely turns his head when he gives me a sideways glance. "Maybe."

"I'll take that maybe."

"But not until after performance week. Kyle will kill us both if we show up with broken legs."

"Deal."

Kyle calls out, "Two minutes. Actors to the stage in two minutes."

Cole starts to gather up our garbage, and I put one hand on his, stopping his movement. "I've got this. You bought the snacks, the least I can do is clean up."

He shrugs and stands. "Okay. I'll see you up there."

"See you."

Cole smiles as he walks away, and I can't help but think of the contradicting look on his face a few minutes ago when I mentioned jumping out of an airplane. Fears are funny things. And Cole has missed out on an amazing experience all these years because of his fear. This awareness slaps me in the face and opens my eyes.

I refuse to live my life in fear. Not in fear of Jake. Not in fear of failure. Not in fear of anything. The new me will live life without fear. I open my notebook and quickly write:

To paint the grass today, I will...
Do something that scares me.

I close the cover of my notebook and head toward the back of the theater. The garbage can rests against the back wall just below a board filled with announcements and bulletins for events around town.

As I make my way to the trash, I picture Cole and try to come up with something that could possibly cause a similar look of fear to cross my face. The kissing scene from yesterday would definitely count. But I can't exactly set a goal to do something I've already done.

I dump the empty cans and chip bags and glance at the board behind it. One flyer in particular catches my eye. Its red cross stands out against a sea of off-white and cream posters. It reads:

Blood drive this Thursday
Memorial Hospital, 1322 W Crawford St.
10:00-3:00

I read the words Memorial Hospital and shiver. The boys are right. Germs and sick people freak me out. I actively avoid them, and I'd never voluntarily walk into a hospital for any reason. The thought of it fills me with such unease, I immediately think of Cole's face when I mentioned sky diving.

And that's when I know what my next goal will be.

I scribble in my notebook as I make my way to the stage.

To paint the grass today, I will...
Do something that scares me.

Beneath my general goal I write:

Volunteer at a hospital.

I snap the book shut and pull hand sanitizer from my pocket. I slather up as I step up onto the stage. This latest idea of mine just might kill me.

THIRTEEN

SUNDAY MORNINGS ARE FOR sleeping in and painting grass. Too bad I have a few calls to make first thing.

The two hospitals directly to the east of my small town turn me down. No openings for volunteers. Two calls, and two no-thank-yous, not exactly the best start.

I look up hospitals near the theater. Since I drive that direction every day, it should work. With a tap of a phone number, I dial the hospital closest to the theater, fully expecting to hear another *no thank you*.

"Excuse me," I say into the phone. "Could you repeat that?" Panic doesn't slowly rise up inside me, it pounces in an instant, shoving my heart down into my stomach where it will be digested slowly for the next several hours.

Please tell me she didn't say yes.

"Yes," the nurse says again. "We'd be happy to have you as a volunteer. We're a bit shorthanded at the moment. How soon could you come fill out paperwork?"

"What? Are you sure? I mean, I've never done anything like this before."

"It's fine. Many of our volunteers don't have much experience. We'll be happy to train you." The sound of keyboard tapping fills the phone. "Does today work for you? I'll be here until four."

"Today?" My voice cracks. "Sure. You bet. Today's great. I'll be there in less than an hour." I hang up the phone and head straight to the hospital before I can talk myself out of it.

After a thirty-minute drive, a two-hour hospital training video, and twenty minutes of paperwork, I'm good to go for the following day.

"As long as nothing flags in your background check, we have an open shift tomorrow afternoon. Should I sign you up?" the receptionist asks.

"Ummm." I want to say yes, but fear takes over my voice, and I can't form the words. I swallow audibly, and the woman behind the desk gives me a strange look.

"Well, can you do it? Do you want the shift?"

"I . . . I think so . . . give me a minute." Suddenly all the time I spent watching training videos and filling out paperwork seems like a waste. What do I do if my heart is willing, but my fears are more than willing?

The woman sighs and shakes her head, clicking out of the open screens.

"Wait!" I'm suddenly able to speak again. "Yes, I want it."

She nods and types something, smiling now.

"I'm painting the grass," I whisper to myself—but obviously not quietly enough.

"I'm sorry?" She tilts her head, looking at me like maybe I need to be in a hospital myself. "I think you might be confused. This is a volunteer position to work with patients at this hospital. There's no paint involved or landscaping needed."

"Yes. Sorry. I understand." I send her my most sane-looking smile. "I'm available after three."

"Perfect." She types on her keyboard, hands me my hospital volunteer badge, and smiles. "We'll see you tomorrow afternoon."

I nod once, suddenly doubting all of my life choices. "Thanks. I think."

Once I'm outside of the building, I take deep breaths of the fresh mountain air. I shove my newly-printed hospital ID badge into my purse and apply a liberal amount of hand sanitizer.

"You can do this. You can do this." But no matter how many times I repeat my new mantra to myself as I drive home, I still find myself dreading tomorrow.

I PULL ON MY grubby clothes, grab a small jar from my craft room, and head out back. Now that I have the system down, unloading the gear from the storage shed goes twice as fast. The three large painted squares make me smile as I position my stencil next to the golden star of the square I painted a few days ago. I didn't get home until after dark on the night of my karaoke debut, so today's the day to paint my square.

A tiny mixing marble rattles inside the paint can as I shake it. No other supplies are needed, so I step up to my square and begin to spray. Shiny silver covers the prickly grass. While the paint is still wet, I take the jar of silver glitter I brought with me from the house and begin to sprinkle it over the square.

The metallic glitter sticks and melds to the drying paint, until the entire square looks like a disco ball. I flip the power switch in the corner of the yard, and light bounces off the glitter shards, dancing through my painted garden. Little light fairies flicker around the weeping willow branches and skip along tree trunks. It's magical. As if my very own team of Tinkerbells have come to brighten my life.

"Perfect," I say aloud. The silver shines just like the microphone Lettie brought to the table for my karaoke debut. It sparkles like the reflection of the moon off the lake on the night we found Scarlett. *Try something new.* From now on, I'm going to be living outside my comfort zone.

I wait a little longer before I move the square frame away, making sure the glitter has time to dry. With both hands and all my body weight, I leverage the template away from the finished painted grass.

Instead of dragging it back to the shed, I slide it over a few feet and put it in position to paint another square. With a box-cutter knife, I cut a piece of black plastic off the roll I bought at the hardware store. The plastic drapes easily across the square template, and in the exact middle, I carve out a freehand heart. The heart takes up nearly the entire four-foot canvas, and I begin to shake the purple paint can.

Ten minutes later, I have a slightly crooked purple heart next to my glitter square. The act of service I did for the woman at the grocery store was such a small thing, hardly anything at all, but that's the beauty of it. My insides well up at the memory of her smile. Kindness is catching—and addicting.

A crash and a curse word sound from behind me, and I turn just in time to see Mrs. Platt looking over the fence. Three of her cotton-headed friends follow her lead. It's bridge club night. They stare at me like I'm an exhibit in a zoo, and their none-too-subtle whispers let me know exactly what they think of my painted grass.

"And there's more to come," I call to them, raising my voice to be sure they hear me. Eventually the Bridge-Club Biddies get tired of spying, and by the time I clean up and lock the shed, I'm alone. I step back to view all my painted squares. Five in total now. It's quite the display. And I can't wait to add more.

MONDAY MORNING MY ALARM chimes after I'm already dressed. My new routine settles around me like a favorite blanket. I follow the same pattern. Get out of bed. Run. Rehearsal.

But today, I get to add another item to my to-do list.

It's hospital volunteer day.

On a scale from one to five, my nervousness jumps to an eight on the elevator ride up to the third floor. Pediatrics! Why didn't I ask what they did on the third floor before I said yes? It's written as clear as day on the directory in the lobby. Third floor: Pediatrics. I didn't sign up to deal with kids. They're the worst when it comes to germs. They never wash their hands or cover their mouths when they cough.

Why did I agree to do this? Will I offend these sick kids if I wear three masks and disinfect them with sanitizing wipes before I say hello? My insides fight to become my outsides on the never-ending trip to the pediatric wing, and I swear any second now I'm going to lose it.

Calm down. It's going to be okay. I attempt to give myself a pep talk.

The elevator dings. The doors slide open. And the little boy waiting on the other side vomits all over the floor.

"Scratch that," I say aloud. "It's not okay."

None of this is okay.

My fingers reach toward the door-close button on the elevator just as a nurse says, "Here let me help you around this mess."

She holds her hand out to me, and I stare at it like it's infested with flesh-eating bacteria.

"Or maybe not," she lowers her hand and laughs. The doors start to close, and she leans forward to block them open with one arm. "If you give me a minute, I'll have someone clean this up for you."

"It's okay, I've got this." I tiptoe around the mess in front of me, trying to pretend germs aren't floating up from the toxic waste that just came out of the cute Japanese boy now smiling at me. Even still, I hold my breath all the way to the nurse's desk.

A tall dark-haired woman glares at a computer screen behind the desk. Her blemish-free brown skin shines under the bright lights above her. When she sees me approaching, her glare transforms to a professional smile.

"Can I help you?" she asks in a well-trained, polite voice.

"Bethany Taylor. I'm here to volunteer. They told me to meet," I glance at the email pulled up on my phone, "Nurse Gables here at three-thirty."

"So, you're my newbie. Happy to have you." She steps around the desk, extending one hand toward me. "Dana Gables. Head nurse. You ready to meet the patients?"

I open my mouth to say yes when the image of the little boy hunched over a pile of vomit enters my mind. "Just a minute."

The head nurse's eyes widen a bit as I pull out hand sanitizer and wipe down my hands and arms. I grab a pair of bright-blue gloves out of the box on the nurse's desk, slip my fingers inside, and snap them on. Then for good measure I dump more sanitizer on top of the gloves and rub it all around. Next, I don two face masks and ask, "Do you have one of those disposable robes that I've seen people wearing? I had a close call—just now—by the elevator."

Nurse Gables stares at me for so long, I start to feel a bit ridiculous.

"I'm sorry," I sigh. "I don't know if I can do this." I pull off one glove and lower my masks with my bare hand. "I'm a bit of a germaphobe, and I'm trying to work through it. I thought this would be good for me, but . . ." I shrug.

Instead of laughing or confirming my feelings of inadequacy, Nurse Gables nods as a one-sided smile slips onto her face. "Actually, I think I have the perfect solution for both of us. We have a very special patient I'd like you to meet. You'd be assigned solely to her room. She's under strict visitor guidelines, and I think you'll be a good fit. Should we go meet her?"

"Her?" I ask.

A little girl! I'd always wanted a little girl to take care of. I love my sons, but I was never able to have a daughter.

"This way." Nurse Gables starts walking down the hall to the left. "Let's go meet Nat."

At the very end of the east hallway, she stops in front of Room 348.

Natalie Cook marks the chart hanging next to the door.

"Natalie is one of our regulars. She's eleven years old and has been in and out of this hospital her entire life. Since her grandmother died a few months ago, that little girl is alone in this world. The state caseworker who checks in here every few weeks is her only visitor. Ever. Until now."

I nod, taking in all the information. "Why is she so sick?"

"She lost the genetic lottery. I'm sure she'll tell you all about it. She understands it better than any of us." Nurse Gables wags her eyebrows and holds up what looks to be a light-blue bedsheet made of paper. "And you even get to wear a gown." As I slide into the gown, Nurse Gables continues. "Nat's been living here full time for the past two months. She could use a little TLC. You ready to go in?"

I give a quick nod. "I won't hurt her, will I?"

Nurse Gables looks me over from head to toe. "How many bottles of sanitizer did you bring with you today?"

"Three. And two travel packs of wipes."

"You'll be fine," she smirks.

I slip my masks back over my nose and mouth and knock softly before I push open the door. The hinges groan as I step inside, adding to the bleak feeling of the dimly lit room. Bits of sunlight leak through the covered windows to dance along the walls, but it does nothing to cheer the colorless space. It's all white on white on pale green and smells very clean. A veritable germ death scene. Like Clorox and Lysol were hosting a party moments before I stepped inside.

The hinges creak again as the door closes behind me.

A child's voice, with a heavy Dracula accent, says, "I vaunt to suck your blood." A small form in the seat by the window starts to giggle.

It's the giggle that does it for me.

In such a sterile place where heartache rules the day and people exit to the next life, this giggle stands out and says, *I am child. Hear me roar.*

A small-framed girl sits in one of two seafoam-green hospital chairs turned toward the window. With feet pulled up onto the chair and arms wrapped around legs, her face rests against her knees as she stares at me. Her pale skin almost glows in the fading sunlight.

"What's with the vampire voice?" I ask.

"It's a bit I like to do with the new volunteers." She continues to stare. "You know, because I'm so pale and have to sit in the dark."

I nod, adjusting my eyes to the dim light of the room. Even though I'm sure her thermostat is strictly regulated, it feels colder in here than it did in the hallway. Cold and devoid of life. So different from the home I raised my boys in. At this age they were in their outer space stage with planets and stars hanging on their bedroom ceiling and walls. So different from the sterile room where this little girl lives.

I clear my throat and say, "Vell, eets very nice to meet chew." My mock vampire voice sounds a bit too forced, but she laughs anyway. Warmth seeps into me, erasing the pity. Her laugh brightens the dark room, and I'm changed from the inside out.

This room . . . this girl . . . they're magic.

Her face flips to mine, thick silvery-white hair falling forward to cover one eye. She wipes the colorless wisps away from her forehead, revealing a definite sparkle in the palest ice-blue irises I've ever seen. Barely pink lips pull into a smile, revealing oddly spaced teeth.

"No one's ever done a vampire voice back," she says. "Today your first day?"

"Yup." I sit in the chair across from hers. "And it really feels like a first day."

"I'm surprised. They usually don't let first-timers visit me." She raises one eyebrow and looks at me expectantly. "It can be hazardous to my health."

I nod. "I totally get that. I find new people hazardous to my health too."

She laughs, and the tension drains from me. Maybe this volunteer gig won't be so bad.

"Nice masks," she says.

"Nice robe," I say back.

She holds out one arm and brushes it with the opposite hand. "The color helps me blend in with my surroundings. Camouflage is the key to survival in here."

I look down at my bright-blue paper robe. "Well, it looks like I'm a goner for sure then."

She lifts one eyebrow. "Why did they let you in here? I'm in one of the restricted rooms. No germs allowed."

I empty my pockets onto the table. Three bottles of hand sanitizer, two small packages of antibacterial wipes, and a travel-sized bottle of Lysol spray. I raise both hands. "I'm a bit of a germaphobe."

She shakes her head. "And you volunteer at the hospital. That makes no sense."

"Well." I repack my pockets with my germ protection. "It's more of a face-your-fears thing for me."

"You're kind of weird."

"So I'm told." I nod.

"It's okay. I like weird." She extends one gloved hand. "I'm Natalie. Natalie Cook."

"Bethany Taylor." I shake her gloved hand with my own gloved hand. "Nice to meet you, Nat. Can I call you Nat?"

"Sure." As she pulls her arm back, she knocks a plastic cup off the windowsill and onto the ground. It flops and clatters its way across the room. She gives a dramatic sigh. "I hate it when I drop stuff. I'm not supposed to crawl on the floor to pick it up."

"Allow me," I say as I flip on the lamp in the corner.

Natalie sucks in air through her teeth and shields her eyes.

I grab the cup and quickly shut off the lamp. "I'm sorry."

"It's okay. The light. It hurts my eyes sometimes. Today's a bad day. Just one of the lucky side effects of Chediak-Higashi Syndrome. It's a special kind of albinism. Don't worry, no one has ever heard of it."

"Well, it just so happens I have heard of it." I take my seat again.

"You have?"

"Yes." I nod. "About ten seconds ago, this gorgeous alabaster beauty queen told me all about it."

She smiles, and the room warms in an instant. "It's a really rare disease. My mom was a carrier. She felt so bad about it, every time she looked at me, she couldn't handle the guilt. So, she left when I was four."

"I'm so sorry."

"S'okay." Nat shrugs. "I've been living with my Gran for the last seven years. Well, really Gran and the hospital have had shared custody. I spend half my time in here and half with her. Until a few months ago." Her voice drifts off, and she looks out the window. "Now I spend all my time here."

"So why the fancy accessories?" I motion to my masks and gloves. "This isn't for light protection."

"CHS causes problems with the immune system too. If I get an infection, I have to come here and live in a bubble while they pump me full of meds. Even still, germs seem to find a way in, and I've been on meds a lot over the last eleven years. I live here full time now, so I'm used to being in the bubble." She props her arms behind her head and leans back in her chair. "It's a pretty cushy life."

"Looks like it."

"Yeah. It's just . . ." Her gaze drifts to the window again.

"It's just, what?"

"I wish I could go somewhere. See something different." She sighs and turns her attention to me again. "This room is always the same."

"Where would you go?"

"Ummmm. The beach maybe. I've never seen the ocean."

"Well, I'll have to see what I can do about that. But for now, what would you like to do today?"

"You want to stay longer? Usually, the volunteers only stay five minutes to check in on me, and then they can't wait to leave."

"I'm here until you get sick of me."

Her smile lights up the room brighter than any lamp ever could. "In that case, how good are you at cards?"

For the next several hours we play Go Fish, War, Slap Jack, and Dominos. Natalie wins more than I do, but her joy in each win far outweighs any frustration at my loss. We're both laughing when a knock at the hallway window gets our attention.

Nurse Gables smiles at us from behind the glass and taps her watch. My time is up.

"Well, that's my cue. Is there anything else I can get you before I leave?"

"A sunset," she sighs, and looks at the covered glass. "My windows at Gran's house faced west, and I miss the sunsets more than anything. I haven't seen one in months."

"Months?"

She nods. "Yes. Months."

"Why can't you go over to the other side of the hospital and watch?"

She makes a circle around her body with one pointer finger. "I have to stay inside the bubble, remember?"

"There has to be . . ." A thought hits me and I hold up one finger. "I'll be right back." I'm out the door and rushing to the other side of the building, hoping I'm not too late. I glance out the huge glass windows along the west-side lobby. If I hurry, I'll make it just in time.

I reach the far-side lobby and stand close to the window as the sky lights up the world. With cell phone camera in hand, I start snapping pictures as fast as I can, from every vantage point possible. When I finish, I have twenty breathtaking sunset photos in my recent albums.

In less than five minutes, I'm back in Nat's room. I settle in front of her and pull out my sanitizing wipes.

"What is it? What did you do?"

"Just a minute." I wipe off my phone, sanitizing every square inch, and then open the photo album in full-screen mode. "What do you think?"

"Whoa." She reaches for my phone. "It was a good one tonight."

"Yeah." I lean in close and point out a spot on the screen. "Look at the gold shimmer. Gorgeous, right?"

She hugs the phone to her chest. "It's perfect. Thank you."

"Tell you what," I say. "Program your email into my phone, and I'll send you the pics. Then you can look at them on your tablet every night. So you won't miss sunsets as much."

"Deal." Her tech savvy fingers tap and slide and tap some more, until she hands my phone back to me.

I open a new email, attach her ten favorite sunset pics, and within seconds, the tablet on the bed dings. "There you go. You're all set."

Nat stands slowly and makes her way to the bed. She settles against the pillows, pulls her tablet onto her lap, and begins to flip through every photo I just sent.

"Can I get you anything else?" I ask.

"Nope." She tilts her head to smile up at me. "Thank you. Will I see you again?"

"Maybe I'll stop by tomorrow." I give her a wink before I slip out of the room and, for the first time since my boys were born, I smile as I walk down the halls of a hospital.

Being with Natalie reminds me of all the good times I had raising my boys, and happy memories play through my mind for the entire thirty-minute drive back to my house.

When I get home, I head straight outside, flip on the yard lights, and pull out my painting supplies. I don't even change into my grubby clothes before I get started. It takes less than ten minutes for me to get a white square painted in the grass.

Instead of keeping it simple like I had planned, I take my time and pull out my inner Rembrandt. I want it to be just right, so I go slowly, ever so carefully. When I finally step back, two, slightly uneven, pale-blue eyes stare up at me from the middle of the white square.

Nat.

The lonely girl in need of someone to take care of her. Maybe I could be that someone.

A smile catches me by surprise as an idea comes to mind. I turn on the outdoor lights, and start to take pictures of every one of my squares. Then I step back and take a wide shot of the whole painted garden. I shuffle through the pictures, loving each one more than the next.

They're perfect.

I shut off all the lights in the backyard and walk to the house in the moonlight. With each step, thoughts of Natalie and the challenges of her life play in my mind.

As I walk into the house and gently close the French doors, I think about all the years of my life when I wanted to see something different, and all the times I wanted to travel and couldn't. But even with all my wanting, I can't even imagine being stuck inside the same room, day in and day out, like Natalie.

So—if she can't go to the ocean, then the ocean will have to come to her.

FOURTEEN

MY MORNING RUN AND today's play practice rush by in a blur as I anticipate going back to the hospital. If my boys could see me now, they'd assume I'd been a victim of brain washing of some sort. They'd never believe their germaphobe of a mother was counting down the minutes until she could go spend time in a hospital room.

Amazing how one person can impact an entire life.

"Cut!" Kyle yells and walks up to the stage. "Bethany, what's going on? You've been a bit off all day."

I pull out my sweetest smile, and give him the truth, albeit a misleading truth. "Sorry. It's just, I have an appointment at the hospital this afternoon, and it has me a little distracted."

Kyle's manner softens immediately. "I'm so sorry to hear that. Nothing too serious, I hope."

"No. I'll be fine."

"Tell you what." Kyle checks his watch. "If we can get through this next scene perfectly, with you completely off book, we'll break early for the day."

"Done!" I throw my book aside and focus on making the scene shine.

Twenty minutes later, I'm in my car on the way to the hospital.

While I was at practice, Jake left another voice message on my phone, and I listen to it as I drive.

"Bethany. It's me. I can't believe you still haven't called me back. Who are you anymore? I feel like I don't even know you. This isn't like you. Call me."

"You're right, Jake." I say aloud in the empty car. "But then again, you never have taken the time to know me, and that was even before I started painting the grass." I shake my head, getting rid of my negative thoughts, and stop at a store for supplies. Hopefully it will have everything I need to transport Natalie to another place for the next few hours.

Natalie lights up when she sees me getting gowned up through the window of her room. It took us twenty minutes, and every available nurse, to decontaminate all my beach-for-a-day items so I can bring them inside. The hospital laundry staff even managed to sanitize the towels I bought on the way over. They're sealed in clear plastic bags, along with the few other items I'm balancing in my arms as Nurse Gables opens the door for me.

"Do you know what today is?" I ask, the minute I step into the room.

"What?" Nat sits up on her knees in bed, excitement shining in every feature of her face.

"It's beach day!" I toss a small beach ball at her and then laugh when she catches it. "First things first—no beach day is complete without—the ocean."

I hold up a Bluetooth speaker and plug it in. I'm no tech genius, but it only takes me a few minutes to open a video of crashing waves on Nat's tablet and link it to the speaker. I prop the "ocean-view" tablet up on the table in front of the window.

Two beach towels, one striped in yellow and blue, the other in orange and pink, add a bright spot on the white floor. I light a piña-colada-scented candle and set out the approved snacks: juice boxes, pineapple, mango and orange slices, and a variety of cheeses and crackers.

All that's missing is the sand.

"Shall we?" I hold out one hand to Nat and guide her over to our private beach. "Which towel would you like?"

"Pink and orange. I love bright colors."

We lay back on the towels, propping pillows behind our necks so we can watch the waves on the screen. The sweet smell of pineapple and coconut goes a long way to sell the illusion, and I hand Natalie a pair of neon-pink sunglasses to complete the set-up. She slides them on her nose, and the contrast of color against her pale skin brightens her happy face even more.

"I can't believe you did all this for me." She pops a bite of pineapple into her mouth and chews as she smiles.

"Totally worth it. I love the beach."

"So, what's your favorite beach you've ever been to?"

"Oh man. There are so many to choose from." I close my eyes and think for a minute while she sips on her juice box. "I guess one of the most interesting beaches I've been to is Whale's Tail beach, in Costa Rica. It's an incredible place. There's ocean on either side of the beach, and the waves move toward each other, creating a land bridge that leads to a rock island. When you walk along the sand bridge there's waves on either side, and on the rock island there are hundreds of tide pools to explore. It's such a different world."

"Why's it called Whale's Tail Beach?" she asks.

"Because it's shaped exactly like a whale's tail." I use one finger to draw the familiar shape in the air.

"I wish I could go there," Nat sighs and leans back on her towel.

"Well . . ." I lay back on my beach towel and motion for her to do the same. "If you close your eyes and listen, we'll go there together." She smiles and reaches over to hold my hand as I begin to set the scene.

"The waves are soft this time of day, a small push and pull of water brushing against the sand." I paint a picture with my words, transporting her to a place on the other side of the world. She clings to my hand.

"With each step you take, your feet sink a little deeper into the wet sand. And look, tiny sand crabs scramble sideways across the ground in front of us. We chase after them and then race each other to the rock island. Ocean water sprays all around us." I open a water bottle and splash a little in her face, and she laughs.

For the next hour, I do my best to help Nat feel the sand beneath her toes and the ocean breeze on her cheeks. We eat juicy pineapple and creamy brie cheese spread on toasted wheat crackers. We flip onto our stomachs, pretending to soak in the sun to work on our imaginary tans.

I almost forget I'm in a hospital.

And I hope she does too.

When the dinner hour rolls around, it's time for me to go. As I pack away all our beach day props, Natalie climbs back onto her bed.

"So where will we be tomorrow?"

"Where do you want to be tomorrow? Any other requests? Or should I surprise you?"

"A surprise! I never get to be surprised."

"Well then, a surprise it is."

I finish gathering up my supplies but let her keep the Bluetooth speaker, and the sound of waves spills into the hallway as I open the door to leave. I blow her a kiss through the window as the door shuts behind me, and this time, it's her smile that lights up my world.

As surprising as it is, I think I'm falling in love with this particular volunteering gig.

Once at my car, my stomach rumbles. Fruit and cheese do not a meal make. I'm starving, but there's no one at home waiting to eat with me. No one to cook for. No family dinner tonight.

It's just me. I'm alone.

As I drive home, I sink into feeling sorry for myself, until I remember where I've been.

Natalie.

She has never once given off a feeling of self-pity. If she can live life alone in a tiny hospital room, I can certainly make do on my own.

My hunger makes the drive home feel twice as long, and the minute I step into my house, I head straight to the take-out menu drawer in the kitchen. I fumble through the stack of pamphlets and browse the variety of food choices.

Lukewarm take-out doesn't sound good.

What I really want is a hibachi platter from my favorite Japanese restaurant, but they don't do take out. I'd usually go out with Jake, but that's not a possibility. And with the boys gone and Lettie busy tonight . . . maybe I'll just have to be my own date.

I glance across the room to my office door. Such a simple and fun idea adds a bounce to my step as I cross the room. I snatch my red-leather notebook off the corner of the desk and open it wide.

With my purple pen, I write . . .

To paint the grass today, I will . . .
Be happy being alone.
Go out to dinner by myself.

With smartphone in hand, it takes only seconds to look up the phone number. The Tanuki Grill is just a fifteen-minute drive away, and I crave their food at least once a week. My phone rings only twice after I press the call button, and a perky girl with a heavy accent answers.

"Tanuki Grill, how can I help you?"

"I'd like to make a reservation, please. For today at five o'clock."

"Yes, ma'am, I can help you with that. Reservation at five. For how many?"

"One," I say with a smile. "Just one."

I take a little extra time getting ready for my date. My date with myself. The idea of sitting at a table alone makes me second guess myself, and I almost call to cancel. Instead, I add a smokey eye, some winged eyeliner, and put on my favorite outfit. Black and white checkered pants and a white blouse with flared sleeves. In less than twenty minutes, I'm ready to go out on the town. I grab my purse, my notebook, and my phone and head for the door.

"Welcome to The Tanuki Grill." The hostess and the sharp scent of ginger greet me as I enter. Soft lights illuminate the natural colors of the restaurant. Tall pots of live bamboo plants separate tables, and a full wall aquarium fills the space behind the bar.

"Do you have a reservation?" the hostess asks.

"Yes."

"For how many?"

"One. It's just me."

She sends me a tight smile and says, "This way please. Follow me."

I wind my way between closely spaced tables and around chairs full of smiling diners. Like a little duckling, I follow the tiny hostess all the way around the back of the restaurant to a table nearest the sushi counter.

"Will this be okay for you?"

"Yes," I smile as I sit. "Thank you."

She hands me a menu and begins to clear away the silverware and napkins set across from me. Twice she drops the fork, and it clatters around the table as she apologizes loudly. My cheeks flush red, and I feel all eyes on me. The faces around the room scream, *Look at the poor lonely woman eating all by herself.* I close my eyes and sigh aloud when the server finally leaves.

I quickly clean my table and the outside of my menu with the wipes from my purse, and then sanitize my hands. When I turn my attention to the menu, it only takes seconds for me to choose. The warming smell of grilled meats helps me in my decision. I order hibachi filet minion with noodles and vegetables, and a salad with ginger dressing on the side.

While I wait for my food to arrive, I watch the sushi chef create his art and allow my ears to wander. The four men sitting directly behind me conduct business over shared sushi rolls. The girls to my right are sisters enjoying a night away from kids. And just in front of me and to my left, a couple celebrates their six-month anniversary. They lean toward each other, holding hands, and kiss across the table.

Wow. Six whole months.

I glance at the table in the corner. The secluded one, reserved for couples celebrating special occasions. For my birthday last year, Jake brought me here, and I remember being more excited about my salad than about my date. He'd been on the phone the entire evening for work, worried a bid would fall through.

At the time I thought, *What happened to us?* And as I sit here alone at my table almost a year later, I'm still wondering the same thing.

My soup and salad get to my table just as the couple orders dessert and a bottle of champagne. I force myself to focus on my meal. To enjoy the night. And revel in this new experience of eating alone.

I smile at the empty seat across from me as I take my first bite. It's quiet and peaceful, and the food is delicious. There's no pressure to come up with topics of discussion, no worry about conversation lulls. There's only great tasting food and my thoughts.

And the couple in my line of sight now feeding each other chocolate-covered strawberries.

With a shake of my head, I open my notebook and read through the goals I've made over the last few days. Remember what you love. Check. Try something new. Check. Show kindness to a stranger. Check. Be happy being alone. I place one final check mark by the latest entry and tap my pen against my lip as I consider what to challenge myself with next.

The server comes and clears away my salad bowl and places a large oblong plate of food in front of me. She hands me a pair of chopsticks and nudges my arm.

Pointing to the couple in front of me, she says, "Aren't they the cutest?"

"They sure are." I nod and pull my lips into a smile.

She offers a long, drawn-out sigh. "Isn't love amazing? It makes everything better. Books, movies, life in general, don't you think?"

"You bet." I nod, hoping my Chatty-Kathy of a server will leave me in peace to enjoy my dinner.

Then she places a hand on my shoulder. "Don't worry, sweetie. You won't *always* have to eat alone. You'll find someone. It's not too late for you."

My mouth drops open at her rude assumption. Before I can correct her, she saunters off to top off the love birds' long-stemmed glasses with sparkling wine. I watch as she crouches next to their table and presses her hand to her heart. The couple smiles and kisses again and says something I can't hear. The waitress leans in and whispers something to both of them, and without warning, all three faces turn to look at me. In unison, their heads tilt to the side, and they each give a small nod in my direction.

They're feeling sorry for me.

The realization hits me all at once, and my smile opens into a laugh. At the harsh sound, the noise level in the restaurant drops to nothing, and I lift my head, biting my lips to keep them quiet. A strange joy fills my chest at the thought of some pathetic baby love-birds feeling bad for me.

I've been happier these past two weeks than I've been in a long time. Sitting here alone in this restaurant, I love the company I'm keeping. Getting to know myself is my next great adventure.

But I don't expect them to understand.

With a happy-with-life smile firmly in place, I lift my glass in a silent toast to them. They return the gesture with sympathy in their eyes and mouths pulled into compassionate frowns.

I laugh again and enjoy the looks of confusion at their table.

The banging of drums from the hibachi-grill side of the restaurant distracts them, and I turn my focus to my open notebook. With my purple pen, I write my next goal.

To paint the grass today, I will...
Celebrate life without romance.

I glance back at the couple, now gazing longingly at each other. It doesn't take any time for me to come up with an idea as I put pen to paper.

Read a book without a love story in it.

I underline "without" three times.

"I don't need a man to be happy," I remind myself.

The kissy-kissy couple finally finishes their meal and leaves the restaurant. They're probably off to the nearest hotel room to reassure each other with fake orgasms.

I eat the rest of my meal in a state of absolute happiness, enjoying each bit of salty steak and perfectly seasoned veggies. I lick my lips between bites and use the chopsticks to savor every last noodle on my plate.

Food has never been so fulfilling.

Without the distraction of socialization, I'm able to enjoy it even more.

When nothing but meat drippings and discarded onions are left on my plate, I pay for my food and make my way to the car. Cool evening air slips around me in the twilight, and I veer away from the parking lot to follow the winding cement path toward my favorite bookshop. If I hurry, I'll make it in just before they close.

The cheerful tinkle of a bell sounds as I open the door to *Book Therapy*. Jodi, the shop owner, has scented candles burning, and a pot of coffee percolating on the back table. The scent of cloves and cinnamon and freshly brewed cappuccino blends seamlessly in the air.

"Hey, Bethany," Jodi says. "Can I help ya find something?"

The steady clack of a laptop keyboard keeps time in the quiet room. The only other customer at this time of night sits on a chair in front of the fireplace, earbuds in her ears and eyes focused on her computer screen.

"Good to see you, Jodi. I'm just going to go look around a bit, but I promise I'll be done before closing."

"No worries. Take your time."

I smile at the woman working by the fire and begin to browse the shelves. My first circle of the store yields no love-free books, but when I come back around, I find just what I've been looking for on the Employee's Favorites table. I lift the small book free from its stand and smooth my hand across its cover. The beautifully exotic face of a woman with intelligent eyes stares up at me. I lean in and smell the dusty scent of fresh pages filled with words.

It's exactly the kind of book I need in my life right now. I read the title and excitement rises up.

The Emperor's Soul. By Brandon Sanderson.

"It's perfect!"

A swift purchase and a quick drive home, and I settle into bed to read a story about life and lies and not love.

FIFTEEN

MORNING BEGINS WITH THE confused and frantic slapping of my
alarm. After the horrid screeching is silenced, I flop back on my pillow
to squeeze a few more seconds of sleep out of the wee-small hours. Snuggling
into my covers, I close my eyes.

For another hour.

"What!" I leap out of bed and run to the bathroom. "No, no, no, no . . ."
My second waking of the day brings panic and a stubbed toe as I rush into the
challenge of getting ready and still being on time to rehearsal. I burn as many
calories during my aerobic shower as I usually do on my morning jog, and then
I apply makeup with one hand as I dry my hair with the other.

"And this is why reading is dangerous," I say to my reflection. I don't
remember what time I finally fell asleep, and even when I did it wasn't by
choice. My eyes just closed mid-sentence. The non-love book I bought proved
to be difficult to put down, and it also proved my point. In the end, the
characters found fulfillment and purpose, and love didn't magically make it
happen for them.

Such a well-told story and so worth reading. The powerful, female protagonist breaks free from the society who judges her, uses her, and tries to kill her. She's currently outsmarting them all.

"Paint the grass, baby!" I yell to the ceiling. Excitement sizzles through me as I fly out the door, grabbing my notebook from off my dresser as I leave. During rehearsal, I'll map out my new goal for the day. My fingers are itching to add another square to my painted garden.

I'm the last one to practice, and I'm pulling my hair back as the music for the opening scene begins, but our run through is almost flawless. We continue on to the working scene for the day, and I'm standing onstage, kissing Cole when the thought hits me. Jake might actually come to this play. He'll be in the audience. He'll see me onstage kissing another man. I start laughing mid-kiss.

"CUT!" The director yells from the front row, both hands on hips.

Cole shakes his head at me. "I've had several women sigh while I was kissing them, and one even cried, but no one has ever laughed before."

"Well, there's a first time for everything." I laugh again, and then turn to our director. "Sorry, Kyle. It won't happen again."

"If I was up there, it wouldn't have happened at all," Piper snips.

"It's fine. There's bound to be a few missteps," Kyle says.

"Are you kidding me? I could have done better than that, even with a broken leg." Piper wobbles toward us, dragging her injured leg behind her. Her cast slams into the stage, clunking against the solid wood. "Help me up there. I'll show you how it's done."

Nervous giggles shake through the chorus, but one look from Piper silences them all.

"Fix it," Cole whispers to me. "Fix it now."

Compassion blooms inside me. Piper has lost something dear to her. This shot at acting. The chance to perform, to do what she loves. It's only available to me because of her injury. Her angry voice masks her pain.

A pain I know well.

"I'm sorry." I crouch down and look her in the eye. "I won't let you down again. I promise. I know how it feels to lose something you love."

Piper stops her struggle and steps away from the stage. "You better not let any of us down," she whispers, then clumps her way back to her seat.

"Okay. Let's reset the scene and take it from the top." Kyle directs the stage crew, while we reposition to our starting places.

I take a second to close my eyes and breathe in air heated by the stage lights. The flurry of the cast around me fuels my determination, and I tune into Kathrine's grit and grace. All thoughts of Jake slide away. I'm no longer Bethany Taylor. I am Lilli Vanessi, famous actress.

"All right, everybody. Ready?" The director calls. "And action!"

With every atom of my body possessed by my character, I take to the stage. I'm fierce in my dedication to get it just right, and this time when Cole's lips meet mine, there's not a chance anyone will be laughing.

When we finish the scene, Kyle jumps out of his chair. "Wonderful! Absolutely wonderful! That's more like it."

Piper Gibson, wounded actress extraordinaire, wobbles to a standing position. While balancing on one foot and one crutch, she points directly at me. "You didn't totally suck. It was almost as good as I could have done it." She holds up one finger. "Almost."

A happy heat floods my chest. Piper complimented me—sort of. Well, as much as she can, anyway. I never thought she'd ever have anything good to say about me, but there she is standing in front of her seat, smiling. A smile and a sort-of compliment in one day, I don't know if I'll ever recover from the shock.

"Okay, okay," Kyle says. "Now we have to get the rest of the scenes up to the same level. And we only have nine days, people. Nine days until opening night." He rubs both hands through his hair until the black strands stand up on end, haphazardly pointing in all directions. "Actors, take a ten-minute break while we set up for the next scene."

As we leave the stage, Cole leans in close to me. "Wow. I've never heard Piper say something so nice before."

"That was nice?" We walk to the back row, and I settle into my normal seat. Cole heads to the vending machines to get us a snack, and I open my notebook. I read through all my recent entries before he gets back and sits next to me.

"So ... what's with the laugh this morning?" Cole asks. "Did my imaginary mustache tickle your lip?"

I close the book and take the diet cola and bag of white-cheddar popcorn he hands me. "Honestly." I smile as I pop open the soda. "I was imagining my husband watching us kiss onstage, and it just kind of slipped out." I shrug.

"Come on, really?" Cole crunches on a chip. "He's never seen you kiss someone onstage before? No way. You're way too good at it for this to be your first time."

I raise one eyebrow at him, and he smiles back innocently.

"What? Tell me I'm wrong."

"You're not wrong." My gaze finds the stage, and so many memories play out before me. "Jake watched me onstage plenty of times before we got together, but he hasn't seen me act for twenty years. I sort of stopped after we got married."

"What? That's crazy." He shakes his head. "Anyone with eyes can see how much you love it."

"I do love it."

"Actors back to the stage," Kyle yells into his bullhorn. "All actors back to the stage."

Cole stands and grabs my hand to pull me to my feet. "You know, nothing should keep you away from something you love. Especially not *someone* you love."

A lump instantly forms in my throat. To hide my sudden tears, I start to gather up our garbage from off the chairs. "I've got it this." I sniff. "You head on up."

Cole squeezes one of my shoulders. "You really are amazing, Bethany Taylor."

I balance two empty soda cans in one hand and crush two snack bags with the other. The trash bin sits at the top of the aisle, and I hurry up the sloped floor to drop the remains of our snack inside. The gaping hole swallows up the garbage and instantly makes me think of my marriage.

I stare and stare and stare at the hollow, black opening of the theater trash bin.

Please tell me I haven't thrown away twenty years of my life.

Nothing should keep you away from something you love. Especially not someone you love. Cole's words hit me like a physical force.

"Bethany to the stage, please."

My director calls my name. I shake away my marriage worries and transform myself to Katherine before I reach the stage. Cole is right about one thing. I'm a damn good actress, and this afternoon, I plan to prove it.

I'M STARVING WHEN I finish my shift at the hospital. Natalie and I traveled to a small-town county fair and rodeo in our imaginary explorations for the day. We rode IV-pole stick horses and barrel raced around buckets of laundry soap in matching cowboy hats all while staying in the safety of her hospital room.

The best part of the night came when she asked, "Where will we be tomorrow?" just like she had the day before. Giving Natalie something to look forward to each day has become my favorite challenge.

I ignore the missed calls on my cell phone as I drive home and walk straight to the kitchen when I step through the door. I chop and boil and strain and mix and always, always sprinkle with cheese. In less than twenty minutes, I have a beautiful plate of pasta to enjoy. I take it out to the back patio and sit facing my painted squares.

As I eat, I plan out the next square I'll paint. A small laugh lifts inside me, and I sigh at the simple pleasure of being here. Home, healthy, and happy—doing exactly what I want to do.

The sun begins to set as I finish up the last bit of cheesy, rich pasta, and use my final crust of bread to mop up the citrus cream sauce. It's so good, I actually consider licking my plate. Since no one's watching, I give into the urge and lift my plate to my lips. With one continuous motion, I run my tongue along the smooth porcelain. Sauce drips down my chin, and my moment of rebellious abandon will always be marked by a sharp lemon flavor.

I slide my plate back onto the patio table and wipe my face with a napkin. With a sigh, I lean back against the cushioned chair and watch the last fingers of sunlight play with the drooping willow branches. The sky blazes orange, clouds kissed with pink float along a world brightened by a golden haze. It's the kind of scene painters wish for. The kind in which new hopes are born, and a lost woman finds herself again.

It's also the kind of scene where pasta sauce dries on plates. I wait until the lasts bits of sunlight snuggle down behind the mountain and then head inside to clean up. As I walk through the kitchen, I turn on my speaker phone and press play on the awaiting voicemails.

"Hey, it's me." Jake's soft voice surprises me. "I thought if I called you again, maybe you'd pick up. How many messages do I have to leave? Come on, B. Talk to me. You can't give up on us after twenty years. I'm coming home in a few days. Call me." There's a pause, and then a soft, "Please, B. We need to talk."

The message stops and the room falls silent. It stays silent as I load the dishwasher and wipe up the kitchen. In the half hour it takes me to clean, I have a full-on Lincoln-Douglas style debate in my mind.

I debate both the pro and con side of the issue, for and against. When I finish, I don't have any answers. But I conclude as a wife of twenty years, ignoring my husband won't make him go away.

And even though he hurt me, and he deserves to be ignored, I still miss talking to him in the evenings. I guess it's bound to happen when you share a life with someone for so long. Even though he's an asshat, I still miss the sound of his voice and the way he says my name.

My phone gets heavier the longer I stare at it, and when I finally settle into the comfiest corner of the sofa in the living room, it's like a weight in my hand. I turn on the lamp, cover myself with a blanket, pull a pillow into my lap, and heft the phone to my ear.

"Hello," he answers after one ring. "You there? I'm glad you called."

"Hey, Jake," I whisper into the phone.

"What's wrong? You sound sad."

"I'm not sad. In fact, I had a great day. I've been crazy busy since you left. And I'm happy. I'm really happy. It's just . . . talking to you makes me sad."

"Ouch, Beth. That hurts."

"You know what else hurts? Picturing you with Alex."

"I'm not with Alex. I've never been with Alex."

"Except for running, in class, at breakfast, and who knows how many other times."

"B, come on." He sighs into the phone. "Can we please talk about something else?"

"Like what?"

"Like you. How are you?"

"I told you. I'm fine. Better than fine. I'm doing great."

"What have you been up to?"

"I've been trying new things and remembering what I love."

"Am I on that list?"

163

I groan into the phone. "Jake, seriously. This isn't about you."

"Okay, fine. Sorry."

There's a lull in the conversation, and I don't try to fill it. I sit quietly, drawing shapes in the nap of the fuzzy blanket on my legs. Heart. Star. Quarter moon. Clover. Diamond. A full bowl of Lucky Charms now covers my blanket.

"I'll be home in a few days." Jake interrupts my doodled masterpiece.

"Yeah, I know. It's on my calendar."

"Can I take you out to dinner when I get back? Somewhere special?"

"That depends," I say.

"On what?"

"On how many times you've texted Alex this trip."

"Bethany, seriously?"

"Yes, seriously. How many times has she called you or sent you pics? How many times have you missed her with no consideration for your wife?"

His sigh is long, drawn out, like he's avoiding this conversation or hiding something or both. "I'm trying, Beth."

"Trying to what?"

"To work things out."

"With who? Work things out with Alex or with me? Or maybe you want both of us. Are you working on how to stay married to me while keeping your special relationship with her? Let me save you the trouble of asking. It's not happening."

"Beth, I need you to understand," he begs. "I am trying. But I can't just break off a five-year friendship without a reason."

"I'm not a good enough reason?" My voice breaks, and tears come to my eyes. I have to end this conversation.

"Please. Let me take you out when I get home. Let's talk every night like we used to. Don't let this come between us."

"She's already between us." I throw the blanket off my legs and stand, gearing up my courage. "And you're the one who put her there. So, feel free to call me back when you're ready to let the other woman in your life go. Bye, Jake."

I tap the red end button and drop my phone on the couch. It hits the leather with a satisfying slap and immediately starts to buzz.

It's Jake.

Instead of answering, I put a pillow over the phone.

"I meant it when I said goodbye," I say to the pillow. "I'm done talking tonight."

Leaving the phone on the couch, I open the French doors off the living room and walk outside. Cool night air and shimmering moonlight help me shake off the frustrating conversation. At the edge of the patio, I kick off my shoes and step out onto the soft lawn. Tiny pricks of grass send energy spiking through me, and I start to run.

I'm running and laughing like a mad woman in the moonlight.

Cold grass under my feet brings to mind the memory of laying sod with my dad in the backyard of my childhood home. I remember him telling me I needed to spin on the grass to get it to stick to the ground. Such a silly little thing, and completely untrue, but that doesn't stop me as I begin to turn in a circle.

I spin across my painted grass. Over a patch of neon green. Pass through a stage, a golden star, and the silver glitter of a microphone. I keep spinning overtop a purple heart and Nat's perfect blue eyes, all with my arms extended like a witch worshiping the moon on Midsummer's Eve.

When I reach the end of the grass, I hold one hand against the sturdy shed until the world stops turning. With unsteady fingers, I lift the latch and pull out the tools of my new hobby.

It's time to paint the grass.

I think back to the night before, going out to eat by myself, then reading late into the night to finish my book. The perfect two squares come to mind, and I grab a can of gold paint.

Ten minutes later, I have a golden plate with a fork and knife and spoon, each on their proper side. The perfect place setting for one.

I flip the square template to the side and begin to spray out a fine mist of midnight.

In less than fifteen minutes I have a dried base of dreamy blue, and I begin to freehand a simple design over top. When I finish, a single diagonal line of white Zs stripes the blue. The universal symbol for drifting off to sleep reminds me of my late-night, non-love-story read-a-thon.

It's perfect.

The metallic scent of spray paint lingers in the air as I lock the supplies back in the shed and head inside for the night. When I reach the patio, I scoop up my shoes and continue into the house barefoot.

As I brush my teeth and wash my face, I think over the day. Play practice. Volunteering at the hospital. A conversation with Jake, which started off bad and ended worse. Spinning on the grass over my garden of painted squares. All in all, not a bad day.

My life isn't perfect by any standard. But I'm through living it for someone else.

I will always be here for my boys. I'm happy to help someone else in need. And I'm open to serving my community and the people around me in any way I can.

But I'm done letting others tell me what to do and how to be. I'm done with people who make me feel small so they can be large and in control. And I'm done with the guilt that comes with making my needs a priority.

Finally.

My life is mine.

And that's exactly what it needs to be.

SIXTEEN

FRIDAY MORNING THE PING of my phone wakes me before my alarm. It's a text from Lettie.

> **Lettie:** My he'd-like-to-think-he's-my-better-half is taking the kids tomorrow night. So, you and I are headed to the Spa Royale. Don't say no. You're the only person I don't feel awkward getting naked around, which includes Eric, the aforementioned wishes-he-was-my-better-half. See you tomorrow.

There is absolutely nothing better to wake up to than the kind of words only a best friend can write. I send a quick text back.

> **Me:** It's a date! Can't wait. See you Saturday night.

Once I'm up and moving, I put on my brightest neon orange sports bra, slide into my favorite gray shorts, and head out for a run.

I hit the pavement at a steady pace, enjoying the morning breeze against my midsection. It's such an incredibly freeing feeling, and I weave my way through the streets with a smile on my face. Left at the first intersection and a right at the next with my favorite music playing through my headphones all the while. My feet keep time to the music, and I don't realize what direction I'm headed until it's too late.

I'm near *her* house.

Involuntarily, I turn my head and examine Alex's newly-painted fence. Thanks to the slope of the yard, I have a clear view of her back porch, where she's currently standing with her teeny-tiny-nightie-clad body wrapped around a bare-chested man. He slides his hands down her backside and under her satin nightgown until I see way more of Alex than I ever wanted to. He cups nearly-bare skin with both hands and kisses her, very thoroughly.

Maybe he'll suck the breath right out of her.

The kissing progresses quickly, and thankfully they dip out of sight as I jog by.

But I have a boost of curious energy for the rest of my run. Seeing her with another man doesn't put my frustrations to rest. Quite the opposite. I wouldn't be surprised if she had several men on speed dial. One guy has never been enough for her. She must collect them like some women collect decorative spoons.

After another mile, my curiosity forces me to turn back. Though I know I shouldn't, I take the long way home. I tell myself it's not so I can run past Alex's house again, but I know myself well enough to recognize when I'm being lied to.

When I get to her street, I stop next to the neighboring house to stretch my hamstrings. Muscle health is very important. And besides, stretching isn't spying. As I bend toward the ground, reaching for the toe of my right leg, I hear her talking on the phone from her side yard.

Her front door opens, startling me, and I almost fall over.

"Careful there." A man rushes down Alex's front steps and reaches out to steady me. His hand touches my elbow, and I see one thing very clearly. The mystery man's wedding ring glinting in the morning sunlight.

He's married.

Alex is not.

I give an awkward laugh and look at the concrete at my feet. "Uh. Thanks."

"You bet. Enjoy your run. And watch out for those tricky moving sidewalks." He winks at me then gets into his fancy Jaguar and drives away.

Alex continues to talk on the phone, and her voice carries over the fence as she paces in her backyard. "I can't wait to see you. I get lonely when you're gone."

Seriously. How many guys does this woman need to have on her string? She should get a revolving door. And nametags. Maybe it's a hobby for her. Something to show to relatives when they stop by. Her man collection. Maybe she mounts their pictures as trophies on her wall.

"This is so stupid." I stretch my other leg, determined to put all the Alex drama aside for the rest of the day.

"So when exactly will you be home, Jake?" she says.

My insides shrivel up and fall to my toes. In my haste to get away from this unwanted reality, I start to run and trip over my own feet, leaving a nice piece of skin on the sidewalk.

"This can't be real," I whisper as I roll onto my back, breathing through the pain.

"Sorry I didn't answer your text yet. I was busy this morning," Alex says.

I snort. "Busy." Then cover my mouth with both hands.

"Yes. Of course. I miss you too. Will you stop by when you get to town?" Alex asks my husband. "Perfect, and if you call me on your drive we can shoot for a new record. We can beat three hours. Right?"

I no longer feel the sun's warmth or the wind against my skin. I don't feel anything at all. Except for the undying need to scream. Spikes of betrayal grow on the underside of my ribcage, and my heart bleeds with each beat.

Can a heart break again so soon after it's mended?

He's such a fraggard, and he doesn't even understand what an idiot he's being. Stupid, stupid man. As I listen to her giggle into the phone, I imagine him being struck by lightning while rabid beasts pull limbs from his body.

With one swipe of my hand, I clear the blood off my knee and jump to my feet. I can't run home fast enough. Once inside, I discard my clothes and let the hot water of the shower wash away my worries.

I've wasted enough tears on Jake.

I refuse to cry.

SOMEHOW, I MANAGE TO get through play practice without shedding a single tear. When images of Jake, or Alex, or intimate lunches comes to my mind, I work even harder. I'm a master at avoiding my feelings through extreme focus.

No one even notices I'm a little off today. I guess that's why they call it acting.

"See you tomorrow, Bethany," Cole says as we walk out to the parking lot together.

"See you tomorrow." I nudge his shoulder. "It's Friday night. Go out and do something fun."

He laughs. "Right back at ya. Go do something that makes you happy."

"Already planning on it." I wave goodbye as I leave, very aware of how strange it is that going to volunteer at a hospital is something that makes me happy.

The afternoon sun's warmth sets the inside of my car to broil, and I'm practically crispy-fried by the time I reach the hospital parking lot. I call the front desk workers by their first names as I enter, completely comfortable as I walk through the hospital hallways.

When I finish wiping down and masking up, I open the door to Natalie's room. Her smile makes the problems in my life fade. If someone with the load of trials she's had to bear can have a smile like that, then so can I.

"Today," I say as I pull out a special orange notebook, "we will be going somewhere even more fantastic than yesterday."

"Where?" Natalie asks, eyes wide with wonder.

I hold up a green pen. "We are traveling into your imagination."

"What?" Nat's smile falls into a frown. "That doesn't sound fun."

"We're going to write a story together. Whatever you can dream up."

"Anything I want?"

"Anything you want."

She smiles and leans back against the pillows at the head of the bed.

I settle into the chair next to her and allow myself to get caught up in Natalie's world. For the next two hours, I'm a happy traveler inside her head. We live in her fantasy world for the afternoon. Traveling to a place where dreams turn into mountains and children fly away from troubles. Complete with an albino princess, a giant turtle, a mischievous mouse wizard, and a shy dragon.

"And the princess and the mouse wizard save the dragon with the power of a dandelion wish. The end." Natalie says, leaning toward me as I write the final two words and hold them up for her approval.

"I love it!" I close the notebook and place it on the table next to her bed as I stand. "I'll read it to you the next time I visit."

"Where will we be tomorrow?" It's her standard question. She asks it every day now.

I laugh at the excitement on her face. If I never do another good deed for the rest of eternity, my life will still have been worthwhile because of the joyful gleam in Nat's eyes.

"How would you like to be on a ship?" I suggest. "I bet you'd love traveling on the water. I'll be the cruise entertainment. I'll sing your favorite song."

"You can sing? How come I've never heard you?" Natalie's smile turns into a yawn and lets me know it's time to go.

"I'll sing for you tomorrow. Sleep well tonight, my little wizard mouse."

"How come I'm not the princess?"

"Because you're magic."

"I wish. I feel so tired tonight, and it's not even dinnertime yet. Why am I so tired?"

"Just listen to your body." I touch her hair as I stand. "If you need to rest, then rest."

"Goodbye, Princess," Nat calls as I open the door.

"So now I'm the princess?"

"Well, someone has to be."

I'm laughing as I leave her room. "See you tomorrow, little mouse."

While I'm waiting for the elevator, the woman next to me holds a phone to her ear. "Of course I miss you," she says. "When are you coming home?"

And suddenly, I remember Jake's call to Alex this morning.

The woman steps inside the elevator and holds the door open for me.

"No thanks." I give her a tight smile. "I'll take the stairs."

SATURDAY MORNING STARTS WITH a short run and a long lecture from Mrs. Platt about paint and grass and HOA inspections. I have to skip my shower so I'll have time to stop at the store to grab a few large plastic totes and two toy microphones for today's adventure with Natalie. But even with my best efforts to hurry, I'm still late to the theater. And after a rough practice, Kyle stops us early and calls for an emergency Sunday morning session the following day.

Realizing I will no longer have my restful Sunday, I take a breath and determine to enjoy my hospital visit with Natalie all the more. We row through the waves of an imaginary ocean in our plastic bin boats, pretending to be tossed among the swells. I take the time to teach her the words to *Fight Song* by Rachel Platten, then hand her a toy microphone. We stand in our small boats, microphones pressed to our lips, and we sing. It takes us three tries to sing it through with no mistakes, and when we do, she announces it's her new favorite song. The joy shining from her face makes me feel like I've just won a Grammy.

We say our goodbyes, and even though I'm not scheduled to volunteer on Saturdays, I promise to come visit her after play practice the next day.

I rush out of the hospital, on my way to meet up with Lettie. Hallelujah for soft music and scented oils. It's time for spa night. I need a massage, but I need to see Lettie even more. The scene at Alex's house yesterday has been weighing on me, and I need to lighten my load. Thank goodness best friends are like wheelbarrows, always there to help carry any troubles that are too heavy for us to manage on our own.

Thirty minutes later, we're on our way to the day spa in Lettie's car. As we drive, I spare no details about what I saw and heard during yesterday's run. Lettie makes all the right shocked sounds at all the right moments.

"You're sure he was married?" she asks.

"Oh yeah." I hold up my left hand and wiggle my finger. "He wore a wedding ring."

"And then Jake called her."

"He did."

"And you just jogged away from her house instead of taking an axe to her front door?"

I shrug. "My axe was in my other pair of running shorts, so I left."

"Solid self-control there, Beth. Seriously like ninja-level self-control."

"I earned my black belt today."

She laughs. "Yes . . . yes you did. You really do need this massage, don't you?"

I sigh and close my eyes. "You have no idea."

Twenty minutes later, I'm lying naked with a sheet covering my lower half as Sara, my favorite masseuse, concentrates on loosening my neck muscles.

The lullaby of tin flutes soothes my nerves, and the trickle of the water feature washes away all my frustrations. Lettie was right. This is exactly what I need. Relaxation. I breathe in air laced with lavender and eucalyptus while breathing out thoughts of husbands and homicide.

For two full hours, I clear my mind, not thinking about anything. And it's the most blissful feeling in all the world.

I TOSS AND TURN most of the night.

My emotions tangle with the events of the past few days, and I can't turn my mind off. The channels in my brain flip so quickly, the images blend together. Jake. Alex. Cole. Piper. Nurse Gables. Play practice. Running. The hospital.

And there my mind stays. In the hospital, with Natalie.

Each time I see that sweet mouse of a girl, I discover another attribute to add to the list of reasons why I love her. Even though I've only known her for a little over a week, I can't imagine not having Nat in my life. Time spent at the hospital rates on the highest level of my happiness scale.

A permanent smile takes up residence on her face no matter what we do. We travel to imaginary destinations each day, read books, play cards, and sing songs. She teaches me to live every minute like it's my last, and I'm convinced her goodness could light the entire world for a month straight.

But when I think about Jake coming home, the light in my world dims. I'm not sure what will happen. The idea of finally finding my life after forty-one years on this earth, only to give it up again, keeps me awake the remainder of the night.

I sleep walk through rehearsal the next day, and for the first time since going off book, I have to ask for help with a line. Before I head to the hospital, I chug a Diet Coke, but it doesn't help. Halfway through our imaginary trip to the African Safari, I fall asleep in our green-chair Jeep.

Poke. Poke. Poke.

Something taps me in the forehead.

"Bethany," Nat whispers. When she giggles, I blink my eyes open.

I stretch both arms and yawn. "Did I really fall asleep?"

"Yeah." She nods. "And it's not even close to dinner time."

"Well, some volunteer I turned out to be."

"Are you kidding? You're the best one I've ever had."

My heart expands like a rubber band, stretching wider and wider, completely enveloping the perfect little imp in front of me. "Thank you." I reach over and gently squeeze her hand. "You're my favorite too." I yawn again as I stand. "But, unless I want to fall asleep on the way home, I better leave now."

"Will you come back tomorrow?"

I nod. "And every day after that."

"I can't wait to see where we'll be tomorrow." She climbs up on her bed, and waves goodbye as I walk out the door.

On the way to the car, my phone buzzes in my pocket. It's a text. From Jake. The more times I read it, the slower my feet move.

> *Jake:* Hey, B. Great news. I get to see you tomorrow. I'm hoping you can get past all the unnecessary hurt feelings so we can celebrate seeing each other after two weeks apart. I've missed you.

But not a lot. I notice he doesn't take the time to type *a lot* to me. To his wife.

Every spectrum of human emotion washes over me, and when I finish reading his text for the tenth time, I'm entirely awake. All desire to hurry home has evaporated into the cool fall air. I lift my phone to my ear—and call Lettie.

Half an hour later, Lettie and I sit in our favorite Italian restaurant eating pasta stuffed with an obscene amount of cheese. Breadsticks appear at our table as if by magic, and I'm eyeing a sinfully rich-looking, chocolate dessert.

The smell of oregano and parmesan drifts around us as Lettie tells a funny story about her most embarrassing moment as a mom. I can't stop smiling. And with the way this day began, that's a miracle in itself. A true miracle, fit for a Bible story.

"Thank you," I say after we order dessert.

"For what?"

"For being such a great friend. For sitting here at dinner with me so I don't have to think about Jake coming home tomorrow."

"Well. You'd do the same for me." She dips a breadstick in red sauce and takes an enormous bite. "Now, tell me." She stops for a minute to chew. "How's the Finding-Bethany list going? Any more squares get painted since I was there?"

I tell her about all my goals and their corresponding squares. When I explain how much I love my new volunteering gig, she drops her fork.

"You're kidding?"

"Nope," I say with a soft laugh. "Crazy, right? But really, it's all because of Natalie."

"Sounds like I need to meet this Natalie." Lettie lifts one hand in the air.

Our server immediately stops by our table.

"Can we please get our desserts to go?" Lettie asks.

"Of course, I'll bring them right out."

"What're you doing?" I ask.

"We're going to the hospital. You as a hospital volunteer is something I have to see for myself."

When we pull into the parking lot, I direct Lettie to a spot closest to the elevators, and we use my volunteer badge to get us up to the pediatric wing after visiting hours. I can't wait for Lettie to meet Nat.

"You'll just love her," I say as we round the corner. "She's the sweetest girl in the world. Even with all she's been through, she's always smiling. I'm telling you, it'll hit ya right here." I tap my chest with one finger and look toward the end of the hall.

Lettie touches my arm. "Is that her room?"

Three doctors and two nurses huddle outside Nat's door.

"Something's wrong." I run the rest of the way, and I'm breathless when I reach the end of the corridor. Lettie follows, right on my heels, and my skittering heart and worry pushes me toward panic. A bright red caution sign is taped to Nat's door.

"What's going on?" I direct my question to the head nurse. "I was just here earlier today. She was fine when I left. What happened?"

Nurse Gables frowns as she answers. "Her fever spiked. She's developed an infection. We put her on strong antibiotics. She'll be okay, she's a fighter. But it'll probably be a few days before she can have visitors again."

"An infection?" My hands start to shake as my mind reviews the past week. "This is all my fault. I brought those props into her room. Did I do this to her?"

Nurse Gables is shaking her head before I finish speaking. "This is not your fault." She steps back and takes one of my hands in her own. "You took every precaution. We sanitized everything that went into her room. There is no reason to blame yourself."

The window into the sterile room shows Nat propped up in bed. Her imperfect body barely makes an impression in the mattress.

"This last week, she's been happier than I've ever seen her," Nurse Gables whispers. "You did that for her."

Nat's covered in a white blanket, and when she turns her head my way, even in her weak state, she sends me a tired smile and lifts one arm to wave.

I raise my hand to my lips and blow her a kiss. Just like she did for me earlier in the day.

"When will I be able to see her?" I ask.

"Not tonight," a doctor says from behind us. "She'll be quarantined until this infection is under control."

"Of course." I nod, then turn to Nurse Gables. "What else can I do?"

She shrugs. "Pray. Pray for her." She smiles toward Natalie, then turns kind eyes to me. "She loves spending time with you. I'll let you know as soon as she's well enough for you to visit again."

"Thank you."

Lettie and I don't speak again until we get to the car.

"She looks like a brave girl," Lettie says.

My heart swells, nearly bursting with all the emotions surging through me. "She's amazing. Honestly, she's probably the kindest person I've ever met. One time, when we were singing together, I told her about the play. She made me promise I'd have someone take a video so she could watch the best actress in the city perform." I have to stop and swallow away the lump in my throat. "I volunteered to help her, but really—she's the one who's helped me."

"I can't wait to meet her."

"When she's feeling better, I'll bring you back."

"Sounds perfect."

We pull up in front of my house, and Lettie stops the car but doesn't shut off the engine. "You gonna be okay?" she asks.

"I'll be fine," I sigh. "Until Jake gets here tomorrow."

"Do you want me to come spend the night? Be Switzerland when Jake gets home?"

I laugh. "No. I'm fine. Go home to your family. I've been stealing you away too often lately. The boys will set fire to the garage or tie Eric to a stake in the back yard if you're not home soon."

She sighs. "Back to my crazy life. Thanks for inviting me out tonight."

"Thanks for meeting me. I needed it."

I walk to the house, and my phone dings as I close the door behind me.

"Please not Jake," I say as I fish my phone from my purse.

It's not Jake. It's Lettie. She's messaged me before she's even left my driveway. I tap on the blue conversation bubble, and my smile pushes through the worries of the day.

> *Lettie:* Seeing you is always a highlight in my day. Love you. I'll say a prayer for Natalie tonight. Sleep well.

Tears fill my eyes, and all the emotions from the day pour out of me at Lettie's sweet text. I cue up a slightly inappropriate gif and send it to her.

I read her text again and let its message sink through my pain and frustration and allow it to replace the anger with hope and something resembling happiness. Amazing how a few small lines of text can have such an effect, but it's the truth.

Words are a powerful healer.

I walk to my office, grab my notebook, and begin to write.

To paint the grass today I will...
Cheer someone up with my words.
Send out twenty kind texts.

And four of them will be to Natalie.

Before I can close the cover of my notebook, there's a knock at the door. Did Lettie forget something? The knocking continues until I cross the room and yank the door wide.

"No need to knock . . ." My voice dies when I see who's on the other side.

Jake stands on the front porch.

One look at him and pain rises like hot air inside me, heating two weeks of emotion to a rolling boil. Anger, hurt, sadness, and guilt churn in my chest.

"Surprise. I took an earlier flight." Jake shoves his hands into his front pocket and lifts his shoulders. "I wasn't sure if you'd want me to just walk in, so I thought I'd knock."

I inhale short, staccatoed bursts of air, nearly hyperventilating as I struggle to maintain control. I've been trying so hard to heal, to move past the pain and replace it with positive change. But one look at him, and the forming scabs rip away. My heart drops, settling somewhere between my knees. Just low enough for Jake to kick around some more.

The door becomes my lifeline. I cling to it with all the tired strength left in me. And even though I've lost both my smile and my voice, my eyes never leave his face.

Jake clears his throat and looks at the ground. "Listen. I know you're mad, but if you just hear me out, we can talk through this. I'm not saying you're wrong exactly, it's just I know how sensitive you are, and I think . . ."

He drones on and on, and I keep standing. Keep staring. The more I watch him, the more my wound festers and puckers with blistering resentment.

". . . if you'll just let me inside. We can sit down and—"

As I listen to him fumble over excuses and form justifications, I finally find my voice.

"No."

"Excuse me?" Jake gives me a look that clearly states he thinks I'm crazy.

"I'm not ready." I stand a little taller, no longer relying on the door for strength. "You'll have to get a hotel or something. I need more time."

"B," Jake says, desperation shifting the tone of his voice into a higher octave. "Come on. Don't do this . . ."

I slam the door on his words.

On him.

"Goodbye, Jake." With a quick turn of the lock, I engage the deadbolt and flip off the porchlight.

As I walk away, I wait for the familiar outpouring of guilt to stop me, to make me turn back. But it doesn't happen.

I feel good. Space is what I need right now, and it's okay if I take it.

The concept is so new to me, my mind becomes a whirl of conflicting emotions as I get ready for bed. Future worries fight with past memories, and there's no truce in sight. By the time I settle onto the mattress, I don't even bother to turn out my bedside lamp.

Why did he have to come back early? I was ready to see him tomorrow, I'd prepared myself. But when I saw him on the porch tonight, reality punched me in the heart. I can't do it. I don't want to see him, to listen to him explain. I don't want anything to do with him right now.

I need to focus on something—anything—to take my mind off the issues battling inside me. With a deep breath in and a loud sigh out, I set my mind on my next goal.

Send out twenty kind texts.

Easy enough. And at least I know where to start. I grab my phone and pull up my contacts list.

Megan Allen.

I wonder how her baby's doing?

I tap *send message* and start to type.

A half-hour later, it's full dark out and my thumbs will forever be stuck in a texting-claw position. But I've done it. I've sent out twenty texts to different friends, and four messages to Nat's tablet. Hopefully, they'll make a difference. Sometimes the smallest gestures have the biggest impact.

With that in mind, I fold my arms and say a quiet prayer for Natalie.

SEVENTEEN

THE NEXT MORNING, I wake up before my alarm and get started on my run a little early. Avoiding Alex's house altogether, I take an entirely new route toward the river at the edge of town.

The sun rises over the mountains and paints the water in pink and orange. I stare at the swirling colors, breathe in the crisp morning air, and let go of my worries.

Today will be a better day than yesterday.

I run home with the sound of rushing waters at my back and imagine a ship with all my worries sinking below the surface. Alex is at the helm and Jake is her first mate. I focus forward and take comfort in the earth beneath me as my mind celebrates shipwrecks.

My feet remain at a steady pace, pounding gently on the pavement, always in time with the music of my headphones. As I run the two miles back to my house, I get lost in my thoughts. Every one of the women I texted last night responded. Some with funny gifs, some with heartfelt words, some with a special memory of us together.

Sometime during the night, Nurse Gables sent me a message telling me Natalie's out of danger for the moment, but no visitors will be allowed for two more days. Sprinkled in among all the memes and tender responses from my friends, this is my favorite message of all.

My pace picks up with the beat of the music, and I think of Natalie. Her beautiful blue eyes form a clear picture in my mind, and I'm reminded of all the powerful women in my life. We could be such a strength to each other. Why don't we get together more often? How can we let life get in the way of something so important?

I run my usual distance, but the minute I set foot on my lawn, I silently wish I had added an extra half mile to my route—or that I had the power to transform myself into an iris.

Mrs. Platt loves her bearded irises.

She's also waiting for me, and the emotion on her face definitely isn't love.

"I spoke with the HOA president."

"Good morning to you too." I laugh as I approach.

"Yes, well, good morning and all, but I just wanted to give you a fair warning." She holds up a piece of paper. "The HOA president reserves the right to come inspect any changes made to any property viewed by the public."

"So, my backyard is viewed by the public now?"

"I can see your backyard."

"Only when you and your bridge club stand on your stools and peer over the fence."

"Well, that's neither here nor there." She folds the paper in her hands and then lowers her hands in front of her. "What time works for you?"

"Works for me for what?"

"For the inspection. Mr. Miller said he'd come over himself."

A laugh slips out. "Inspection. It sounds so official." Mrs. Platt's look tells me she's not going to drop it. "Set it up for any evening this week," I sigh. "I'm done with play practice around two and then head to the hospital for an hour or two after that."

"Alright then," she says. "Are you sure you don't want to set it up yourself?"

"Of course not. You'll enjoy it so much more than I will." I step up on the porch. "Have a great day, Mrs. Platt."

I open the front door, slide inside, and close it behind me.

My shoulders sag, and I release a heavy breath into the room, allowing myself just a moment to rest against the door. If Mrs. Platt didn't make such fine soups and keep a hawk-eye watch over the neighborhood, living next door to her would be a pain in the ass.

Why a little paint on the grass gets her so hot and bothered is beyond me. I let go one more sigh and push away from the door.

My running shoes stay in the front entry, so I slip into the kitchen in my stocking feet. When I step around the corner, an impressive vase of flowers fills my view. But the sight doesn't make me smile.

Jake.

Why? Why does he think flowers can fix this? Slapping a Band-Aid on the severed artery of our relationship isn't going to work.

I shake my head even as I grab the card and tear open the envelope.

B,

I WANT TO WORK THINGS OUT. WE JUST NEED TO BE REASONABLE ABOUT THIS. I'M SURE AFTER TALKING TO ME, YOU'LL SEE THIS ISN'T THAT BIG OF A DEAL. PLEASE. LET ME COME HOME. LET'S TALK.

LOVE,
Jake

Classic Jake double talk. *I want to work things out.* Translation: I'm the only one who does. *We just need to be reasonable.* Translation: You need to be reasonable. *You'll see this isn't a big deal.* Translation: You're making this into a big deal.

His words prep the fire, and my anger flames to life.

I snatch the vase from off the table, grab a set of kitchen shears, and get to work.

Snip. Snip. Snip.

Heavy blooms roll along the countertop and flop to the floor. With every flower I behead, my determination grows. I will not be a doormat. Snip! I will not be taken for granted. Snip! I won't be told my feelings aren't valid. Snip! I won't be anyone's second choice! Snip!

When I place the scissors aside, a cluster of naked stalks fills the vase, and a pile of twenty-four flower heads roll along the flat surfaces surrounding me. I take a deep breath in and release it slowly.

My hands steady. My mind clears.

A little destruction's always good to build composure.

I pick up the blooms at my feet and stack them into a pile on the counter. Using one arm, I sweep them all onto an empty plate. With sure strides and growing confidence, I walk the dead heads down the hallway and out the front door. Once on the front porch, I tip the plate and dump them all onto the top step. They slump together, forming a hill of petals and florets. I hold the plate under my arm while I tear his note into tiny bits and sprinkle the confetti onto the pile of rose blossoms.

Even for a husband as dense as mine, it sends a pretty clear message.

When I walk back into the kitchen, flowerless green stems stand tall in the glass vase. Even without their flower heads, they look sturdy and strong. The life-giving stalks reach high, straight and steady, even when they don't have to. Ever ready and always willing to support the blossoms I removed.

"I want to be like them," I say aloud. To lift others up. To hold them higher than they can hold themselves. I want to support and be supported. And most of all, I want to be there for others.

I walk to my bedside table where I left my notebook the night before. The soft red-leather whispers beneath my fingertips as I open the book.

> To paint the grass today I will...
> Support and appreciate the women in my life.
> Time for a girls' night in!

I type out a quick Evite to everyone I texted last night, including Lettie, and ask them to come over for a girls' night on Tuesday. *Give me two hours*, I tell everyone. We deserve two hours to eat and laugh and paint each other's toenails.

I'm smiling as I hit send.

Before I rush off to play practice, I head to my backyard to paint my grass. I start by spraying a base of dark gray and then add a bright red heart to the center. Showing kindness to those I love will be on my permanent list of things to do from now on.

My drive passes quickly, and when I reach the theater, Cole meets me at the door with a cup of warm lemon tea. I take a sip and sigh.

"Perfect." I smack my lips together. "Great tartness to sweetness ratio. Very warm, but not too hot. It's perfect. You have a gift."

He laughs. "The lady at the coffee cart down the street has a gift. I'm just the delivery boy."

"Well, I'll take it." We continue into a theater filled with chaos and costumes. More costumes than I've ever seen in one place at one time. "What's all this?"

"It's the reason for the tea." Cole nods toward a woman wearing a measuring tape as a scarf. "Today's the final fitting for costumes. It's always a bit stressful."

"Not for me," I say with confidence. "I refuse to let anything stress me out today."

"Famous last words," Cole says as we step up onstage.

Silk skirts and satin bodices, colorful bows and black ties, floppy hats and high heels are yanked on and off my body for the next two hours. Pins prick my skin, and I'm left standing in my bra and underwear so often, no one even says anything about my undressed state anymore.

Well, almost no one.

"Suck it in, Bethany," Piper smirks. "No one wants a frumpy star."

Her rude words stir up a fire inside me, and I let my better judgement slide. "Well then, it's a good thing they replaced you with me, isn't it?"

The former star's face twitches its way into a spasm before she clomps away, smacking her casted leg on the theater chairs as she goes.

Piper doesn't taunt me for the rest of the day. I'll take that too.

At the end of practice, Cole and I stay to run through our problematic dance scene until we get it right. The theater is nearly empty when we finally leave, and the sky is clear of clouds as we walk through the parking lot together.

My phone buzzes. It's a text from Jake. A photo of our front porch piled with dead flower heads.

Underneath the picture he's typed a single word.

Jake: Really?

Yes, Jake, really.

My phone buzzes again. Now he's calling.

Nope.

I press ignore.

"Who was that?" Cole asks.

"My husband."

"What did he do?"

"Something stupid." I force a smile.

"Something stupid or someone stupid?"

188

I laugh even as my shoulders sink. "Both, maybe. I'm not sure." The warm afternoon heats my skin, but the wind stirs up goosebumps on my arms. "I'm not sure about all the details. But he hurt me, and I don't know what to do about it." We reach my car, and I lean against it, facing Cole.

"Well, I know it probably doesn't feel like it now, but there may be a day when you wish you had him around even though he does stupid things." He looks up at the sky. "There are a lot of days I wish my wife was here."

"You have a wife? How come you never told me? I want to meet her."

"Leslie would've loved you."

"Would've loved me?"

He nods. "She died. Two years ago, next month."

"Cole, I'm so sorry. I had no idea."

"It's okay. I've had years to move past the really awful pain." He pauses, and silence stirs in the air around us. "But you know, I'm still here. Doing what I love. She'd want me to keep acting. It's my passion, and she knew it. And she would have really liked you."

I smile. "You think so?"

"Oh yeah. You would have been friends for sure. Probably best friends."

I turn to face him. "Well, she would've definitely been invited to my girls' night."

"Girls' night, huh? Guess I'm not invited then."

"Only if you're interested in being set-up. I have a few single friends."

"You found out I'm a widower exactly thirty seconds ago, and you're already playing matchmaker." He gives a sad sort of laugh and shakes his head. "Now you sound like my sisters. They're always pushing me to meet someone."

"You'd make someone really happy." I shrug my shoulders.

He sighs. "Yeah. I guess. When the time's right." He looks at his watch. "I'd better get out of here. I have a very important night of television binging and microwaveable meals ahead of me."

He reaches across me and opens my car door for me. I sit behind the steering wheel, and Cole shuts the door. With a press of a button, I lower the driver's side window so I can look up at him. "She'd want you to be happy, Cole. She wouldn't want you to be alone. I mean, if she's anything like me anyway. I'd want that for someone I loved."

His head droops, and he nods three times...slowly. "You're right. I know you're right. She would want me to be happy." He reaches out and squeezes my hand. "See you tomorrow."

"See ya." As he walks away, I put my car into drive and head home. At the last minute, I turn toward the hospital. Even though I can't visit Nat, I decide to stop on my way home to write her a note.

The gift shop near the front door has stationary, and I buy a few sheets in a bright color. It takes only a few seconds to write: *You're more beautiful than a thousand sunsets. Close your eyes and imagine the sun setting behind an ancient volcano. That's where we'll be today.* I head up to the third floor and find her room. As I tape the message to the window, she looks up at me. I wave and see her smile grow as she reads the words I've written. She immediately closes her eyes, and I hope she's imagining the most beautiful sunset in all the world. She deserves it. I close my eyes and join her in her imaginary sunset gazing. After a few minutes I open my eyes and blow her a kiss, all while praying she'll be well enough for me to visit soon.

My prayer continues for the entire drive home, but when I pull up to the house, it turns into a curse.

"Dammit."

Jake's waiting for me.

He sits on the front porch as I pull into the garage and close the door behind me. What if I just ignore him? What if I pretend I didn't see him? Sitting on our porch. Waving like a madman as I drove up. Holding another gift, which I assume is for me.

Did we learn nothing from the flower incident?

As I climb out of the car, I huff and puff and grumble loud enough, I half expect my house to blow down. Stomping all the way up the garage steps, I step inside the kitchen. I'm not sure I'd mourn the loss of this house. It's full of too many memories.

A soft knock sounds from the front entry. Jake isn't going to let me ignore him. I place my car keys on the designated hook and set my purse on the table beneath it. Seconds later, I grit my teeth and pull open the door.

Jake holds a dolce-de-leche cheesecake in one hand and two forks in the other.

"You can't resist this. It's your favorite." He holds the dessert closer so I can smell the sweet goodness. "Come on, B. Doesn't this at least get me a few checkmarks in the he's-not-a-total-asshole column?"

"Yes, it actually does."

Jake sighs. "Finally."

I reach through the doorway and lift the cheesecake out of his hands. "Thank you."

He smiles. "You're welcome."

"This will be perfect for my girls' night tomorrow." I take a step back, and with a soft kick, the door slams shut—on Jake's shocked face.

EIGHTEEN

KYLE CUTS REHEARSAL SHORT on Tuesday morning, and it's just after noon when I stop by the hospital to write Natalie another note for the day.

Even if I can't officially visit her, I still want to cheer her spirits.

The note reads: *You're stronger than a thousand diamonds. Today, we're deep in the earth, searching a hidden mine in South Africa for a lost diamond.* I wave to her and blow her a kiss in greeting. I pretend to fasten a diamond necklace behind my neck, and she puts a hand to her chest and nods, miming that my invisible diamond is beautiful.

She pretends to find her own necklace, and I signal that the diamond is so bright it's hurting my eyes. We laugh for a few minutes, and I'm glad she looks like she's feeling better.

"See you tomorrow," I say through the glass.

After I leave the hospital, I head out to shop. Three stores and as many hours later, I finally have everything I need. It takes another hour to get everything set up at the house, but it turns out even better than I could have hoped. I hang up the *It's a Girl* sign and I add an S' and put another sign below it that reads *Night In.* The wall facing the door of my house now says— *It's a Girls' Night In.*

Soft candlelight glows from every surface, bringing the spicy scent of cinnamon to the air. Pink and silver balloons cover the floor, and twenty different colors of nail polish line the edge of the pedicure station. Drinks of all flavors and potencies fill both counter tops, placating both non-drinkers and heavy drinkers alike. My vase of stems decorates the food table, and the treats surrounding it tempt me to dig in before guests arrive. Especially Jake's donated cheesecake.

I laugh to myself as the front door opens, and Lettie barrels into the room.

"I know I'm early, but it's the right of the best friend..."

"Come on in. The party starts as soon as you get here."

Lettie pours us each a drink and holds up her glass. "To my Bestie!"

"I'll drink to that." I raise my glass to hers with a clink.

The sound of car doors slamming drifts through the open windows.

"They're here!" I set my drink down, and we hurry to the door to greet our guests.

Lettie throws the door open wide. "Come on in, ladies!" She slaps a crown on her head. "Buckle up! It's gonna be an epic girls' night in."

The warmth of the night calls to us. Stars shine bright overhead, and once our toenails are fully dry, we take the party out to the backyard. With bare feet and drinks in hand, twelve women line up on the patio and pose for a photo. They say a picture is worth a thousand words, but this one, packed full of such amazing women, could easily spit out ten thousand words in a glance.

We leave our shoes off and step onto the lawn, delighting in the cool green between our toes. A few ladies gather around my painted garden, looking at different squares, guessing at what they mean. Several others lay on blankets and look up at the night sky, pointing out where Cassiopeia might be.

I weave my way over to my sons' tree swing hanging from the largest willow in the far corner of the yard. As I sit on the unsteady surface, strength stirs inside me.

Here in my yard, in the company of these incredible women, I'm surrounded by support and love.

No judgments.

No anger.

No belittling comments.

No one making me feel less than.

Just simple acts of kindness and smiles all around.

All women need a support group like this. Strong women who will lift them up when people try to tear them down. As long as there are other women in the world, we never need to feel alone.

Lettie comes up behind me and gives me a single push high into the air, then runs underneath me. I squeal, just like Ryan used to do, and kick my feet toward the sky. The wind presses against my face, and all my sadness slips away from me.

As I watch Lettie make her way across the yard, I let go of the hurt holding me down and imagine it floating off into the night like a lost balloon. I swing up again, lift my feet to touch the clouds, listen to my girlfriends laugh, and savor this perfect moment.

When moments like these happen in my life, I hold them in my memory until the image stains the surface for good. On the hard days, I'll want to remember how I feel right now. And when I doubt myself, or when someone makes me feel small, I'll have this feeling waiting for me. I'll pull it out, wrap my arms around it, and smile.

"Hey, B! Come here," Lettie calls. "I have the best idea."

She's over at the shed, and I jump out of the swing like a six-year-old in pigtails and run across the grass. By the time I get there, three ladies are already inside the shed with her, and Lettie is directing them.

"Take this." She points at my grass stencil. "And we'll need all of these." She grabs six colors of paint and hands them off before grabbing six more colors.

"What are you doing?" I ask.

Lettie smiles into my eyes and says, "I'm painting the grass. You should know. You taught me how."

We walk over to my painted garden and create a square together.

A bright-green base, covered in twenty-four handprints—in every different color imaginable. Some are half one color and half another. Some have dots. Some are solid. Some have fingers in each separate hue. All are unique. All are beautiful.

As we turn on the hose to wash paint off our hands, Lettie says, "Hey, B! We have some unexpected visitors." She motions to the far side of the yard.

Four sets of eyes peer over the fence. Mrs. Platt and her bridge club, all shaking their heads at us. They're back again this week.

I smile my brightest smile and wave an orange-painted hand her way. "Hey, Mrs. Platt. Want to join us?"

Mrs. Platt gasps, and the four heads disappear behind the fence all at once. Off to play bridge, and to gossip about the horrid neighbors.

Lettie laughs. "Well, I guess we'll take that as a no."

"Tonight, I don't even care." I laugh with Lettie as we look at the newest square in my painted garden.

My friends and I have created a masterpiece.

Together.

When it's time for everyone to leave, we stand at the door and high-five each other with our stained hands. As if we're competitors in a high school sporting event. As if we're young and free of worries.

"Goodnight," I call out again and again. "Thanks for coming! . . . Yes, I promise." I blow a kiss. "We'll do it again soon."

When the last car pulls out of the driveway, Lettie gives me the biggest hug ever known to womankind. "You are the most amazing friend a girl could ask for. You know?"

"Back at ya," I say.

She steps off the front porch. "You did a good thing tonight. I've never seen so many smiles in all my life." As she drives away, she yells, "Love you, B."

"Love you back."

A few minutes later, I curl up in bed and sleep better than I have in years.

I WALK INTO PLAY practice the next morning with a smile on my face and sass in my step. The set's colors are brighter, the chorus is singing on key, and even the musty smell of the theater isn't as bad today. I close my eyes and breathe in my surroundings, then exhale with a sigh.

"Someone's happy this morning," Cole says from behind me. "I take it the party went well."

"It was a hit."

"Of course." With a stretch of his arms behind his back, he sticks out his chest. "It must've been all those good vibes I sent your way from my couch." He nods as we make our way toward the stage.

I laugh and follow him. "That must have been it."

A flurry of chorus girls surrounds us, and we squeeze closer together to make our way through the crowd.

"So . . . what'd you end up doing last night?" I ask.

"Oh, you know." He shrugs. "There was a Bourne marathon on, so I learned how to take out the bad guys."

"Nice." I nod and smile. "Should come in handy if a rogue government agency ever comes after you."

"I'll be more than ready."

Out of the corner of my eye, I notice a dark-haired chorus girl step forward, toward us, then back away. She smiles shyly and stares at Cole. Of course, he doesn't even look her way.

We start going through our morning warm up. Tongue twisters. Scales. Opening lines. I watch the chorus girl the entire time. She never takes her eyes off Cole.

After our warm up, Cole turns toward backstage and gets set for the first scene.

"Hi, Cole," the chorus girl all but shouts out at him. "How are you?"

Cole smiles politely. "Good. I'm good. How are you, Taahira?"

Taahira steps out of the backstage shadows, and I have to stop myself from saying wow out loud. She's a natural beauty. Her deep sienna skin compliments her long black hair like the colors of a sunset compliment the sky. And when she looks at Cole, her eyes say she'd like to spend more than a few offstage hours with him.

Cole is oblivious to it all. He starts to walk away, and Taahira's smile slips.

Time to step in.

"Cole," I say, and he turns toward me. "It's rude not to introduce me to your friend."

"Oh, I'm sorry." Cole shakes his head. "Bethany, this is Taahira Madan. Taahira, this is Bethany Taylor."

We shake hands. Her skin is even softer than it looks.

"It's so nice to meet you," she says. "Thanks for saving our show."

"Oh, please." I wave a dismissive hand in front of my face. "We'll see how much saving's being done on opening night."

"Stop it," she says. "You're so talented."

Her sincerity touches my heart. "Thank you. And can I just say, you are so beautiful. I'm incredibly jealous of your skin tone."

"Really?"

"Yes. It's gorgeous." I gesture to my face. "Take it from someone whose complexion is one step up from corpse, you're the envy of all us pasty folk."

She laughs just as Kyle calls out, "Actors, get set for the opening scene."

"It was nice to meet you, Taahira," I say.

"We better get set." Cole motions toward backstage. When he doesn't say anything to Taahira, I open my eyes wide and tilt my head in her direction.

"Oh... yeah," he stutters. "Good to see you again. Enjoy the rest of your day."

"When's the chorus back on?" I ask.

"We rehearse during your lunch break." She looks wistfully at Cole. "So I'll be back then."

I sigh. Cole isn't even looking at her. Men are so blind.

He grabs my hand and pulls me to my spot.

I send an apologetic look to Taahira. "See you after lunch," I call out and send her a wink.

We have a few minutes before our entrance, so I lean close and speak quietly to Cole. "What do you think of Taahira?"

"She's nice, I guess. Why?"

"She is totally into you."

His gaze darts to her receding figure, and he laughs. "Uh. No, she's not."

"Uh. Yes, she is."

"She's like seven years younger than me and could have her pick of guys. There's no way."

"Does she talk to you every rehearsal?"

"Yes. But just because I'm always here."

"Does she make it a point to touch your arm or shoulder?"

"Um. Yeah. I guess so."

"Does she laugh no matter what stupid thing you say."

"She does. But only because I'm funny."

"You're not that funny." I shake my head. "Maybe there's another reason she talks to you every day, touches your arm, and laughs at your corny jokes." I raise one eyebrow and let my words sink in, watching as realization dawns on him.

He stares at Taahira onstage, then sighs and leans against the back wall. "You really think so? It's been so long. I . . . I didn't even notice. I . . ." He shakes his head.

I laugh and take a step toward him. "Well, now that you know, the question is, do you want to do something about it?"

THREE HOURS LATER WE'RE seated at my favorite table in my favorite Mexican restaurant. "The enchiladas are incredible," I say as I take a bite of cabbage salsa. "But really, you'll be happy with whatever you get."

The server brings us our drinks and takes our orders. Once she leaves, I dive right in. "Okay. So . . . are you interested in asking Taahira out?"

Cole nods his head as he swallows. "Most definitely."

"Perfect. Just wanted to make sure I wasn't pushing you into anything."

"Push away." He smiles and dips another chip into the spicy salsa.

"Well, we know you guys have acting in common, so there's a good start. Common ground. Do you know anything else about her?"

"Only that her grandmother still lives in India, and she visits her once a year. She missed rehearsals last month for a week."

"Good. Very good. We know she likes to travel, which means it's a pretty safe bet she'll be up for something a little more adventurous."

"Like what?"

"Well, what are some things you like to do when you have an evening free?"

"I like to go to the symphony, and they have a concert tonight."

I'm already shaking my head. "Nope."

"What? Why? Too boring?"

"No. How are you going to talk during Handel's Water Music?"

"Good point. Well, I also like to go rock climbing at the place just outside of town."

"That's perfect! Do you need a reservation? Or can you just walk in?"

"Either. But I have a membership, so I'm sure I could get us in."

"Done and done."

"But what if she doesn't like rock climbing?"

"Trust me." I nod at Cole as steaming enchiladas are placed in front of us. "The way she was looking at you today, you could ask her to go shopping for burial plots, and she'd say yes."

Laughter sounds from the other side of the table, and when I look up, soda's dripping off Cole's chin.

"Burial plots? Really?" He smiles.

"I'm telling ya. She's just that into you."

WE'RE STANDING BACKSTAGE WHEN the chorus begins to gather up their things for the day. I clear my throat as Taahira walks by.

"Cole, what was the place you were telling me about at lunch?" I ask.

Nothing but a blank stare from Cole.

"You know, where you have the membership."

Relief washes over Cole's face as he catches on, and I almost laugh out loud. "Oh yeah. *Cliffside.* It's a rock-climbing place. I still think you should try it out. I'm planning on going there later tonight."

Nice! I think.

"In fact." He turns to Taahira. "Are you busy tonight?"

"What? Me? No, I'm not busy." Her smile lights up the stage.

Cole stands there a little too long, so I nudge him from behind. "Well. Would you like to come with me?"

"Really? I'd love to. I've never been rock climbing. Sounds fun."

"It's the best. Really." He smiles. "Pick you up at six?"

"Perfect. I'll be ready." She's all but floating as she walks away.

Cole turns to me and gives me a thumbs up.

"Her number," I hiss.

"Oh yeah." He turns and jogs after Taahira, and I laugh when he trips and tries to recover all Rico Suave like.

He's back onstage ten minutes later, and he surprises me with a hug as we're getting set for Act Three.

"What was that for?"

"It's a thank you hug," he says. "And I'm giving it to you now because after the date, I might not be so thankful."

"You'll thank me, today, tomorrow, and for the rest of your life. Have a little faith in you. You'll be great."

He sighs. "If you say so."

We walk out on stage, and I whisper, "By the way. I'm coming over to your place after rehearsal to pick out your outfit."

"I've been picking out my own clothes since I was five."

"Yup. And that's why I'm coming over. Trust me."

He rolls his eyes and gives in.

IT'S NEARLY TWO-THIRTY by the time we reach his house, and if I can't spend the afternoon with Natalie, helping a friend is the next best thing. When we step inside, Cole leads me right to his closet. I start pulling shirts off of hangers and shorts out of drawers. When I'm finished, three different outfits lay on his bed.

"Okay. Now..." I point to the first outfit. "This one says, I'm fun and playful and have a bright personality." Then I turn to the second outfit. "This one says, I know how to have a good time, but I'm also serious when I need to be." I motion to the last outfit. "And this says, look at my muscular arms, let me spot you." I smile up at him.

He rolls his eyes. "Wow, really? My clothes are so talkative."

I motion toward them. "Which one do you like?"

"Does it really matter?"

"Nope." I pick up outfit number three. "This is the one." I toss him the shirt. "Plus, it will make your blue eyes stand out, which never hurts."

He puts away the other two outfits, and walks me to the door. "Thanks, Beth."

I turn to face him. "You're welcome. Have fun tonight. You deserve it."

"I will," he says and nudges me out the front door. "Now get out of here. I've got to get ready or I'll be late."

I look at my watch. "You've got your work cut out for you. Only three and a half hours. Think it'll be enough time?"

Cole slams the door in my face.

"See you tomorrow," I yell and then smile all the way to my car.

NINETEEN

THE HUM OF TIRES on the road and the constant drone of the air conditioner relaxes me as I drive across town toward home. The quiet ride plus the image of Cole all jittery and nervous for his first date takes me back twenty years.

Jake had really wanted to impress me on our first date, so he took me up on a scenic glider ride. He'd only had his glider's license for a little over a month, but he managed to get us into some good currents in the air. We rode the thermals for more than forty minutes. I've still never seen a more beautiful view than the summer mountains through the bubble canopy of the glider.

When we rolled to a stop on the grass runway, he had a limo waiting for us on the tarmac. First class treatment all the way. We feasted on Indian food and then cooled our mouths with ice cream. We debated the finer points of movies and recited lines from our favorite scenes. By the end of the night my sides hurt from laughing, and every time I looked at Jake, I knew my life had changed forever.

A swell of emotion builds in my chest, pressing my heart into my ribcage.

Of course, at the time, I thought I'd won the relationship lottery. But now, thinking back, I wonder if he did those special things for me—with only my happiness in mind. After every tender moment, he'd always ask if I told my sisters about it, if I'd shared pictures online, or if I'd let the other spouses from work know about the impressive night he'd planned.

I'm not sure I was a necessary part of the process. Anyone else could have filled my place and given him exactly what he wanted—a good ego boost.

Has he ever really seen me? Or has he only ever seen what I can be *for him*?

I pull into the garage and step out of the car like I'm exiting an emotional rollercoaster. When I shut the door, I lock the memories inside. With an overly dramatic sigh, I lean my head on the roof of the car. No more tears. No more memories.

My cell phone rings as I turn and settle back against the car door.

"Hello," I answer.

"Bethany. It's Nurse Gables."

At the sound of her voice, all my senses snap to attention. "How's Natalie?" Everything else in the world disappears. All I want is for Nat to be okay.

"Better today. I saw her smile this afternoon, so that's something. Reading those notes you've taped to the window has helped more than you know."

"Thank you, God. Seriously . . ." I step out onto the driveway so I can pace as I talk. "I'm so glad you called to let me know."

"Of course. I promised her I would. She wanted me to ask you when you could come see her."

Tears flood my face and my voice is a swamp of emotion. "I can come visit? Is she well enough? Are you sure?"

"Doctor's orders. She won't ever leave this hospital, Beth. But a visit from you will sure brighten her day."

"I'll be there. Tomorrow afternoon. I promise."

I hang up the phone and let out a squeal of happiness. Nat's doing better. This calls for a celebration. I start toward the house looming before me, but its emptiness only adds to the hollow place inside me. For the first time since this painted journey began, I wish I had someone to come home to.

Footsteps sound behind me, and someone clears their throat.

"Hello, Mrs. Taylor?" A skinny man wearing a polo shirt and carrying a clipboard stands in my driveway.

Next to him, Mrs. Platt smiles at me.

"This is Kurt Miller from the HOA association. He'd like to inspect your grass."

"Of course he would."

Mr. Miller follows me to the backyard, and when I motion to my painted squares, he surprises me with a laugh. "I can honestly say I've never seen anything like this before."

For some reason the comment makes me smile.

His inspection takes less than ten minutes, and consists of checking privacy fences and grass height. Mr. Miller wanders around my yard three times before he makes his way back to the patio.

He holds his clipboard in front of him. "I'll admit, this is a strange complaint. Half the reason I came out here was to see it for myself." He shakes his head. "But truth be told, back yards don't fall under the same scrutiny as front yards, so there's nothing illegal about your painted garden." He points his clipboard at me. "But your grass height is getting close to being outside regulations, so I'd think about mowing soon."

"That's it? The spray paint stays?" Mrs. Platt's not happy.

Mr. Miller opens his mouth. "With the agreement that Ms. Taylor mows

---

her yard at the end of the week to keep the grass regulation height."

Mrs. Platt smiles. "Assuming Bethany here will agree to that."

"Fine." I hold up my hands in defeat. "When I mow the front, I'll mow off the squares here in the back too. This isn't meant to be a permanent thing. More symbolic, really."

It's impossible to mow away the real changes I've made, and I'll continue to paint my grass from the inside out.

I turn to Mrs. Platt and hold out my hand. "Truce?"

Mrs. Platt grasps my hand with her gloved fingers. "I suppose I can stand the squares for another week or so, as long as you trim this time before you mow. Scraggly edges on a yard make me crazy."

"Agreed," I say.

"Well, it looks like I'm not needed here any longer," Mr. Miller says. "Nice to meet you, Ms. Taylor."

"You as well," I say.

"I'll lead him out and shut the gate," Mrs. Platt says. "You go on and enjoy your painted squares for the little time you have left with them."

"Thanks for the concern," I call out as they disappear around the corner. When I enter the house, the kiss of cool air-conditioning against my skin is a welcome relief. With slow, deliberate motions, I stretch my neck and sigh as I step into the kitchen.

There's an envelope on the table.

Inside are two symphony tickets. With a note.

PICK YOU UP AT 7:00 ~ LOVE, *Jake*

I rub the slick paper between my fingers and close my eyes. I can almost hear the music. Jake knows how much I love the symphony. He knows I can't pass up these seats.

And I won't.

My notebook rests on the counter where I left it. I move to where I can reach it and flip open the soft cover.

To paint the grass today I will...
Do something nice just for me.
Dress up and go to the symphony!

Excitement ripples through me. The symphony is always a good idea. But it's a good idea I plan on enjoying alone.

I rip the second ticket in half and tape each half to the front door at eye level. I consider leaving a note, but decide against it. I'm hoping my message is clear this time. Nothing you buy me will fix this, Jake.

It's almost 5:00. An hour and forty-five minutes. Plenty of time to shower, get ready, and leave before Jake shows up at the door.

The dress I choose looks like something Audrey Hepburn would wear in the movie *Breakfast at Tiffany's*. It's a classic black sheath with two white stripes just below the bustline, and a wide circular neckline, also in white, with short, capped sleeves. It's perfect.

"Tonight," I say to my reflection. "I'm going to wear what I want to wear and make some new memories."

Tonight, my happiness comes first.

My high heels rest on the floor of my car as I drive to the Watson Event Center. Although it's the nicest building within thirty miles of my home, there's still no valet parking. I take my time finding the closest parking spot and finally slip into a place someone vacates just before the sun sends its last glinting rays over the building. The sky lights up with color, and I snap a quick picture of the beautiful sunset and send it to Natalie just to make her smile.

As I enter the building, the echoes of my footsteps chase each other through the tiled entry way until they're muffled by the faux-velvet red carpet leading into the lobby. Several well-dressed men glance my way. Smiles and appreciative looks follow me as I make my way into the concert hall. I pull my shoulders back and hold my head high.

Still got it.

Two sets of press-bar entry doors lead to the concert space, and I follow my own personal red carpet through the one indicating it leads to Section B. A young man dressed in a tuxedo greets me on the other side of the final door.

"Welcome to tonight's performance. Would the lady like a program?"

"The lady would like that very much. Thank you."

He hands me a thick program and offers to lead me to my seat. The ticket Jake bought gives me access to the center floor section, six rows back from the stage. With careful steps and almost no high-heel wobble at all, I make my way to my seat.

After a quick chair wipe down, I settle in and glance up at the rows of music stands set before empty chairs. I'll be able to count the wrinkles in the conductor's jacket from this angle. A bubble of happiness rises in my chest and bursts into a thousand goose bumps that cascade down both my arms. I smile at the stage, and with the satin banner hanging just so, the stage smiles right back.

I'm holding my breath when the lights dim—once and then twice. The conversations buzzing around the crowd hush to a quiet murmur and then stop altogether when the concert master steps out onstage. She carries her violin with regal grace and leads the entire orchestra to their places. Scrapes and shuffles fill the now quiet theater as the musicians get set and ready.

A single note pierces the air, followed by a flurry of sound as the players tune their instruments. And then the maestro himself walks on stage, brandishing his conducting wand like a sword.

Without a word he turns his back to the audience and waves his baton in an accentuated downbeat. The music begins. Softly at first with just the strings section, and then one by one, the brass and then the woodwinds join in. Finally, the percussion splashes into the fray with a crash of the cymbals. I close my eyes and feel the music pour over me.

I'm transported to a perfectly tuned heaven.

IT'S DARK OUT WHEN I exit the building. I'm humming Claire de Lune as I make my way to my car. The night has turned cold, and a shiver catches me off guard. I pull my coat in tighter, wishing I'd worn a more sensible dress.

The lights of the parking lot glint off my wedding ring. I almost laugh as I think about what the evening would've been like with Jake at my side. Getting all fancied up to go to a symphony concert would be about as fun for him as attending a funeral. He would never intentionally attend the symphony, and he would've snored through the entire thing.

I glance inside the empty car, but still . . .

At least he'd be here. At least I wouldn't be alone. I tilt my head to the stars and send a sigh into the night.

Something brushes up against my elbow, and my sigh becomes a scream. I turn on the spot.

A well-dressed man around my age is smiling at me. I press my hand to my chest to keep my heart from jumping out and send a weak smile back at him.

"Ciao, bella. I am sorry to startle you, but . . ." He pulls my red silk scarf out from under his suit jacket. "You dropped this on your way out."

"Oh. Thank you. I didn't even notice it fell off." I slip the scarf around my neck. "Thanks for returning it."

He extends his hand toward me. "I am Peter, and you are?" His voice has a heavy Italian accent.

"I'm Bethany." I shake his hand. "It's nice to meet you."

When I try to pull my hand away, he clasps it tighter and pulls it toward his chest, covering it with his other hand. His European manners are showing.

"You must go to drinks with me tonight." His voice is deep, sexy even, and his smile is something mothers warn their teenage daughters about.

"I'd love to, but I'm married." I hold up my left hand as proof, letting my wedding ring speak for itself.

His smile grows wider, and his accent thickens. "It's okay with me. I do not mind."

My mouth falls open.

"Please," he continues. "Come out with me. Such a beautiful woman should not be alone on a night like this." He kisses my hand, like a gentleman of old, but there's nothing gentlemanly about his words. "I promise I will make you happy in every way tonight. No strings attached."

I use my other hand to leverage my fingers out of his grasp and lean away from him. "No strings at all. I'm not going out with another man. I'm married."

He brings his fingertips to his lips and kisses them, then shakes them toward the sky. "The stars will cry for you tonight. And I will have to drink alone."

As he walks away, I breathe out an unsteady breath.

He stops and says, "You are sure?"

I nod. "Very sure."

He shakes his head and mutters in Italian, and I sigh again. I think back on all those years of dating, of men hitting on me. Truth is, I was glad to leave it all behind. Truth is . . .

"I like being married," I say out loud as I unlock my car. With a single lift of the handle, I pull the door wide and slide into the seat. The gear shift moves easily into drive, and I start toward home.

Alone.

I walk inside my house.

Alone.

I paint the grass with a cream-colored square and a music note.

Alone.

I clean up.

Alone.

Then I go to bed.

Alone.

TWENTY

"HOW DID IT GO last night?" I ask Cole the second I see him at practice the next morning.

"Hey, what kind of a guy do you think I am? I don't kiss and tell."

"So, there was kissing. That's promising."

His face flares red, and then he leans in and hugs me. "Thank you. It's been a while for me. And last night . . . well . . . it felt good to be out there again."

"You look happy." I smile at him as he walks out onstage for his opening scene.

He turns back and blows me a kiss. "You know it."

While I wait for my entrance, my thoughts wander to the last month with Jake and the Italian man's offer last night. Will I be out there again soon? No matter how much I fight against it, the tactless idea marches through my brain. I shake it away and get set onstage to become someone else for a few hours.

It's all the therapy I need.

At the end of practice, I notice Taahira approach Cole. He smiles at me and nods toward her to make sure I'm noticing. I laugh and mouth, "Have fun."

I walk out to my car by myself.

My phone shows one message, and it's from the hospital. By the time I finish listening, I'm rushing to the car with excitement. It's from a nurse on the pediatric floor wondering when I'll be arriving. Natalie keeps asking for me.

On my way to the hospital, I stop to buy a bag of chocolates and a few other sweets. All are on Nat's list of approved treats, and all are needed for today's adventure.

I exit the elevator and walk down the hallway as if I'm about to win the gold medal in an Olympic speed-walking event. As I stride past the nurse's station, Nurse Gables actually claps her hands.

"Oh, she'll be so excited you're here."

There's no need to elaborate on who she is. Everyone here knows who I've come to see.

I'm panting by the time I reach her door, and tiny prickles of sweat creep down my hairline as I gear up. A nurse helps me change into a sterile set of scrubs before I enter Natalie's clean room. They have the system down, and I'm grateful for the well-practiced hands keeping Natalie safe.

"Welcome to Natalie's Chocolate Factory." I step into the room with a sealed bag of sanitized sweets in each hand. The door swings shut, and I expect Nat to be overcome with happiness, to jump out of bed and hug me.

But Natalie doesn't jump or move at all.

She does smile though. And her smile is enough.

Her frail body barely makes a bump in the white blanket covering her from the waist down. I return her smile, tucking away the fear surely showing in my eyes. She's thinner and paler than the last time I saw her. How is it even possible?

Still, I'm thrilled to be with her. I've never been so happy to see a person I didn't create myself.

I don't hesitate as I sit on the bed next to her, covered from head to toe with a mask, gown, and gloves. I hold out one red-wrapped chocolate truffle and watch her eyes brighten at the treat. She pulls on the two ends of the wrapper and laughs when the chocolate ball drops into her lap. Before I can suggest she get a new one, she pops the creamy chocolate sphere into her mouth.

"They sanitize my bedding every morning," she says as she chews.

I pull down my mask to pop a truffle in my mouth and sigh as rich chocolatey goodness oozes over my tongue. "These are the best."

Nat holds out an empty hand and nods.

I dump an entire bag of red and gold wrapped truffles into her open palm. They spill out across her bed, and we both laugh.

After she eats three more, she finally asks. "So how bad do I look?"

Both my eyebrows shoot up of their own accord. "What? You don't look bad. You're an alabaster beauty queen."

She sends me a knowing smile. "One thing you learn real quick in here is to judge faces, especially when people first look at me. I saw your face. It was what-flowers-am-I-going-to-bring-to-the-funeral bad." She flops back onto her pillows. "I look awful."

"Not awful." I force a smile, trying to stall. "You look . . ." I leave my mouth hanging open, hoping the perfect words will magically appear in my mind, but I wait a bit too long.

"That's what I thought." Nat pulls the covers up to her chin.

I watch her lip quiver and realize more than anything in the world right now, I want to hear her laugh. She needs something to laugh about. "Okay, fine then . . . just in case. What are your favorite flowers?"

Her eyes flash to mine, wild with surprise. She hadn't expected those words.

I tilt my chin down and send her my most innocent look. "Just curious, you know. No other reason." I shrug and smile.

A sweet laugh bursts out of Natalie. It's the best sound I've ever heard.

Full and joyous and catching.

"It's definitely not because I want to buy a large quantity of them for any specific occasion," I add.

"Yeah, sure." Nat pops another truffle into her mouth.

I swallow down my last bite of chocolate. "I mean that would be totally inappropriate, with you still breathing and all. Plus, I've heard it's bad form to bring someone a funeral arrangement before they actually die."

She gives me one of her patented exaggerated eye-rolls I've learned to love over the course of my visits.

I reach across the bed and give her a quick hug. "I'm glad I came."

"Me too," she whispers. "And for the record." She looks me right in the eye. "Hydrangeas. My favorite flowers are white hydrangeas. But I'm allergic to all kinds of flowers, so I can't have any in the room."

"Duly noted." I nod once, turning serious now. "I'll be sure not to bring you flowers the next time I visit. If you see so much as a single petal around me over the next few weeks, you have my permission to give me the shocked adult look."

She demonstrates her shocked look for me, and I can't help but laugh.

"Now that's a good look for you." I lift my phone and take a pic. Then turn the screen toward her so she can see it. "*Vogue* cover material right there."

Another eye roll, and I laugh again.

"So are you up for some cards?" I ask. "I think I saw the nurses sanitizing some when I came in."

Natalie pushes the chocolate wrappers aside and pats the blanket. "Have a seat. Just don't cry when I beat you at Uno."

"Uno, huh?" I smile as a nurse enters carrying a stack of cards. "I see I've properly scared you with my Phase Ten skills. You might actually stand a chance with Uno."

We play games until Nat starts to drift off. Her head drops to her chest, and I try to slip away. Her eyes immediately flash open.

"No!" she calls. "Don't leave. Please don't leave."

215

The panic in her voice has me back at her bedside in an instant. "Hey." I hug her close. "It's okay. I'm not leaving for good. Just to give you some time to rest." I cradle her sweet face in my hands. "And when I come back to visit, can I bring my friend, Lettie? Would you like to meet her? She's pretty amazing."

Natalie yawns, and some of the panic fades from her face. I breathe easier. She lays back and snuggles deep into her pillows. "Okay, I guess. I am pretty tired."

She's asleep before I leave the room.

"It's wonderful for you to visit," Nurse Gables says as I walk by the nurses' station. "It'll make things easier for her, now . . ."

At her words, my smile melts away. "What do you mean, now?"

Nurse Gables holds my gaze. "The doctors have done all they can, Bethany. Natalie will be leaving us soon."

"What?" I'm shaking my head. "They can't just let her die. There has to be something else they can try."

She sends me the soft, knowing smile of a seasoned nurse. "They've tried everything. Trust me. We all love her. And I know it's hard to hear, but Natalie has been living this half-life for a long time. She's ready."

"How long?"

"What?"

"How long does she have?"

"Weeks? Days? However long her body decides to hold out."

"Can I do anything for her? Anything at all?"

"She said she wants to see the sunset one last time."

One last time. I thought I knew how it felt to have my heart broken on that day two weeks ago when I saw those texts on Jake's phone. But now, when Nat sleeps quietly a few yards away—when she knows she's dying and spends an entire afternoon playing cards with me—now when her only wish in the world is to see one final sunset—now when someone I love is dying.

Now I understand a whole new level of heartbreak.

"Will the doctors let her?" I ask.

"Let her what?"

"Will they let her see the sunset one more time?"

Nurse Gables lifts her shoulders. "She can't go outside, but we're trying to find a portable respirator small enough for her so she can watch it somewhere on the pediatric floor."

I nod, my mind working faster than my feet can move. "Work on finding that respirator. Let me know when you do." I call back to Nurse Gables as I walk away. "I have an idea. I'll take care of everything else." I'm dialing Lettie's number as I exit the building. "I need your help."

IT TAKES JUST OVER twenty-four hours for us to gather everything we need. Thankfully Lettie is on the arts and education board for the county, and she has some pull at the local college.

When evening comes, there's only one item left on my to-do list. *Make a gift for Natalie.* I'm determined to give her something that will make her happy. Something that will lift her spirits and let her know someone loves her.

Which is why I continue pacing in my kitchen trying to come up with an idea to make her smile again. Nothing. Nothing. Nothing. My steps echo my failure back to me. I bump the table with my hip, and the vase of stems wobbles and tips over, spilling water everywhere.

"Dammit," I sigh. "I should have thrown these things away days ago." I grab the vase to do just that, but stop myself when I come up with a better plan for the left-over stalks. Simple. Easy. "And she'll love it."

An hour later, Lettie and I walk into the hospital, each carrying homemade bouquets. Bunches of tall stems wrapped in layers of winding ribbon. As promised, not a single petal tops the stalks, no flowers to remind her of funerals. No blooms to set off her allergies.

The perfect gift.

And tonight, everything has to be perfect.

For most kids, the night's activity would probably be more of a chore or an assignment. But I'm hoping she'll love it. I can't wait to see her face when she hears what we get to do.

Lettie's by my side as we take the elevator up to the pediatric wing. We're both giggling like elves on Christmas Eve, so excited are we for this epic surprise.

"Is everything ready?" I ask Nurse Gables.

The nurses are all smiles as she answers. "It's all set up, and we're so excited. Such a great idea. She'll never forget this."

"That's the plan," I say as I make my way to her room. Nurse Gables follows. "Do you have the respirator?"

She nods. "The doctor dropped it off in her room an hour ago."

"Perfect." We stop in front of Natalie's door, and I turn to Lettie. "You ready to meet the most amazing eleven-year-old in the world?"

"Considering I've lived with eleven-year-olds, the bar's set pretty low. As long as she doesn't throw spit wads at me, she'll surpass all expectations."

"She will," I whisper, then open the door, and we step inside.

Natalie instantly falls in love with Lettie. And their love affair is mutual. I've never seen so many adoring smiles pass between two people in my life. I'm almost jealous. But the more people to love this sweet girl, the better.

I hand Nat my green-stalk bouquet, and she makes a show of smelling the non-existent flowers. "They're beautiful." Lettie hands her the second bouquet. "Prettiest non-flowers I've ever seen."

"You ready for an adventure?" I ask.

"An adventure? I think you have me mixed-up with a normal kid." Nat motions to her sterile environment. "Unless you have an adventure hidden somewhere in this room."

I smile.

Lettie smiles.

Nurse Gables smiles.

The question hangs on Natalie's confused face before she asks, "What's going on?"

"Well..." I sit next to her. "I've been making goals for myself these last few weeks, and I need your help."

"Help with what?"

I turn my notebook to show her my latest goal.

To paint the grass today, I will...
Learn a new skill.

"What do you want to learn? Like cooking or something? 'Cause I'm not making sushi. No raw fish." Nat sticks out her tongue and pretends to gag.

Lettie laughs.

"Where is it?" I ask Nurse Gables.

She disappears into the attached bathroom and comes back with a mask and filter connected to a portable oxygen bottle.

"What's that?" Natalie asks.

"It's your ticket to freedom for the night." I smile as Nurse Gables hooks Natalie up to the breathing apparatus. My heart flips and flutters like a baby bird learning to fly, and it feels as fragile as Natalie's touch. I hope this works. I hope she loves it.

When Nurse Gables steps back, Nat looks like a character from a futuristic movie, and she's practically bouncing in her wheelchair. As carefully as I can, I wheel her out the door and follow Lettie to where our surprise awaits.

"Time for me to learn something new," I say as we turn the final corner.

Natalie's head swivels left and then right. Her eyes open wide, ready for anything that might come her way. But nothing prepares her for the sight of the entire pediatric wing staff dressed in artist frocks standing in the west lobby.

The blinds have been raised, and the hazy pink beginning of a sunset tints the room in an orange hue. As we enter, twelve easels with canvasses, resting and ready for paint, stand tall. A short man with a long beard comes forward.

"Hello, Natalie." Crouching down to her level, he shakes her hand. "I'm Professor Bloom, and I'll be your instructor this evening." He motions to the wall of windows facing west. "Tonight, the sunset will be our subject, so let's get our brushes ready."

I set Nat up at the easel between mine and Lettie's. "I've always wanted to learn how to paint," I confess.

"I love painting," Natalie whispers, almost reverently. "I used to stare out the window at my Gran's house and paint whatever I could see."

"Well," Lettie says. "Then you're going to be way better at this than we are."

I lift my brush and dip it in water, then look at Lettie. "Ready to be shown up by an eleven-year-old?"

"Ha!" Lettie answers. "Like that's never happened to me before." She winks at Nat, and we set brush to canvas and start to paint.

It's a glorious sunset.

I find myself thanking God for the beautiful colors, for the wispy clouds holding onto the light, for the way the horizon cradles the sun, and most importantly for the smile that never leaves Natalie's face.

She paints for over an hour—and creates a masterpiece. Finer than any artwork displayed in any gallery in all the world.

We finish just as the last bits of light fade from the sky, but no one's painting comes close to Nat's in beauty or skill. She has poured her heart onto the canvas.

At Nurse Gables' suggestion, we all pose for a photo, and then she snaps one of Natalie hugging me. Natalie takes the time to thank the professor and says goodnight to everyone, calling them each by name. I forget how long she's been here. These nurses are her family.

No one minds the muffled sound of her voice, or hugging her around her respirator. Each and every person here basks in the joy on Nat's face.

I wheel her down to the far end of the hallway and allow the nurses to go through their sanitizing routine once again. While they take care of Nat, I situate three of the canvases on easels in her room. Mine, Lettie's, and hers. They're all completely different, and my favorite by far came from the hand of the youngest artist in the group. The paintings bring a much-needed spot of color to cheer the sterile room.

"There," I say to Nat as she situates herself in her bed. "Now you can see the sunset whenever you want." I walk to her bedside, and she throws her arms around my neck.

She clings to me like she's the horizon, and I'm the sun.

"Thank you," she whispers, and tears drip down my cheek. I can't tell if they're hers or mine because we've both started to cry.

I kiss her nose and fluff her pillows as she gets comfortable in bed.

"Best night ever," she says. "Thank you so much."

"You're welcome so much." I smile at her, and notice someone's put my bundle of flowerless stalks in a vase by her bed.

"Where will we be tomorrow?" she whispers.

"Wherever you want to be." I send her my brightest smile and gather up my things. When a nurse enters to help her get ready for bed, Lettie and I head toward the door.

"Good night, Nat."

"Good night, Queen B," she says.

"Queen B," Lettie laughs. "It fits her." She waves to Nat. "It was nice to meet you."

"You can come back tomorrow too if you want."

"Wouldn't miss it," Lettie says.

We walk to the elevator in silence, except for the few times I have to sniff back my tears.

"Thanks for making this happen," I say as the doors close behind us.

"Hey..." Lettie holds up both hands. "It was your idea. I just pulled a few strings and bought some paint."

I smile. "She's great, isn't she? Impressive, I mean. And brave. So brave."

"Yes," Lettie nods. "She's amazing. And it's true what they say."

"What's that?"

"Strong women build up everyone around them."

"Well, I agree," I say. "She definitely brings out something in me."

"You're the strong woman I was talking about."

I open my mouth to argue, but Lettie stops me with one raised hand. "It's not up for debate." She loops her arm through mine, and we step off the elevator and head to her car. "Now how about we go paint something else. Grass, maybe?"

TWENTY-ONE

OUR SUNSET SQUARE IN honor of Nat is now my favorite in the painted garden. Red, orange, yellow, and pink blend seamlessly together and fade into deep-blue, creating the perfect layers of colored sky across my back lawn. It's a beautiful depiction of my goal to try something new, which transformed into Nat's best night ever.

Lettie only stays for a few minutes before she has to go tend to her boys, the little ones and the big one.

I smile at her when she leaves. I smile while I clean up. I'm still smiling when I get ready for bed. I'm even smiling when the phone rings.

Jake's face stares at me from the Caller ID.

I wait for my anger to spike or for sadness to weigh me down, but it doesn't happen.

I'm just too happy.

"Hello," I chirp into the phone.

"Well, someone sounds happy," Jake says. "I haven't heard this Bethany in a while."

"I had a great day," I say. "I met this really amazing girl, and I've been spending a lot of time with her."

Jake's deep chuckle sounds over the phone. "Are you trying to tell me something? Have you replaced me with a woman then?"

"Oh. Come on. You have the maturity of a fourteen-year-old. Seriously, Jake. She's eleven, and she's amazing."

"Eleven? Where did you meet an eleven-year-old girl?"

"Volunteering at the hospital."

"You're a volunteer at the hospital? How many vials of hand sanitizer did you go through on your first day?"

"A lot. But I'm doing a good thing, and I'm loving it."

"Good. I'm glad you're finding your passion, B. And that you're happy." He clears his throat. "And I'm really glad you're not replacing me."

"I'm not the one who's pushing so hard to spend time with someone else."

"Come on, B. Things were going so well . . ."

Unwanted emotion rises up and I swallow it down. "You know, Jake. I'm in a really great mood, and I don't want to ruin it with this conversation. So, I'm going to hang up now."

"Can I come over?"

"Not tonight. Maybe tomorrow. Today, I'm too busy being happy." I end the call before he can say another word.

I'm still smiling when I set the phone on the table. After talking to Jake, I still have a smile on my face.

Which may just resemble something that looks a lot like a miracle.

Soft morning light slips through my window, brightening my room after a peaceful night. I reach over and turn off the alarm on my phone and stretch as I climb out of bed. I'm still smiling.

I rub my sore cheeks and wonder if I smiled all through the night. Then I shake my head at the ridiculous image of a Joker smile pasted on my face as I slept. A giggle slips out as I change into my running clothes.

To avoid Alex's house, I choose my route, taking a detour through the neighborhood one block over. It's totally worth it. Nothing's going to ruin my mood today.

My feet pound the sidewalk, and I feel the contact deep inside. *Hap-py. Hap-py. Hap-py.*

Having Little Miss Natalie in my life has been an incredibly mood-altering experience. I take so much for granted. I find myself thinking of how much time I waste on things that just don't matter.

But not today, I think as I run. Today I'm going to be happy. I'm going to be grateful. I'm going to grin like I've just won a Nobel Prize all day long. In honor of my new friend. My heart beats, my legs burn, and my smile stays in place. I think of Natalie and her beautiful sunset painting the entire thirty minutes of my run.

I'm dripping with sweat by the time I make it back to the house, and I strip off my clothes on my way to the shower. Under the hot spray, my muscles let go of the tension brought on by exercise, and an idea turns around inside my mind. A simple idea to brighten my day.

After a quick shower, I pull my hair back into a tight bun, put on a bright-turquoise top and black yoga pants, then go in search of my notebook. It takes almost no time to write my goal for the day.

> To paint the grass today, I will...
> Share some happiness with others.

I grin to myself before I add:

> Smile at everyone I see. (For Natalie.)

With one hand, I flip my notebook closed and slide it into my purse. Everywhere I go today, I'm going to spread the joy Natalie has brought into my life. She can't leave her hospital room, so it will be up to me to share her smile with everyone else.

My car door sticks a little as I open it, and I remind myself to tell Jake about it. Except, I can't tell Jake. Not after what's happened. I feel my smile slip a little, so I think of Natalie. I hold onto the image of her rowing a plastic bin boat through her hospital room, and my smile slides firmly into place once again.

I smile and wave to the other drivers as I make my way to the theater. I smile at Cole and Taahira as I step up onstage. I smile at Kyle as we begin our opening routine. I never stop smiling, and my happiness is contagious.

Kyle doesn't yell when Heather misses a critical line in the second act. Cole buys me my favorite chocolate bar and bag of chips during intermission. And Piper Baker hands me an audition flyer for another play with a start date two months from now.

"I think you'd be perfect for this. Just don't try out for the lead. Hopefully I'll be off the crutches by then. We can play opposite each other. We'll bring down the house. Together. If you can manage to not suck." She smiles as she limps away.

"I've just witnessed a miracle," Cole says, and I punch him in the arm.

Happiness must be in the air at our little theater.

After rehearsal, I stop by the hospital to see Nat. But today, when I get to her room, she's sound asleep.

"Your painting activity wore her clean out," Nurse Gables says.

I smile at Nurse Gables and leave Nat a book and two props to go with the story, a plastic mustache, and a bight-pink hair bow. "Tell her I'll come by tomorrow and stay twice as long."

When I leave the hospital, I'm not ready to go home. Instead, I drive to town and park on Main Street, wanting to find a few more people to smile at today. I climb out of the car and smile at a garbage man, high up in his truck.

"Hello," I call out.

He looks at me like I'm crazy, but he smiles and waves back.

I smile at the grocery store clerk and the bank teller. I smile at the server who brings me a late lunch. I smile at a postal worker behind the counter at the post office. I smile at the man walking his dog and another stranger on the street.

I smile and smile and smile.

Only one person asks if I'm crazy.

I laugh and answer, "Maybe."

But still, he smiles back at me.

I smile all day, even on my way home. In fact, I smile right up until the time I throw up in Mrs. Platt's front yard.

It's almost impossible to smile when you're doubled over, heaving your lunch onto the neighbor's lawn. Crouched in this position, no one would see my smile anyway.

Mrs. Platt rushes outside, most likely to see what damage I've done to her lawn, or to keep me away from her rare, reblooming irises. She shakes her head as I offer her a weak apology. "None of that now," she says.

She cups her hand to my forehead, just like my mom used to do. Ladies of a certain age do not need thermometers to judge temperature. They can feel a fever just like they can feel a storm coming in. I wonder if Mrs. Platt can feel both in me today.

"You aren't feverish, but you look terrible. Let me help you inside."

With one arm around my back, she lifts me off the ground and gets me to my feet. She supports me as we walk up the stairs and through my front door. Instead of taking me to my room, Mrs. Platt walks me to the sofa in the living room. Then she disappears into my bedroom and returns carrying a pillow and blanket from my bed.

She gently lifts my head and places the pillow behind it, then removes my shoes and tucks the blanket in around me. "When I was young," she says.

"My mother would make us a bed on the couch whenever we were sick. It was the only time we were allowed soda in the living room. I'll bring you some ginger ale later on if you'd like." Her mothering hands fuss over me like I'm one of her own children, and I'm surprised and comforted by her kindness.

I feel loved.

"Thank you, Mrs. Platt," I whisper.

"Oh, please," she clucks. "Call me Sonia. We've been through a battle and come out on the other side. I think that warrants a first-name basis."

"Thanks, Sonia." I offer a weak smile. "I just can't be sick. I have to get better. I have to." I lean back against the pillow but still try to make her understand. "There's this sweet girl in the hospital, and she's not doing well and . . . and she needs me. I visit her every day. I'm all she has."

"Of course, dear." She smiles at me. "I'll get you feeling better faster than pansies sprout in spring. We mothers have to take care of each other." She leans in and kisses my forehead, and her wrinkled lips bring even more comfort. After she closes the blinds, she puts a large plastic bowl beside the couch and hands me the remote to the television. "Here you go. The bowl's for in case you get sick again. Now find a nice movie, something happy, and don't get up the rest of the day. That's an order. I'll be back at dinner with some soup and ginger ale. You have your phone?"

I hold up my cell phone.

"Good." She nods once. "You call me if you need anything else. Is Jake going to be home soon?"

For some reason, at the sound of Jake's name tears fill my eyes. "I don't know," I whisper.

"Well, never you mind, then. You get feeling better. Hopefully it's just something you ate. A bit of food poisoning should only last a few hours, a day at most. Once it gets out of your system, you'll be right as rain."

"Thank you."

"No need to thank me. You go on and rest. I'll see myself out."

The door clicks behind Mrs. Platt, and I allow my head to sink deeper into the pillows. My stomach cramps, and my entire lower abdomen rumbles. I place both my hands over my tummy and groan. Probably not the best idea to eat lobster and scallops at a waffle house in a town seven hundred miles away from any ocean.

The thought of eating makes me gag, and I hang over the side of the couch and dry heave into the bowl. Thankfully my stomach's empty. There's nothing left to come up. I wipe one hand across my mouth and curl up on my side facing the back of the couch.

My forehead touches the soft brown leather, and I think of all the times I've force-fed medicine to my boys. All the times I've cleaned up piles of throw-up and wiped snot-crusted noses. When anyone in the family gets sick, the mother takes care of everything. She makes magic soups and heats up rice packs for sore backs. She buys whatever fluids are requested and spoons medicine into mouths. She moves heaven and earth to get everyone well again. But when the mother gets sick, she sucks it up or suffers in silence.

My pity-party slips to new levels, but it doesn't make me feel any better. Using my phone, I look up how long food poisoning lasts. I'm no doctor, but it certainly feels like I've been poisoned. After I type in a few keywords, I read food poisoning can last anywhere from a few hours to a few days. Maybe, since I only ate two scallops and a teeny, tiny lobster tail, mine will be the shorter version.

I snuggle deeper into my pillow and pull the soft blanket up to my chin. Maybe if I close my eyes, I can sleep away all the awful feelings. It's the last thought I have before I drift off.

The sound of the doorknob turning wakes me. I open my eyes. It's full dark in the house. How long have I been sleeping? A light flips on in the hallway. With both hands braced against the couch, I slide myself up into a sitting position and click on the table-lamp next to the sofa.

"I'm still on the couch where you left me, Mrs. Pla . . . I mean . . . Sonia," I call out.

There's no answer.

"Maybe with your help I can make it to the table to eat. I don't want to drip soup on my favorite blanket."

Everything goes still after I speak.

Again, no answer.

My heart digs into my chest, as my mind flips through scenes from every crime drama known to man. "Sonia?"

But it's not Sonia who answers.

Jake steps into the room. "Really, babe? I know we've been on the outs lately, but I think after twenty years you'd recognize your own husband."

TWENTY-TWO

M Y NAUSEA RETURNS THE minute I recognize his voice. "What are you doing here?"

"Yesterday you said to come over tomorrow. It's tomorrow." Jake walks into the living room and smiles down at me. "I saw Mrs. Platt in the yard. She told me you weren't feeling well so she's making you some soup. I figured you'd either welcome my TLC or attack one of my essential body parts with scissors." He shrugs. "I took a chance."

I can't help it. I grunt out a short laugh. He always was good at making me feel better.

Suddenly, I'm self-conscious. I know I look a mess and probably have dried vomit on the side of my face. Still, I try to smooth my hair behind my ears and fix my bangs. Old habits die hard.

"You look gorgeous," Jake says, charming as always.

"Shut up. I do not." I roll my eyes at him. "And I feel even worse than I look."

I try to stand up, wobble a little, then almost fall over.

"Whoa." Jake guides me back to the sofa. "Don't get up. How long has it been since you've had water? You're probably dehydrated."

I lay back down and listen to his footsteps as he makes his way to the kitchen. He brings me a glass. There's a straw sticking out of the top, and I'm grateful I don't have to tip it as I slowly sip the water. When I'm done, he takes the glass from me and puts it on the side table, making sure he uses a coaster. He really is on his best behavior.

"Why are you still here?" I flop my face back onto the pillow. "I don't want to see you." With one hand I pull the blanket over my head.

Jake sits on the wood-slab coffee table and leans forward, elbows on knees. "Okay," Jake says. "But since I'm here, maybe we could talk."

"No. I'm sick."

"I know you are." He stands. "I'll let you rest, and I'll be back to check on you after I grab a few things out of my office. But before I leave, I'm feeding you soup. You need sustenance."

He walks away, and I don't try to follow him. I also don't sleep. How can I sleep when *he's* in the next room? What am I supposed to say to him? How does he expect me to act?

I lay on the couch, my spirits as empty as my cramping stomach. For the past twenty years, I've been living an invisible life. And I have no idea what to do to get Jake to see me.

For the better part of an hour, I stew in my worries until they're fork tender. And still, I have no idea what I'm going to do. When a knock sounds from the door, I sit up, but before I can stand, Sonia pushes her way inside the house.

"Don't get up." She motions me back down on the couch with her chin. In her hands she holds the largest pot of soup I've ever seen. "I made my special homemade noodles too. My kids say they're magic." She hauls the pot onto my stove. "This will fix you right up."

"Well, hello, Mrs. Platt." Jake comes out of the bedroom and greets us. "Thanks so much for looking after Beth while I was gone."

She looks at me and gives me a questioning glance, then turns a smile to Jake. "Glad you're back. Now I don't have to worry about her all night long." She sets a six-pack of ginger ale on the counter. "Keep her hydrated."

"Yes, ma'am," Jake says.

I sit up tall on the couch and holler toward the door. "Thank you for the soup."

"You just get to feeling better." She sends me a knowing smile, and it feels like a hug even from across the room. Then she opens the door. "I'll leave you two be. Welcome home, Jake."

"It's good to be back. And thanks again."

The door closes and two heartbeats later, Jake is standing in front of the stove ladling soup into a bowl. He digs some saltine crackers out of the cupboard and places everything on a wooden TV tray. I stay on the couch and watch him side-step the kitchen table to carry everything over to me. But instead of setting it on my lap, he lowers it onto the coffee table and pulls up a chair.

"What are you doing?"

In answer, he picks up the bowl, dips a spoon into the soup, and extends it toward me.

"Are you serious?"

He touches the spoon to my closed lips. "Open up before it drips."

I eat the soup and grab for the spoon.

Jake easily evades my grasp.

"I can feed myself," I complain.

"Let me do it. Please. I never get to take care of you."

"I don't feel good. I can't deal with this right now."

"Then just eat." He holds up another spoonful.

He's still an ass, I think as I eat the second bite.

The warm broth whispers down my raw throat like a heavenly blessing, and the starchy noodles settle my stomach. Sonia's kids are right; this soup is magic. With Jake's unwanted help, I eat three crackers and the entire bowl of soup, all without speaking to him. He simply feeds me one spoonful at a time, periodically handing me a cracker as needed. When I'm finished, he stands up and lifts the tray from off the table.

"I'll just get this cleaned up. See if you can get some sleep." He walks to the kitchen, rinses the dishes, and packs left-over soup into storage containers.

I pull the covers over my head, but sleep is a faithless friend. I can't even close my eyes with Jake in the next room. Why does he have to be kind now? It only makes his betrayal hurt worse somehow.

I'm vulnerable, and he knows it.

I grab my phone and text Lettie.

Me: SOS. Jake came over. I need you.

In less than thirty seconds she responds.

Lettie: I'll be over in ten minutes and stay as long as you need me to.

Me: Thank you.

I hit send on my text, and close my eyes so Jake thinks I'm sleeping.

He dims the lights and walks into the bedroom.

Our bedroom.

Does he think he's going to sleep here tonight?

That is not going to happen! Feeding me soup is one thing. But he can just go on back to the hotel so one of the maids can clean up after him, and he can have a restaurant chef cook for him. And he can just leave me out of it.

The sick feeling in my stomach joins with the sick feeling in my heart makes for a terrible combination. I'm so exhausted. Tired of fighting. Tired of not knowing what to do. Tired of feeling like I'm going to throw up if I move too quickly.

My hands shake, and I wish I felt well enough to smash something. The only thing I see is a pillow, so I throw it across the room for good measure.

It lands with a muffled thud under the mountain picture hanging on the far wall.

I stare at the beautiful painting and wish I could transport myself there. The gorgeous artwork depicts one of my happy places. A place filled with mountains and trees and sunshine. Here on the couch, sick and sad, and with my cheating husband in the next room, there's no sunshine to be seen.

It's a hard reality to be faced with. And even though I've had plenty of time to get my angry on, sadness still clings behind my eyes. He let someone come between us. And even though I didn't catch them in bed together, emotional connections form stronger bonds and require more trust than sex ever could.

Crazy how a non-physical affair can hurt like a physical cut to the heart.

There's a quick knock on the door, and then it swings wide. Lettie and I have a knock-once-and-open rule at each other's houses. She takes three steps into the room, notices the tears in my eyes, and hurries to my side.

I make room for her on the couch as she sinks in next to me, positioning my head so it lays on her shoulder just as Jake comes into the room.

"Hey, Lettie."

"Hey, asshole."

"Lettie," I gasp. But then I can't help but laugh. My best friend has my back.

"What, are we not using the new nickname yet? 'Cause I think it fits him." She sends a wicked smile Jake's way.

"I take it you heard about our disagreement," Jake says.

"If by disagreement you mean how you disregarded and took for granted the most amazing woman in the world, then yeah, I heard about it."

"Okay. Enough. I don't feel like getting into this right now." I force myself to stand, and Lettie helps me stay on my feet. I find my legs don't wobble nearly as much. The soup has made me stronger.

Thank you, Sonia.

I glare at Jake, then grab Lettie's hand and look her in the eye. "Come paint another square with me. I'm feeling strong enough. Will you help?"

Lettie smiles. "Fine. I'll just pretend like he's not here."

But Jake doesn't take the hint. He follows us outside instead. "What are you painting? What squares?"

I flip on the yard lights I've strung between the trees, and he sees my painted garden for the first time.

"What the hell?"

"If you know what's good for you, you'll smile and say it looks wonderful," Lettie snaps through clenched teeth.

Jake mimics a smile and says, "It looks wonderful. What is it?"

"It's my painted grass," I say, like it explains everything. Then Lettie and I pull the supplies out of the shed.

We ignore Jake completely. Lettie because I'm sure she doesn't trust herself to be civil, and me because I have no idea how to act around him now. My cup runneth over with awkwardness, and I feel like he's about to see me naked for the first time.

How can I ever get past this?

Jake finally leaves us alone and heads back inside the house. Lettie and I paint a blue square with a smiling mouth on it to celebrate my day of smiles. But only because my best friend's got talent.

"You could be one of those graffiti artists," I say as we clean up.

"Yeah. And a great role model for the kids too. They'd be like, 'Dad, where's Mom?' And Eric would say, 'She'll be home late. The cops arrested her for tagging a building again, now eat your peas before they get cold.'"

I'm laughing as she finishes her ridiculous story, and it feels great to laugh. "Hey." I stop and put my hand on my stomach. "I laughed without puking."

"I'm so proud. Not everyone has those skills."

We're standing inside the shed, and I hug her tight. "You always make me feel better. Always. Thank you."

She shrugs. "What can I say, it's my super power."

I close the shed and lean up against the doors. "I don't know what to do. I don't want to talk to him, even though I know I need to. It's just—I have no idea what to say. There's no compromise, you know. It's me or her. That's how it has to be."

"It's you." Lettie leans next to me. "And if he can't see that, then you're better off without him." She nudges my shoulder. "You need to choose you. Or nobody else will."

I nod. She's right, of course she's right. "We have twenty years together."

"Yeah, you do."

I look at Lettie square in the face. "Even after twenty years . . ." I take a deep breath. "I wouldn't be surprised if he stopped over at Alex's first before he even came home."

"He wouldn't dare. Does he know I own an axe *and* a meat grinder?"

I laugh again and sink to the ground. "What am I going to do?"

She sits next to me. "You're going to talk to him." I open my mouth to protest, but Lettie holds up one finger. "Not tonight. Tonight, you're going to shower away the vomit and sleep off whatever nastiness tried to kill you today, and then tomorrow—when you feel human again— you'll talk to him."

"But what am I going to say?"

"You've been married to him forever. It isn't like you're asking the guy to give you a kidney on a blind date. You'll figure it out."

"A kidney?"

"Well." She shrugs. "You know what I mean."

"I think I'd rather lose a kidney than deal with this." I rest my forehead on my knees. "I feel like such an idiot. How could I not have known?"

"Because." Lettie puts her arm around me. "No woman, especially not one as amazing as you, should ever have to wonder about their spouse's loyalty. You have nothing to feel stupid about. If he really does have feelings for this other woman—"

"Alex," I add.

"Alex," she says. "If he really does have feelings for her, then it's on him. And he'll lose you, and get to regret it for the rest of his life. Believe me, he will regret it. Everyone who knows you will remind him of it, and I'll be at the top of the list."

I lean against her and sigh. "That's why you're my best friend. You always know the perfect thing to say." I tilt my head up so I can see her face. "Couldn't you just talk to Jake for me?"

Lettie flashes her wicked grin again. "Only if I can bring my meat grinder."

WHEN LETTIE WALKS OUT my front door, she takes my buffer with her. Jake and I are now alone in the house, and I'd rather be anywhere else in the world. I allow myself to hide in the front entry for five minutes, then I put on my big girl panties and go face the music of my marriage.

I delay a little longer by cleaning up the couch. With the meticulous precision of a Martha Stewart groupie, I fold the blankets and stack the pillows. I wash the puke bowl and even get the vacuum out. I'm staring at the curtains when I hear Jake behind me.

"You going to look up how to dry clean those yourself? 'Cause I'm betting it will buy you a lot of time."

I don't move a muscle. I don't say a word.

Jake walks around the room and stands in front of me.

"Come on, B. Talk to me."

"I don't know how to talk to you right now."

"It's still me. I'm the same guy." He reaches for me, and I push his hands away.

"No, you're not the same." I back up, putting some distance between us. "The man I fell in love with would never say I love you to another woman, or go out with someone who sends inappropriate pictures of herself to him." I grab my blanket and pillows from off the couch and head toward our bedroom. "But since you do those things and don't see a problem with it, it's made *me* see the bigger picture."

Jake follows me. "What bigger picture?"

I pause at the bedroom door. "The bigger picture of our relationship."

"What? That's ridiculous."

Anger flares to life, and I whirl around to face him. "Don't tell me it's ridiculous."

Jake takes a deep breath. "Look, I don't want to fight with you. Can't we just go back to how things were?"

"Of course you'd want that, but . . . I don't." My voice chokes and the words die. I swallow down tears and force myself to look at him. "I don't want things to be how they were. I want them to be better. But I can't talk about this anymore tonight. I have early practice, and I need to get to bed."

"Practice for what?"

"I'm the lead in a play. 'Kiss Me, Kate.'"

At the news, his face lights up, and my heart performs a dance number inside my chest.

Stupid fickle heart. I hate it. If it wasn't necessary for life, I'd bury it inside my house and listen to it beat beneath the floorboards.

"I can't wait to see it," Jake says. "I'll be there. Front and center on opening night."

My betraying heart continues to dance and sing inside me, fluttering away like a caged goose hours before it's cooked in a nice port-wine sauce and sliced up for dinner.

"Good night, Jake. I'm sure your hotel will keep a light on for you."

I close the bedroom door in his face and listen as he walks down the hallway and out the front door. When the lock clicks into place, I retreat to the bathroom to get ready for bed.

As I wash my face, I look in the mirror and see my mom. Such a strong woman who lived through so much and still came out smiling. My mother once told me it takes an inner toughness to forgive someone. She took me out to dinner, just the two of us, and told me love is the strongest substance known to man, though no scientist will ever be able to prove it.

Love can do impossible things, she said. It allows you to forgive someone who hurt you, even if they hurt you on purpose. Forgiveness shows strength. Love is the source of that strength.

I look at my sad eyes and wonder if I have strength enough to forgive Jake. After all he's done, after twenty years together, is my love strong enough to forgive?

Do I even want it to be?

With a flip of my wrist, I turn on the shower, step beneath the cleansing spray, and allow the hot water to wash away all my wonderings.

TWENTY-THREE

I WAKE UP THE NEXT morning to sunshine, birdsongs, and thoughts of Natalie. A quick dial of my phone connects me to the nurse's desk at the hospital. Nurse Gables answers on the first ring.

"How's Nat?" I ask.

"Hey, Bethany. Nat was so sad she slept through your visit yesterday. I'm under strict orders to wake her when you come by today."

"I'll have to see how I'm feeling. Had a bit of food poisoning last night. But I'll send her something this morning and try to come visit this evening. Will that work?"

"You bet. I'll tell her," Nurse Gables says. "She'll be so happy."

"How's she feeling?"

"Weak. She's still really weak."

"Well then, I'll just have to send her some of my strength, won't I?"

I hang up the phone and make a call to a florist shop. When I ask them to deliver six bouquets of stems to the pediatric wing of Deaconess hospital, the woman who takes my order says it's the weirdest request she's ever had.

"You want me to cut off the blooms?" she asks.

"Yes," I say. "Or just use your spare stems. If you could arrange them with leaves, ribbons, and bows and address them to Natalie that would be great. Nurse Gables at the pediatric desk will take them to her."

"Okay. It's your money. You want stems. You got 'em."

Doing something for Natalie, even something small, makes me feel a lot better.

When I put on my running gear, the stiffness in my muscles reminds me I spent most the previous day lying on the couch. I stretch my legs and can't wait to get moving again. The sun shines through my bedroom window, luring me out into the day. Don't mind if I do.

I exit the bedroom and step out into a world scented with bacon.

The wood floor gleams with a fresh mopping, and I follow the tempting smells down the hallway and into the kitchen.

Jake's here again, and he made me breakfast.

I've always loved the homey feel of our great room, and today it's even more beautiful. Jake has set a romantic table for two. Complete with a vase of roses and three tall tapered candles. Orange juice fills crystal goblets, and as I walk into the room, he's carrying french toast over from the stove.

When he turns around and sees me in my running gear, his whistle breaks the silence between us. The carefully nurtured smile drops from his face, and his eyes open wide.

"Whoa. You look amazing. I've never seen you like that." He clears his throat and gives his head a small shake. "I mean, good morning. Are you feeling better?"

All I can do is stare at him. When did he sneak back into the house? Why is he here?

Then I remember the why. A bowl of strawberries on the table reminds me of the reason for all of this. There's a guilty explanation and it starts with the scarlet letter—A.

For Alex.

"I made breakfast."

"I see that. Expecting someone special?"

"Just you." Jake sets the plates on the table.

"This isn't going to work, Jake. You can't just romance me into forgetting everything that's happened."

He holds up both hands as if I'm trying to rob him. "No pressure. Just sit down for a minute and eat something."

I close my eyes. "I'm not hungry."

Jake sighs. "Fine . . . no breakfast. That's fine." He takes the plate of food back to the kitchen. "You going on a run?"

I chance looking at him. "Yes."

"Can I come along?"

"Uh . . . no."

"Why not?"

"We've never gone on a run together before."

He shrugs. "There's a first time for everything. Can I come?"

My sigh could knock Alex's skinny ass over. "Fine," I snap. "But only if you don't talk."

"Deal."

While he changes, I stretch again, making sure every part of my body is ready to move. Maybe this won't be so bad. Maybe it will be a chance for Jake to get a glimpse of the new me.

Jake opens the door, and we step out onto the front porch.

"Ready?" I ask.

He nods, keeping his word about not speaking.

We start off down the sidewalk. He runs behind me, and I can feel him analyzing my every move, judging how I place my feet and swing my arms. But I don't care.

Let him judge. I'm over it.

After ten minutes of his inspection, he runs up beside me. "I'm impressed.

I know we said no talking, but you've got some good form, babe. You're a natural runner. Who knew?"

Without my permission, my cheeks flood with color at his praise. Before I can stop myself, my voice sends a breathy, "Thanks," his way.

My entire body is a traitor.

I mentally slap myself for the effect his words have on me and focus on putting one foot in front of the other. We run side by side. He lets me set the pace. Wanting to impress him, I set a pretty fast pace, and I'm making good time. Steady even strides, nice controlled breathing, I'm a running machine. I continue along my usual route, not thinking of what's ahead. Not thinking of whose house we're coming up on. Until we're right in front of it.

Jake cranes his neck to gape as we run past Alex's house. I roll my eyes and try to pretend I don't notice. The sliding glass door in the backyard opens, and a deep voice speaks. Jake slows his pace, then stops all together, leaning down to stretch. I slow my stride a bit and look into her yard. It's the same guy. The same guy I saw her with the other day. The one with the wedding ring.

"That's her ex-husband," Jake says. "Alex didn't say anything about getting back together with him."

I stop in the middle of the sidewalk and turn to him. "I don't care. We going to finish our run or not?"

"Sure." Jake nods as we start down the street once again.

But he's completely distracted, and pretty soon he pulls ahead. I'm too tired to keep up with his well-trained strides. In minutes, he's a quarter mile in front of me, and I'm staring at his tiny figure receding in the distance.

I look at the back of his head, getting angrier with each step. He rounds the end of a cul-de-sac and starts to head back my way. He isn't smiling when he reaches me, and I can tell his mind is elsewhere. Gee, I wonder who he's thinking about?

As he passes me, he holds up one hand for me to high-five.

I ignore it and run past him, keeping up my pace until I too round the cul-de-sac and head back toward him. He's standing in the same spot. I slow down when I get close to him and stop to stretch my legs.

A strange look clouds his face. It's as if I'm a creature he's never seen before.

"You okay?" he asks.

I shrug. "Feeling good."

"Your pace is really impressive. Nice and steady and pretty fast for a beginner."

"I don't care about speed. I run because I like how it makes me feel."

"Good for you. I'm glad you're enjoying it."

"Me too." I finish stretching. "You ready to head back? I usually take the shortcut through the park."

"Sure. Makes sense." He looks down the street. "But maybe I should run back the way we came. You know. Get in a little extra."

My nostrils flare, and I don't even try to stop the fire-breathing monster from settling in behind my ribcage. I huff out an unhappy laugh, and my voice goes flat. "Whatever, Jake. Obviously, what I think doesn't matter."

I turn to take the short-cut home, and Jake doesn't follow.

My feet hit the pavement in a numbing rhythm. One. Two. One. Two. One. Two. The steady beat pounds through my soles, calming me with every step. One. Two. One. Two. I breathe in the fresh morning air, soak in the sunshine, and enjoy the wind against my skin.

And refuse to let Jake ruin my day.

When I get home, I strip out of my sweaty clothes and hit the shower. I take my time getting ready and choose to wear my feel-good outfit. Black-patterned pants and a form-fitting red top with my red Italian leather shoes to match. A touch of makeup and a spritz of perfume, and I'm ready to go.

Jake never comes back to the house.

I try not to imagine him with Alex as I get into my car and drive to play practice. By the time I walk into the theater and onto the stage, I think—*Jake who?* The entire cast goes through our morning warm up, and then we start practice with the top of Act I. It's my best performance yet, and the room is alive with anticipation for the coming week.

"Run through it again," Kyle yells through the bullhorn.

"Come on, Kyle," Cole complains. "It was perfect. What more do you want from us?"

"I want you to run it again," he says. "If it's perfect, then it shouldn't be a problem."

"Got it, boss," Cole says, and we get set to go again.

It's even better the second time through.

"Run it again," Kyle calls out.

Every person onstage glares at the director, a mob ready to storm the castle.

Kyle starts laughing, and his laugh sounds like a deranged robot coming through the mechanical bullhorn. "Got ya," he says. "Actors, take ten minutes. Stage crew, front and center. Let's go over placements for Act Two."

Cole and I make our way to the back row of the theater. He grabs snacks from the vending machines and sits next to me, firmly established in our routine.

I'm flipping through pages in my notebook when the creak of another chair catches my attention. Taahira sits down, smiling shyly at me. She takes the seat on the other side of Cole, and he drapes one arm over her shoulders.

I smile. "Hey, Taahira." I toss her a bag of chips. "If you're going to sit with us, you have to eat with us too. It's part of the gig."

She opens the bag and pops a crunchy snack into her mouth. "Thanks," she says. "You were amazing today."

"Nah," I laugh. "Cole just makes me look good."

A twinkle blinks to life in her eye, and she leans toward the man sitting between us. "He does tend to make people look good." When she leans forward again, her earrings sway, and Cole bats at them with one finger.

A single diamond flower rests directly on her earlobe with buds extending up toward the top of the ear, and vines dangling down below her lobe. They're gorgeous.

"I love your earrings," I tell her.

Instinctively, she reaches up to touch them. "Thanks. I bought them after a really bad breakup. I decided I needed something to make me feel beautiful. So rather than waiting for someone to give me something, I went shopping and bought these for myself."

"Such a great idea." I tap my notebook. "Mind if I steal it?"

"Steal away," Taahira says.

In my notebook, I write . . .

To paint the grass today, I will...
Buy something that makes me feel beautiful.

I flip the book closed. "Thanks."

"Is that your journal?" Taahira asks.

I'm about to answer when Kyle yells, "Actors to the stage."

"Sort of." I take care of the empty snack wrappers and walk toward the stage, giving Cole a few stolen seconds of alone time with Taahira.

Act two goes just as smoothly, and Kyle doesn't have us run it again. Instead, we all sit on the edge of the stage to listen to his instructions for opening week.

"Dress rehearsal all day tomorrow, starting bright and early," Kyle says. "We'll be in full costumes, and hopefully have a completely painted set. Prepare to run it over and over again until we get all the kinks knocked out. Make sure you block out the entire day. And remember, on opening night, we have a promotional photo shoot after the show. Wear something nice for your close-up, folks. I want some good press on this one!"

Cole and Taahira walk me to my car. Smiles never leave their faces, and they find an excuse to touch each other with every breath. It's too cute to be sickening.

"Come to dinner and out shopping with us," Taahira insists. "I still have to find a dress for opening night."

I'm touched by her invite and laugh at the don't-you-dare look Cole tries valiantly to hide. "Don't remind me. I have to find one too. And I hate shopping. But I can't tonight, I'm headed up to visit a friend in the hospital. Maybe during our never-ending rehearsal tomorrow, we could all grab lunch and you can show me your dress."

"Perfect." Taahira lifts her phone and adds it to her calendar. "It's a date."

"I have a feeling I'll need the break. Sounds like it's going to be intense." I open my car door and put one foot inside. "See you guys tomorrow. Enjoy your evening."

They both wave at me as I drive away. I turn left out of the parking lot and set my sights on spending time with Nat. On my way to the hospital, I stop by the flower section of a grocery store and buy her flowers. I look for the ones with the nicest stems, then ask if I can borrow a pair of scissors. Once the blooms are removed, I dress up my stems with a bit of lace and a bright orange and pink bow. The store has a vendor table set up out front selling costume jewelry, and I find a small tiara for Nat. It's a crown fit for my alabaster queen.

It takes ten minutes to drive from the store to the hospital and ten more to get cleared to enter Natalie's hallway in the pediatric wing. The nurses sanitize my gifts for Nat, take my temperature, wipe down my hands and face with sanitizing wipes, and wrap me in a gown and mask. When I'm finally ready to head into Nat's room, I see she's sleeping again. I don't wake her. I simply pull a chair close to her bedside and settle in to read the book I always carry in my purse.

Twenty minutes later, I'm less than one hundred pages to the end of my book when Natalie opens her eyes. A smile forms the minute she sees me, and I lean in to soak up its rays for as long as I can.

"I missed you yesterday," she whispers. "Can't believe I was asleep when you came to visit." Her tired voice crackles, and she starts to cough.

I grab the jug of water from off her bedside table and hold it up in front of her. As she sips from the oversized straw, her coughing fit passes.

"Better?" I ask.

"Better."

She points to the bouquet of stems in my lap and smiles. "Are those for me?"

"Yes." I lay them in her arms, and she holds them Miss America style, as if they're the grandest flowers in all the world. "Of course the look isn't complete without this," I say as I place the tiara on her head. "You look lovely, Your Majesty."

She smiles. "So today we're in a palace, and I'm the queen."

"You are the queen for sure, and I'm at your service." I bow low, bending down on one knee.

Soft giggles burst from Natalie, and she lifts her head a bit higher. "Then as my first act as queen, I ask you to take care of the royal stem garden." She lifts the stem bouquet to her nose, inhaling deeply. "They smell green, and fresh. Will you put this one with the rest?"

"Your wish is my command, Majesty." I lift the bouquet from her hand and move to the other side of the room.

When I reach the window, sudden tears water my face, and every emotion known to man sprouts up inside me. More than a dozen stem bouquets are arranged on a silver tray. She has kept every one I've given her.

Every single one.

They're artistically arranged near the windowsill. Bows of all colors decorate the stems and bring some much-needed color to the room.

"They look perfect," I whisper. My voice is soft, reverent in this space where Natalie lives.

"No one else has a stem garden like mine." Her labored smile brightens her pale eyes, and I'm captivated.

"A garden fit for a queen," I say. "But nothing beats this." I motion to her painting of the sunset in the far corner of the room. "This is my favorite thing in the room. Well," I clarify. "My favorite thing in the room that isn't named Queen Natalie." I wink at her and grab a deck of cards from the windowsill. "You up to learning a new game, Your Majesty?"

"As long as you're up to losing." She laughs at her own joke, and I join in.

I slide the table between us, sit in a plastic chair, and start to shuffle. "I guess we'll see how well royalty can play."

An hour into our card game, all my troubles fade away. In Nat's tiny corner of the hospital, there's no room for Jake. No room for regrets. No room for my building nerves for opening night. There is nothing but a tiara, a loveable girl, and a deck of cards. I laugh and tease and call her on her bluffs. She's a fast learner and beats me several times. We play the evening away.

And I don't regret it for one second.

When the last rays of sunlight begin to fade outside Nat's windows, I catch a yawn coming from her.

"Somebody's worn out." I stand and start to clean up. "I think it's close to dinner, Your Majesty. Do you have any requests?"

Nat shakes her head. "No. They'll bring me my dinner in a little bit. It's not like I get much of a choice. There's only ever like six things on the menu, but I'm used to it by now."

"Well, maybe I can talk Nurse Gables into letting me bring you your favorite food sometime."

"Awesome." Natalie's voice fades faster than she does, and her eyes soon follow suit.

I lean in and tuck her blanket around her. "Rest for a bit, my queen. I'll tell them to keep your dinner warm."

"Okay," Nat sighs. "But just for a minute."

She closes her eyes.

I touch her soft hand and look across the room at her painted sunset. As she drifts toward sleep, she squeezes my hand ever so gently, and I hold onto this moment for as long as I can. Each sound, each smell, each feeling will be locked away in my memory. My heart fills up, drip by drip with each tender moment, and when it's full to bursting my eyes burn with the need to cry.

One day all too soon, memories will be all I have left of her.

TWENTY-FOUR

AS I LEAVE THE HOSPITAL, the sun lazily lingers in the sky, and I decide to take advantage of the last bits of light as day gives way to night. I walk along the shops lining the streets surrounding the hospital. Window shopping isn't something I do often, but the lights in the stores glisten from behind sheets of pristine glass, and my latest goal comes to mind.

Buy something that makes me feel beautiful.

Challenge accepted.

Cooling air nips at my cheeks as I walk toward the welcoming lights of the next store. Jewels of all colors glitter up at me and snatch my breath away. Every piece is unique and beautiful, a true artist collection. Any woman would be happy to own a single bobble in this display. My favorite is a simple diamond tennis bracelet set with silver accents.

But I don't need any jewelry. What I need is...

"That dress," I sigh aloud.

My voice is as soft and breathy as a child's wish. I gaze across the street toward the bright lights of *Violet's Dresser*, and my eyes stay focused on my target as I make my way to the beautiful boutique. A car horn sounds when a driver has to slow down to let me pass, but I ignore it and keep moving forward.

Within minutes I'm pressing my hands against the glass, smiling up at the dress like I'm about to propose. It's a deep eggplant purple, and it shimmers beneath the lights of the window, the full-length fabric looking as if it's woven from water. Crystal beads cover the bodice and the single capped sleeve, and a gentle flare at the bottom balances out the embellished top. Rich purple fabric skims the collarbone and flows seamlessly into the skirt, leaving the right shoulder gloriously bare.

I'm captivated.

I'm blown-away.

I am so trying it on.

A bell chimes as I enter the small shop. Designer gowns and elegant outfits dress every mannequin inside. Accessories of all kinds cover the tables and countertops in the tasteful space. From the moment a customer steps inside, *Violet's Dresser* expertly lulls them into opening their wallets.

I slide my hand inside my purse to locate a small envelope. It's the money I earned from the play. I've been carrying it around with me ever since I cashed the check. Today is a great day to spend it.

"Can I help you with something?" An immaculately dressed store clerk approaches.

I smile and point to the window. "The dark purple dress..."

"Oh," She clasps her hands together. "I was hoping you'd want to try it on. It's going to look stunning on you, with your hair and skin tone." She starts to walk away, then motions me to follow. "Come this way. We'll get you set up in a dressing room, and then I'll bring you the dress."

I step into a dressing room full of plush extravagance. A trio of mirrors line the walls, and a cream-colored arm chair sits in the corner, nestled atop the dark mahogany wood floor.

"Here you go," the sales-lady says. "I'm Cadence. So just get yourself into this slip, and I'll be right back with the dress. I'll bring you a few sizes."

I remove my everyday wear and slide the slip overhead. Minutes later, there's a knock at the dressing room door.

"I have the dresses for you. Are you ready?" Cadence asks.

"Ready." Before I even finish speaking, the dressing room door opens just wide enough for a hand to reach inside. Hanging from the hand are three dresses. Identical in every way but size.

"Thank you."

"Step out once you have it on and we'll get some accessories for you."

The first dress bunches around my shoulders, obviously too tight. But the second dress flows like liquid as it coats my body. It slithers down around my skin with only the slightest layer of a satin undergarments in between. With both hands, I adjust the dress until it lays just so. Then I turn around and look in the mirror.

My breath stops.

The reflection before me looks nothing like a washed-up, over-forty housewife. Cadence was right. The color compliments my skin tone perfectly and accents my hair at the same time. This is it. This is the one.

"Wow," I whisper to my reflection. "It definitely makes me feel beautiful."

"I have some heels and jewelry out here if you want to try them too," Cadence says.

I step out of the dressing room, and she's all smiles.

"I knew it! This dress was made for you." She walks around me, smoothing and adjusting, until everything falls just so. "These metallic heels and dangling earrings will complement it perfectly."

She adds the finishing touches, and I barely recognize myself as I stand before the mirror in the elegant dressing area. I'm glowing. Classy. Fashionable. Gorgeous. Adulations run through my mind as I stare at myself in the full-length mirror.

"It's perfect on you. And it's on sale," Cadence adds. "I'm not going to have to work very hard to get you to buy it, am I?"

"Nope. I'll take it. I'll take it all."

I SING MY PERFORMANCE songs on the way home, making sure I have the words and music down pat. If I wasn't driving, I'd give myself a standing ovation. My voice is strong, and my pitch is spot on.

I'm ready.

"You've got this, B," I tell myself.

My pep-talk serves a dual purpose as I pull up to the house and remember that Jake is probably here. Last night, I'd granted myself a small reprieve and delayed the conversation, but there will be no avoiding it tonight.

I step out of the car, and I'm surrounded by darkness. The small sliver of a moon is stingy with its light, making it twice as hard to find all my purchases in the backseat. The bags grow twice as heavy in my hands as I walk through the garage and into the house.

"There's my beautiful lady," Jake says. "I was wondering if you were ever going to come home."

"Stop. Okay. Just . . . stop."

"Stop what?"

"Stop pretending like nothing's wrong."

"It's called moving on, B. What else are we supposed to do?"

I shrug. "I vote for making some changes. Lots of changes." I shoulder my way past him and head to the closet to hang up my new dress.

"What's that?" he asks.

"Something that won't interest you." I turn and smile. "How's Alex doing?"

"Come on, B. Really? Not this again."

"It's a fair question. You were really interested in her on our run this morning."

"I was worried about a friend. I think she's making a mistake."

My lips pull tight, and I nod to myself. Is this thing always going to be between us now? Because if so, I don't think I can do this anymore.

"This isn't going to work," I tell him.

"What's not going to work?"

"Me talking to you. It's impossible for you to see things from any other viewpoint but your own."

"What do you mean? I always have you in mind when I think of things."

"Actually, *you* always have *you* in mind when you think about things. You think about *me* when you want me to help you with something."

"You're my wife, and the mother of our kids. I didn't think supporting your husband was a bad thing."

"It isn't. But I have more to offer. I'm more than just what I do for you or the boys."

"Where is this coming from?" He glares at me and shakes his head.

"From a lifetime of living in the background."

"I don't understand." Jake slams a palm against the wall, and turns his back to me. His shoulders tremble as pent-up frustrations begin pouring out.

I fold my arms across my chest and wait for him to calm down. I'm very used to Jake blowing off steam.

When he takes a deep breath and turns to face me again, his voice is softer. "You've been here front and center, taking care of us all these years. Why do you think you've been in the background?"

"Because I *have* been in the background. Who I am, my thoughts, my ideas, my values—all the things that make up me—have been pushed aside for years. Our whole life has revolved around you, and what I can do for you. But I'm more than just an extension of you, Jake. I have a lot to offer the world."

I walk to the bedroom doorway and turn back toward him. "I'm going to make myself a priority, since for the twenty years we've been married, you never have." With one hand I motion for him to leave the house. "Now if you'll excuse me, I have some grass to paint."

TWENTY-FIVE

SUNDAY MORNING COMES WITH the last bits of a storm fading away to sunshine. I opt for a zen moment after I'm fully awake and forgo my morning run to enjoy a relaxing cup of cinnamon tea. I take the tea outside and settle into a chair next to my painted garden.

Jake isn't here. He went back to the hotel last night and hasn't shown up yet this morning. Maybe he went running with his "friend," maybe he didn't. I really don't care—or at least I'm trying not to. But I just can't think about that right now. To help myself focus on the important happenings in my life, I have to compartmentalize.

Which means . . . no thoughts of Jake or Alex.

At all.

Instead, I focus on the deep purple square I painted last night. It adds an amazing contrast to the green grass while perfectly representing my something beautiful. When I think of myself in my new dress, a smile fills me from the inside out. I close my eyes and inhale the gorgeous morning, then exhale out all my frustrations with life.

Again and again.

Inhale the beauty. Exhale the stress.

This is my theme for the day.

I sip the last of my tea, savoring every silky, warm drop, trying to delay the inevitable ending of my moment of relaxation. I know once I leave this peaceful backyard garden, the whirlwind of craziness will begin.

It's dress rehearsal day.

DRESS REHEARSAL SUNDAYS ARE a tradition in smaller theaters.

Monday is Broadway's dark day, giving Off-Broadway theaters a chance to shine. Smaller productions often schedule their opening shows on Monday nights to take advantage of the one day a week where they don't have to compete with Broadway.

Monday nights are ours; the day small theaters have an advantage over the larger, more grandiose performances.

And so began the religion of Sunday dress rehearsals. One I haven't been devoted to in twenty years. But today, I'm reconverted.

The theater already bustles with activity when I walk through the door. Stage crew members place props in their marked positions throughout the stage and adjust curtains and tables to exact specifications. Back stage, the costume manager hangs finished outfits on racks labeled with each actor's name. Director Kyle runs around talking to everyone as he prepares for our big day. The performers gather together for our daily warm up routine. I put my phone and my purse on the table in my dressing area backstage and join them in the circle.

Ten minutes later, the chorus opens Act One with our first big musical number. Cole and I manage to enter the scene at the right time, but for the rest of the morning, I'm off my game. I forget lines, stumble through my blocking, and even miss the entrance for my first big song.

"CUT!" Kyle yells for the third time.

"I'm sorry," I say. "I'm sorry. I'll get it together, I promise."

"No hurry." Piper smirks. "What's tomorrow again? Oh yeah, opening night."

"Take a five-minute break, everyone. Then get set to run it from the beginning." Kyle looks directly at me. "Again."

Cole comes over and nudges my arm. "Hey. You okay?"

I answer with an overly dramatic sigh. "I can't focus. I'm not sure why, I just feel . . . off."

He shrugs. "No biggie. You know what they say. Die in dress rehearsal, kill it on opening night."

We find a corner of the stage and sit down next to each other on the stage floor.

"Yeah, well, I'm mastering the dying part."

He laughs. "And the killing it part will come too. Tomorrow night." He waves to Taahira, and she smiles back as she gets set to open the scene with the rest of the chorus. "So," Cole says, focusing on me again. "What's bugging you? If you talk about it, maybe you'll be able to let it go."

"It's kind of personal."

"Yeah, 'cause we never talk about personal things." He points to Taahira. "You got me to open up about my wife who passed away, and now I'm out in the dating world again. It doesn't get more personal than that. I owe you."

"I guess. But—you have to promise not to joke around about this."

"This is really bothering you."

I nod.

"Okay. No teasing. I promise."

I close my eyes. "My husband is seeing another woman."

"What? Are you sure? He can't be that stupid."

I lift my shoulders, and it feels like the helpless gesture it is. When I open my eyes again, I focus on Cole. "He says she's just a friend. But the way he touches her, and the way she looks at him, and he says he misses her when they're not together. It's just . . ." I look down at my lap. "I feel so unwanted and unappreciated. He came home a few days ago, and we talked last night."

"Talked?"

"The dreaded relationship talk. You'd think after twenty years of marriage, I wouldn't have to deal with this." I force a fake laugh. "Lucky me."

"Damn." Cole shakes his head. "No wonder you're off today. You've got a lot on your plate."

"Too much. I'd like to break the plate, actually. Maybe a whole stack of them."

"Actors to the stage," Kyle yells through his bullhorn.

Cole stands and pulls me to my feet. "Let go of the hurt and trust yourself to be amazing." He gives me a quick hug. "Because you are. And if you weren't married and I wasn't dating Taahira—" He leans in. "I'd take the time to show you just how amazing I think you are." When he steps back, he sends a wink my way.

I smile. My first real smile of the day. "Thanks. That means a lot," I say. "Especially since I'm like ten years older than you."

"The heart wants what the heart wants." He flashes me his most innocent look.

I'm laughing as we walk backstage.

We get set for the beginning of Act One again, and after my talk with Cole, I'm much better. Not perfect. But better.

Kyle's demeanor goes from deadly fire-breathing dragon to angry toddler with a water pistol. I take it as a good sign.

My performance gets stronger as the day goes on, and by the time we finish up the last scene, I've conquered all my demons. I haven't missed a line since morning break, and Cole's compliments have given me the confidence boost I needed.

Opening night, here I come.

Kyle calls us together and gives the details for the following day.

"Actors." He points toward the group. "Wardrobe and makeup begin at three o'clock sharp. Do not be late. For our warm-up for the day, we'll run through the opening scene. Warm-up will start at exactly four-thirty and I need everyone there and ready. Doors open at six and curtain goes up at seven. Any questions?"

We all shake our heads simultaneously, anxious to get out and blow off some steam before another busy day tomorrow. With a sigh and a stumble, I grab my purse and phone and walk outside with Cole and Taahira. We're just discussing lunch plans when Taahira's phone chimes.

She looks at the message, and the more she reads, the farther her shoulders droop. When she meets my eye, her lips press together and she sighs. "I am so sorry." With a shake of her head, she looks at me. "It's work. There's an emergency. I'll have to take a rain check on our late lunch."

I send her a soft smile. "Not a problem. Where's work?"

"I'm a vet. Well, almost a vet. I'm doing my clinicals right now," Taahira says. "It's not like I'm going to change the world or anything, but yesterday I saved a cat during surgery. And they asked me to come in today to assist with another. So, in a way, I'm making my life count, I guess."

"Incredible. You're incredible," I say.

"Yes, she is." Cole's entire face lights up. "Raincheck. Celebratory dinner after opening night?"

I nod.

Taahira smiles and Cole opens the car door for her. "Here," he says. "I'll drive you."

I say my goodbyes and walk to my car, thinking about what Taahira said. Making her life count. How many people in this world can truly claim such a thing? When I settle into my car, I pull my notebook out of my purse and write.

To paint the grass today, I will...
Find a way to make my life count.

It's my vaguest goal yet, and I have no idea how I'm going to accomplish it, but I've always liked a challenge. And I've got time. Forty-one years old or not, it's never too late to find a way to make a difference in the world.

I start the car and make my way to the hospital. On the way, I stop at my favorite florist shop but still pull into the hospital with plenty of time for my visit with Nat. Five minutes later, I'm standing in front of Nurse Gables with stem bouquet in hand.

As soon as she sees me, worry etches into the planes of her face. "Where have you been? I've been trying to call you."

"We had rehearsal all day. My phone's still on silent. Why? What's wrong?"

"It's Nat . . ." She pauses. "You need to say your goodbyes."

At the word *goodbye*, my world tilts off balance and wobbles in a sickeningly slow circle. The stem bouquet slips from my hand and falls to the floor. I thought I'd have a little more time at least. Time to prepare. I'd give up my entire painted garden of experiences just to have a few more days with her.

"Pull it together, Bethany," Nurse Gables whispers. "She needs your strength today."

In the next breath, I pick up the fallen bouquet and straighten my shoulders. I wipe my tears away and swallow down my sadness. Ready to be her rock. "Take me to her."

Seconds later we're standing outside Nat's door, looking through the small window. Her tiny form lies motionless in the bed and dozens of tubes and wires silently snake their way to her, recording her every breath, her every heartbeat. My hands automatically reach out to her, touching the glass. She looks so different from the vibrant girl I know, so quiet and still. I wish I could fix this and take away her pain.

"How has she gone downhill so fast?" My voice is shaky, heavy with tears.

"The infection's in her bloodstream. She's septic. Antibiotics are no longer helping, it might be a day or two, but . . ."

There are no words. I have nothing to say.

My chest aches. Physically aches. I massage a spot just below my collar bone and breathe. Just breathe.

Nat's swaddled form lies so still.

Unmoving.

Completely still.

Breathe.

"I'm glad you're here," Nurse Gables whispers.

I pull my lips into a tight line and focus on not crying. "What do I do?"

"Talk to her." She wraps one arm around my shoulders. "Make her feel loved. She understands what's happening. Just be there for her."

I force a swallow and nod my understanding. Nurse Gables helps me through the sanitation process, holds a fresh gown out for me to slide into, then heads back to the front desk.

A single tear makes its way down my face. It trickles from eyes that watched one last sunset with Natalie. Slides around a nose that smelled fresh cut stem bouquets with her. Slips past a mouth that laughed with her. And drips off a chin that will never stop trembling.

I take a deep breath, pull a mask over my mouth, and open the door.

Nat's asleep, and I don't want to disturb her, but as soon as I sit in the chair by the window, she opens her eyes.

And smiles.

I cross the room and settle onto the bed next to her. With great effort, she manages to turn her head my way. Her smile. Her face. Her beautiful pale-blue eyes. She's amazing to me. I will always be grateful for the time I've spent with her.

"Where will we be today?" she whispers. Her voice sounds as weak as her body looks, but her strong spirit shines through her expression.

Her sweet words clog my throat with unshed tears, and it's a few minutes before I can say, "I'm happy right here with you." I hold up the newest stem bouquet. "I brought you something."

She lifts her hand and touches the bright purple bow. "I love it."

"Can I put it with your collection?"

With a slow nod, she gives her permission, and I stand. I take a few minutes to situate her non-floral arrangements and then turn back toward the bed. Forcing a bounce into my step and brightness into my face, I try to act like it's just any other day. I pretend I don't know what's coming. And I promise myself I won't cry.

"So, what would you like to do today?"

She sees right through me.

"You don't have to be so happy. I know how bad it is. And I . . ." She holds her thin fingers out to me, and I grasp onto them like they're my lifeline. "I'm glad someone here will cry for me . . . when I'm gone."

I bring her hand to rest against my cheek as I sit next to her. The minute her fingers brush my skin, my tears start to fall. All the stresses of life pour through me. Jake, Alex, Mrs. Platt, the HOA board, my invisible life, the play, and now Nat.

In this moment it's all too much.

I lay my head in her lap and allow my heart to burst open. I cry freely, and she places one hand on my head.

"Each tear is for a day I'll miss you." I sit up to look her in the eye. "I just want more time."

"Me too," she whispers. She slides her hand under the blanket and pulls out a book. "How about we take one last adventure together? Will you read to me? It's my favorite."

"Of course." I lift the thin book and smooth my hand over the cover. *Bridge to Terabithia*. My throat closes up again, as I realize why this particular novel must mean so much to her. I swallow three times before I'm able to speak, and when I do, my voice sounds like sandpaper scratching stone. "Should we take it from the top?"

Nat nods.

I clear my throat and begin at page one.

We both melt into the story as we travel to Terabithia. My voice grows stronger the longer I read, and soon the sadness drifts away with the words. I'm enjoying my time with her. She's enjoying her time with me. And it's all that matters.

She falls asleep during chapter ten, and I quietly let myself out of her room. I stop by the nurse's desk to make sure they know to contact me if she takes a turn for the worse. My tired feet slide along the floor as I head toward the elevator. Nurse Gables calls out to me just as I press the down button.

I turn toward her.

She surprises me with a hug. "Thank you, Bethany. For everything you've done for our Nat." She hands me a pamphlet. "I thought you might like this."

It's a recruiting flyer for the local nursing college. I read it and shake my head. "Nursing school? You do realize I'm forty-one. And you know how hard it is for me to do this—with all the germs and sick people. They wouldn't take me. I can't."

I try to hand the pamphlet back to her.

"You *are* doing it though, and you're good. Really good." She nods to the flyer in my hand. "You keep it. Just in case. We need good people like you. People who care." She smiles. "Everyone needs a second act. Why not you?"

Nurse Gables' words do their best to convince me of a possible new life as I drive home.

A strange new fluttering wonder stretches to life inside me. I never thought working in a hospital would be a possibility for me. But I've always loved taking care of people. My mother said it's what I was born to do.

Why not me?

How many Natalies could I help?

My drive ends sooner than my thoughts are able to quiet down. I pull into my garage and sit in the car. Doubts and questions swirl inside me until I finally pull up the college website on my phone. I find the link mentioned in the pamphlet. Before I leave the car, I've filled out the online forms to join the new CNA classes starting next month.

"Nurse Taylor." Alone in my car, I test the title out loud. A smile catches me by surprise. I reach into my purse, grab my notebook, and flip it open to my latest goal.

> To paint the grass today, I will...
> Find a way to make my life count.

Beneath it I write:

> Take classes to become a Nurse.

I close my eyes and whisper, "I'm going to make my life count, Nat."

TWENTY-SIX

"**S**URPRISE."

A chorus of voices shouts the single word to me as I step into the kitchen. My emotions roll to life again. Shocked laughter and happy tears turn me into a jumbled mess, but it makes my mom and sons enjoy the surprise all the more. They hold up a homemade banner between them.

CONGRATS ON YOUR OPENING NIGHT

I'm so blown away; I can't form a coherent sentence. I haven't even told them about the play. Before any words come out of my mouth, I'm tackled with hugs. My two boys lift me off the ground and sandwich me between them.

"Wait. Careful." I'm still smiling as they set me down. "I didn't expect this. What are you guys doing here?"

Jake steps forward, and for a minute we stand in a circle. A happy family, or at least the shadow of one. "I thought it was important for them to watch you onstage." At my dazed look, he continues. "It's a big moment in your new life."

My mouth falls open. Jake did something thoughtful—for me.

After all that's gone on these past few months, and after all I've discovered about myself these past few weeks, I'm not sure how to react. Not sure what to do.

Then his phone dings.

A text pops up, and he tries to hide who it's from, but he's not fast enough.

Jake clears his throat and pushes his phone into his back pocket.

"Who's Alex?" Robert asks.

Jake closes his eyes. "Alex is a friend of mine."

"Your friend," Ryan says. "Not Mom's?"

"No," I say. "She is not my friend."

"She?" the boys say in unison.

Jake's shoulders sink.

Mom steps forward and puts her arm around me. "Boys, why don't you go out and get me a quart of my favorite frozen custard? You know the kind I like." She turns to Jake. "You can drive."

Jake sighs. "You bet." He looks at me. "I hope you liked my surprise. We'll be back in a little while."

Three minutes later, they're gone.

"So, is it as bad as I think it is?" Mom asks.

"Depends. How bad are you thinking?"

"Well, you've been completely incommunicado the past month, and you went all van Gogh out on your lawn." Mom nods toward the back lawn. "And after that awkward little surprise party, I'm guessing it's pretty bad."

My chin sinks to my chest, and I can't bring myself to answer her.

She nudges my shoulder and motions out the window to my painted grass. "So, is that spray paint?"

"Yes." I smile and lift my head. "It's my painted garden. A square for each experience in my new life."

"Seems like there's a bit more to the story."

Mom's words break through the perfect-little wall I've built up around my life. There's no need to hide it anymore, so I tell her everything. It's like I'm fourteen again and just found the note from my best friend to my boyfriend telling him to break up with me and go out with her. My wandering words don't always make sense, but Mom never interrupts. She listens to the entire story. I go into detail about his relationship with Alex, how it made me realize I've been living as an empty shell of a person, and what I've done in the past two weeks to fill the void inside myself.

When I finish, Mom's quiet for a few minutes. Then she takes both my hands in hers and pulls me close. "Come here, sweet girl." It's the same tone she used when I crashed my bike at age ten. "You've really had a rough time. Why didn't you call me?"

I lean back, settling onto a stool of my own. "You've always really liked Jake. I didn't want to ruin that."

"Are you going to leave him?"

I shrug and sigh. "Right now, I don't want to be with him. But we've been married twenty years. It's hard to throw all that away."

Mom smiles. "You're the only one who can know what to do here, honey."

I pull my knees up to my chest and rest my face against my legs. "I just want to be happy."

Mom leans forward and kisses the top of my head. "Sweetheart. You can be happy—with or without Jake. You just have to look in the right place." She tilts my face up and taps the spot just above my heart. "In here. Happiness is so hard to find because people are always looking for it in the wrong place."

I lean my forehead against hers, and we sit in silence for a few moments. I'm not sure what my life will look like moving forward. A life alone, or a life with Jake. Each choice contrasts so drastically, I have no idea which direction I should go. I'm still debating the choice inside my head when Mom stands.

"Now, come show me what this painted garden is all about." She grabs my hand and pulls me to my feet. "I've never heard of such a thing."

We step outside, and the coolness of the night drifts around me. I inhale crisp air and confidence. I'm proud of my new life. My heart beats faster, matching time with my footsteps as I grab my mom's hand and pull her along.

Together, we stop in front of my painted grass, and I plug in the garden lights.

"Here it is. Each square represents a new goal I've made for my life. Each one is a part of me now." I begin with the top left corner and explain each square. Mom laughs when I talk about my karaoke night. And tears up when I tell her about Lettie crying over Scarlett. When I explain my volunteering gig at the hospital and how much I've loved spending time with Nat, she brings her hand to her mouth and tells me she's proud.

Each square shares a bit of my story with her, and each moment brings us closer together. We laugh, lean into each other, and fight off tears. I tell her about my plans to become a nurse, and she's the first to congratulate me on registering for my class.

Then I hand her a can of spray paint, and together we add to my garden. Lights flip on inside the house, and I hear the sounds of boys coming home, but they don't come out to bother us. Mom and I work side by side. When my paint can runs dry, I start to clean up, letting Mom finish our square.

I stand in the middle of the yard and look up, listening to the spritz of the spray can in the background as Mom paints the grass. Blackness and bright stars fill my gaze, but all I see are endless possibilities—endless new goals—endless forms of happiness.

Just waiting for me.

I've been working hard to become someone I can be proud of—someone I want to be. And right now, in this moment, I'm choosing to be happy. It's time I remember where I'll find it.

Inside myself.

"Okay," Mom says. "All finished. What do you think?"

I step next to her and put my arm around her waist, looking at the finished square. A white background with red cross, signifying my newest goal. I'm going to become a nurse. I'm going to help people.

"It's perfect," I say.

Mom squeezes me tight and sighs. "I think you've really got something here. A painted garden, all about you. I love it. I may just start one of my own."

I laugh and kiss her face. "I hope you do. I'd love to see a painted garden all about you. Of course, we'd have to censor some squares if the stories I've heard are true."

A twinkle flashes in her eyes, and it reminds me of the stars. "I can neither confirm nor deny any and all stories pertaining to me."

The glass door to the house opens, and I hear Jake call, "Frozen custard is here and melting."

"Well, we can't have it melt now, can we?" Mom hugs me and steps toward the house. "You coming?"

"Go ahead. I need a minute to put this stuff away." I clean up the rest of the yard and close up the shed. The smell of spray paint lingers in the night air, and anticipation hums through me. All this newness in my life is fresh and exciting and resembles something that feels a lot like hope.

No matter what happens with Jake, I'll be all right.

I'll be me.

With one last look at my painted garden, I turn and walk toward the lights of the house.

WHEN THE FROZEN CUSTARD bowls are empty and the dishes done, the boys head out to visit some friends from high school, and Mom goes to bed early.

Jake and I are alone in the kitchen, and I wonder how it's possible for two people to be so awkward together after twenty years of marriage.

"The boys were happy to see you," Jake says.

"I'm glad they came. I love it when they visit."

Jake clears his throat. "They gave me hell about Alex."

In spite of everything, I smile. My boys will always have my back. "Good for them."

Jake shakes his head. "I am really close with Alex, but I don't see the problem. And I can't move backwards in a relationship. It just doesn't work."

A sad smile barely lifts the corners of my mouth. "That says a lot."

"I want to be close friends with her, but I'd never let it get physical."

"Physical? That's the line for you? An emotional connection can be just as hurtful as a sexual affair. You can turn off feelings during sex, but you've admitted that you're in love with Alex."

"But it's not—"

I hold up one hand. "No, Jake. Just stop it with the denials." I lean toward him, not bothering to keep my voice low. "Don't make it sound like your relationship with her means nothing. For years, I've been plugging into someone who didn't really try to connect with me. And because of that bad connection, my confidence in myself completely drained away. And since I thought the lack of connection was my fault, I put even more energy into making you happy, into making your life easier. But pretty soon, I forgot to make myself happy. I forgot to live my own life."

"What are you talking about? I've always had a great connection with you. I still do."

"Oh, really? And how do you keep that connection strong? By spending time with another woman? By asking me to help out at work for free? By expecting the house to run perfectly, and then belittling what I do to fill my days?" I shrug, lost for words. "I'm done with the excuses, Jake. And I'm going to be happy. I'm going to find a way to live my life. And if you want to be a part of it, you'll have to find a way to plug in."

"What? I'm not..." He starts into the denials again, but stops himself and sighs instead. "I actually don't know what I want. But I know I never meant to hurt you."

"Well, the world is full of assholes who never meant to hurt people. I just didn't think you were one of them."

"What can I do?"

"Make a decision, and let me make mine."

He nods once, and I point toward the door.

"And sleep somewhere else tonight."

TWENTY-SEVEN

I WAKE UP ALONE IN BED, and for just a moment, I miss Jake's warmth. Until the reason why I woke up becomes clear. My phone flashes and rings, breaking the silence of the night. I glance at the number at the top of the screen.

It's from the hospital.

Natalie!

"Hello." I press the phone hard against my ear. "Hello, this is Bethany."

"Beth." Nurse Gables' voice is heavy with tears. "You need to get here now. She'll be leaving us tonight."

No!

It can't be.

Not this soon.

The world goes fuzzy, my brain can't focus, and every breath I pull in takes too much effort. I don't know what to do. How can I possibly help? What can I say to her?

But even still, I know I have to be there.

"I'm on my way." I hang up the phone as I jump out of bed. "Hospital. I need to go to the hospital." I'm knocking things over and turning on lights, trying to hurry as I tie back my hair, pull on the first pair of pants I touch, throw a shirt over my head, and slide shoes on my feet. I slam the bedroom door open and grab the keys off the hook on the wall. As I fumble for the keys, I accidently flip on the flood lights in the backyard.

Jake stumbles into the kitchen rubbing the sleep out of his eyes, still wearing his clothes from yesterday. "B, what are you doing? It's two in the morning?"

"What the hell?" I'm shaking and crying, and I drop my car keys twice. "What are you doing here?"

"I slept on the couch. I figured I'd sneak out before you got up."

"What?"

"You can yell at me later. What are you doing?"

"It's Nat. I need to go . . ." My voice chokes and dies. I can't speak, but Jake seems to understand me anyway.

"Here. Let me." He takes the keys from my trembling hands. "B, let me help."

I don't argue. I'm in no condition to drive. Memories and dreams blur under my tears as I picture her sweet face. I just need to get there.

Jake leads me to the car, and I buckle myself into the passenger's seat. We start to back out of the driveway, but as we roll past the front yard, I see Sonia's beautiful flower garden.

"Wait," I yell. I'm already opening the car door as he steps on the brake. "I need stems. Just a minute. I need to get her some stems."

It takes only seconds for me to make Nat's final bouquet from the irises Mrs. Platt has so lovingly tended into a fall bloom. I break off the bearded-flower heads with my fingers and secure the long stems with my hair tie. Then I rush back to the car, leaving the discarded blossoms laying in Sonia's perfect yard.

We drive to the hospital in silence. As each mile passes, I pray I'm not too late to say goodbye.

DISINFECTANT AND CUT-GREEN STEMS. Those are Natalie's smells. As distinctive as a custom perfume and just as sweet. Fresh and clean and pure, just like she is. From now until the day I die, I will forever see her face when I step into a newly cleaned room or walk by a just-pruned flower garden.

I sit next to her on the bed in my mismatched, wrinkled outfit, my skin still wet from sanitizer, a mask secure over my mouth and nose. I watch her shallow breaths, counting each precious one like a treasure. She's warm, very warm. Her feverish body tired from battling infections without the proper tools to do so. What a fighter, she's been. An albino warrior princess, with a flower stem for a sword.

She has yet to open her eyes, but I don't mind. She can save her strength for as long as she needs. I'm not going anywhere.

Holding Nat's hand in mine, I glance out the window facing the hallway. Nurse Gables looks back at me and sends me a comforting smile. Jake stands next to her, his face full of concern and worry. He's never met Nat, but he saw my tears when I first entered, heard Nurse Gables talk about her. The only thing I've said to him since we left the house was— "Call Lettie. She'll want to know."

Now he stands, just outside the glass, knowing I'm hurting, wanting to make it stop. The pain in his eyes matches my own. Pain for a young girl he's never met, but one he knows I love.

My pain is his pain.

The moment I recognize this truth is the moment I know I'll be able to forgive him.

Someday. Somehow.

I don't know that we'll ever truly be together again—but I won't hate him forever.

I'm strong enough to forgive.

Natalie has taught me that.

Strength in the hardest of times.

A soft rustle of sheets grabs my attention, and I turn my gaze back to the bed. Back to the little girl lying so perfect and still in front of me.

Natalie's eyelids flutter softly and open halfway. I lean down to make sure she sees me, and I'm gifted with a smile. Pale lips part to reveal even paler teeth, and another shallow breath escapes. I wish she could hold onto each of those.

"Hey." Her voice is a sigh, quiet and warm.

"Hey, back," I whisper.

"Where will . . . we . . . be today?" She gives a shaky laugh, and all the cathedral bells in all the world could never sound so sweet or so grand.

"Wherever you want to be. Just name it." I swallow hard, and my smile shakes. "I'll tell you all about it, and we can go there together."

She tries to hold onto her smile, but it slips a little as she closes her eyes, pain washing over her features.

My eyes flip to the monitors, and one hand finds her face. "Should I call Nurse Gables?"

Nat gives the slightest shake of her head, and her eyes meet mine. "There's no . . ." she gasps. "Calling . . . the nurse . . . tonight."

Holding back tears, I nod. All her machine alarms have been turned down.

She reaches for my hand, and I entwine my fingers with hers.

"Promise me . . . you'll stay . . . with me."

"Of course." A single tear escapes from each eye. "Germ-infested wild-horses couldn't drag me away." I pull the mask off my face and lower my lips to the back of her hand, placing a soft kiss just above her small fingers. "I'm not leaving for anything."

"Thank you . . . I want someone . . . who loves me . . . to be . . . here."

Her words, combined with the gentle tug on my hands, almost undo me. But I give her a watery smile. "You have that, Nat. I love you. I'm here."

The smile she sends back at me will be forever etched into my memory.

"And . . . promise . . . me . . ." She struggles to pull in a breath. "You'll keep finding . . . amazing places . . . to be . . . for me."

This time I have to force brightness into my voice for her benefit. "I promise."

Over the next few hours, I read to her, taking her to a land far away from this stark hospital room. She tells me more about her gran and asks if I think she'll see her in heaven. At her request, I place all her flower-stalk bouquets at the end of her bed. I whisper comforting words and let her know how strong she is, stronger than anyone I've ever known.

Night surrounds the quiet room, and it's as if we're the only people in the world. Nurse Gables and the others stand near the door, but no one else exists in this moment.

No one but Natalie and me.

I've lost track of the hours just sitting here watching her breathe, feeling the sweet pounding of her heart. Nothing else matters. I wish Natalie could enjoy one more sunset, one more sunrise. One more everything. I wish I could give her more.

She opens her eyes, focusing on me, and I can tell it's a struggle for her to concentrate. "Tomorrow . . . I'll be . . . in heaven." One small finger points at the window, tilted toward the sky. "Where . . . will you . . . be?" She squeezes my hand.

I bring her fingers to my lips. "I'll be onstage. For opening night."

"Good answer." She smiles. "Sing to me . . . one . . . last . . . song."

It's impossible for me to answer, but I'll do anything she asks me, so I nod. After a prayer for strength, and another calming breath, I begin to sing.

"Why should I feel discouraged?
Why should the shadows come?
Why should my heart feel lonely?
And long for heav'n and home?"

It's a beautiful song, full of hope and faith. One I used to sing to my boys when I rocked them to sleep at night. As I go into the chorus, Natalie turns her head and looks toward the three sunset paintings in the room.

"I sing because I'm happy
I sing because I'm free
For His eye is on the Sparrow.
And I know He watches me."

She stares at the canvases we painted together and listens to my shaky voice. A soft smile lifts the corners of her mouth, and I'm captivated.

"Whenever I am tempted, whenever clouds arise,
When songs give place to sighing. When hope within me dies,
I draw the closer to Him. From care He sets me free.
His eye is on the sparrow, and I know He watches me."

I keep singing even after her eyes close. After her small breaths stop. After her grip loosens under my own, and her hand falls limp in mine. Still, I sing. I carry the song through until the final clear note, finishing my tribute to the perfect angel who took her last breath while holding my hand.

My voice breaks on the final note and tumbles into tears. I lay my head on Nat's chest as sobs wrack my body.

Nurse Gables comes up behind me and places one hand on my back. "Sleep well, little angel." The sound of tears hangs on her words as she whispers, "Now you're free, baby."

Free.

Nothing can hurt Nat ever again.

She's free.

TWENTY-EIGHT

W E WALK INTO THE house just as dawn stretches across the sky. The rising colors flood through the living room windows and into the kitchen, painting the floors in sunrise orange. I stare at the morning light glinting back at me and think of Nat. It's like a final wave goodbye. She loved the colors of the sky.

I'm fighting hard to keep the tears at bay. Nat wouldn't want me to be sad. Her body failed her, and she's at peace now. Even though it's a simple truth to understand, it doesn't keep the ache away. I try to focus on moving forward, but instead, I see her smile in the pattern of colors skipping along the ground.

"Do you want breakfast?" Lettie asks. She didn't get Jake's message in time to go to the hospital, but she's here now. "If I leave you in Jake's hands, who knows what you'll end up eating."

"Thanks, but . . ." I shake my head. "I'm not hungry. Just tired. Worn out."

"That's the understatement of the century." She pulls me into a hug. "You gonna be okay?"

"Yeah." I nod against her shoulder. "Eventually."

Lettie leans back so she can look at my face. "Well, try to get some sleep today so you're ready for tonight. I know you won't cancel. The show must go on and all that."

I send Lettie a sad smile and look out the window to watch the sunrise. "She'd want me to be somewhere incredible. Like on the stage."

"She was one amazing kiddo." Lettie kisses my cheek.

"Before you go." I reach over and grab her hand. "There's something I need to do. Will you help me?"

"Of course. Anything."

Lettie follows me as we walk outside to my painted grass. She's helped me often enough she knows exactly what supplies to grab.

Jake sees us over the fence. He's been talking to Sonia. Explaining the decapitated irises, I imagine. He comes over to help just as I'm dragging my giant stencil out of the shed.

"Here," Jakes says. "Let me."

Thankfully he lifts the hefty frame out of my hand just in time. My limbs are tired and I'm emotionally worn to the bone, but I need to do this one last thing before I let myself sleep.

We wrestle the stencil into place, and I paint a pure white square. While the paint dries, Lettie helps me cut out another stencil. Thanks to her artistic talent, it turns out exactly as I imagined.

I shake a can of silver spray paint while Lettie lays the new stencil in place. Everything needs to be perfect.

For Natalie.

A hand clasps my elbow, and I turn. Sonia stands next to me. In her hands she carries a can of spray paint with a ribbon attached to it. She shoves the unexpected gift my way and wipes at the tears rolling down my cheeks.

"Sonia." The minute I see her, my guilt over ruining her flowers starts a fresh batch of tears. "I'm sorry," I sob. "I'm sorry about your flowers. I know how much you love them."

"Don't you worry about it. Jake came by and explained everything. Your special girl needed them more than I did. They'll bloom again next year. And I can even show you how to plant your own." She pats my hand and nods toward our newest painted square. "Can I help?" Then she surprises us all when she takes the can of spray paint from me and aims it at the grass. Sonia finishes up the last few detailed strokes. When she's done painting, she steps next to us.

Jake lifts the stencils away to reveal a beautiful white square bordered on one side by yellowing grass. A pair of silver angel's wings centers the square and sparkles in the rising sunlight. The morning breeze rustles the newly painted blades, and the edge of the wings flutter, taking flight.

We stand in silence looking at our newest creation.

"Thank you," I say, smiling at Sonia. "It's perfect." I reach over and squeeze Lettie's hand. "Nat would've loved it."

"I'M GONNA GO, THEN." After she's made sure I've eaten a little breakfast, Lettie gathers up her things. "I'll be at the theater tonight. We got a babysitter for the rugrats, so Eric will be there with me."

I nod once and hug her goodbye. "Thanks for everything."

As Lettie walks out, she points to Jake. "Take care of her. Make her get some sleep. And don't be an ass."

"Yes, ma'am," Jake says.

The door closes behind her, and I set my dishes in the sink, too tired to care about washing them. It's barely after sunrise. The silence in the house tells me the boys and Mom are still sleeping, and my body urges me to join them.

I slide my feet along the wood floor, so tired my knees won't even bend to walk. My aching eyes fight to close, but I'm worried if they do, I'll see Nat's face. I stumble over the hallway rug, trip forward, and catch myself with one hand on the wall.

Before I can slide another step, my feet lift out from underneath me, and my face presses into a solid chest. Jake carries me into our room, and I don't have the strength to argue. He sets me on the bed and pulls off my shoes and socks, knowing full well I can never sleep with anything covering my feet.

"Do you want to change?" he asks.

Even though my thrown-together, middle-of-the-night outfit is hardly ideal, I shake my head.

He pulls the blanket around me and sits next to me on the bed. "You going to be okay?"

I shrug. "Even my happy thoughts hurt right now," I mumble, which makes no sense. But Jake seems to understand. He doesn't kiss me, or hold me, or touch me in any way. He just sits next to me, letting me know I'm not alone.

And it's enough.

Sleep doesn't come for a long while, and when I finally drift off, I dream of Natalie hugging her gran in a meadow filled with flowers in full bloom. She pulls off her oxygen mask and waves it above her head, then tilts her head back and laughs.

I wake well rested and at peace—with a man's arm draped across my breasts.

The minute I move, Jake is up. He's fully dressed, shoes and all, as he slides off the top of the covers. "Sorry." He pushes away from the bed. "I must have dozed off. I didn't mean to. . . Uh . . . I mean, I tried not to, but . . ." He stops his muttering and faces me. "How are you? Do you need anything?"

I'm suddenly restless and ready to be alone. "Shower. A toothbrush. Something to drink. In that order." I swing my legs over the bed, rub my face with my hands, and stand up.

Jake backs his way toward the door. "Enjoy your shower. Find your toothbrush. I'll have some tea waiting for you."

The hot spray clears away some of my sadness and calms my jumpy nerves. I take my time getting ready, and after an hour, Jake brings me a mug of lemon tea and a blueberry scone. I hold the scone up and send him a question in my glance. "My favorite."

He looks at the ground. "I know. I ran to the coffee shop. Thought it might help today."

"Thank you," I whisper.

An awkward silence fills the room, and I stare at my husband, not knowing quite what to say. When the silence stretches longer than I can stand, I open my mouth.

But before I can say anything, my phone rings.

Jake clears his throat. "Answer that. And eat something if you want. I'll be out here." He closes the door behind him as he leaves, and I slide my finger across the screen to accept the call.

"How we doing?" Lettie's voice cheers me.

"I'm hanging in."

"Still going to wow us all onstage tonight?"

I find my first smile of the day. Leave it to my best friend to cheer me up. "That's the plan."

"Perfect. Just calling to see if you need anything."

"Thank you for checking on me. I guess that's why I keep you around."

"That, and because my sexy body attracts just the right amount of attention when we go out together."

A genuine laugh frees a bit of my sadness, and I can't be more grateful for Lettie. "What time will you be there? I need you to sit in the first few rows. Front and center. That way if I start to panic, I'll look at you, and you can give me a thumbs up or something."

"Even better, I'll flash you. It's about time someone in the audience gave the actors something nice to look at. Am I right?"

"Perfect. It'll work exactly one time, until the bouncers come and toss you out."

"They have bouncers at the theater?"

"Only when you're in the audience."

"Good thing I have an in with the star of the show then, isn't it?"

"Star of the show. That's me." The minute the words leave my mouth, my chest and chin lift together as my heart swells. Me. I'm the lead in the play. "I can't believe I'm doing this after all these years."

"You'll be brilliant. Honestly. You have nothing to worry about."

"Easy for you to say. You're not about to get up on a stage."

"Fair point. But you shouldn't worry, either. You're the most amazing babe this side of Bozeman, Montana."

And I'm laughing again.

"Come on. You know it's true. Say it with me."

"I'm the most amazing babe this side of Bozeman, Montana." We chant together.

"Good," Lettie says. "Now start believing it. Lettie doesn't lie. What time do you want me there?"

"Doors open an hour before curtain, but the family of the cast and crew can take their seats a half hour before that—so maybe 5:30?"

"I'll be there at 5:29. Love you."

"Love you too. See you tonight."

"Most definitely. I'll be the one cheering like a mad lady from the front row."

Lettie ends the call, and I glance out my window to the backyard. I can just make out my painted grass between the willow trees. Each square is a building block, and when snapped together, they form a new creation.

Me.

My fresh, new life is built on squares of painted grass. The greenest grass in the world. A lighted stage. A golden star. Silver glitter galore. A purple heart. Soft blue eyes. A solitary plate. Sleepy Zzzzzs. Colorful handprints of the women I love. A music note. The perfect sunset. A toothy smile. Purple to make me feel beautiful. A red cross of healing. And angel's wings taking flight. Every individual part stacked together makes up me—the new me. I smile. This is just another step in my transformation.

And I'm ready to take it, with my angel Natalie watching me from the other side.

After one final deep breath, I pack away all my fear and move my sadness aside. I'm ready to conquer opening night.

I take my time getting ready. Tonight, I need to look perfect.

By the time I'm dressed and all made up, I'm in a rush to leave for the theater. The cast and crew will be arriving early. It will be all-hands-on-deck to get everything ready for the show. I grab my purple dress out of the closet and head for the door. When I step out into the living room, my family's waiting for me.

The boys whistle.

"Oh, honey. You look gorgeous." Mom pulls me into a hug.

"Thanks." I smile over her head toward the boys.

Mom squeezes both my hands. "Jake told us about sweet, little Natalie. Is there anything we can do?"

I hold tight to the tears wanting to fall and swallow as I shake my head.

A firm hand clasps one shoulder. Another identical hand clasps the other. "She was lucky to know you," Robbie says.

"We all are," Ryan adds.

And then the tears win out.

I'm trying my best to calm myself as I pull them into a hug. "I love you boys."

"We love you more," they say together, just like when they were little.

I pull away from them and wipe my face. "I have to get going or I'll be late. See you guys when you get there. Five-thirty sharp."

"We won't be late," Robbie says.

"I washed the car for you. Thought you'd like a nice clean car for your big night," Jake says as he leans against the far wall. "It's in the driveway."

"Thanks," I manage. The edge of a real smile flashes onto my face at his thoughtfulness. "I meant to do that yesterday."

He shrugs. "Well, now you don't have to."

They all walk me to the door. Ryan opens it for me and tells me good luck. As I back out onto the porch, I step into the warm sunshine—and bump right into Alex.

She's standing on our front porch, hand raised and ready to knock. "Hey," she says. "I was just stopping by to talk to Jake." She notices him standing behind me and waves. "Hi."

My throat swells to three times its normal size as I swallow down a biting remark. My boys are with me, so I force myself to be polite.

"Alex . . . hey," Jake says.

"So this is Alex," Robbie says, and Mom smacks him in the back of the head.

My face flushes and my heart beats way too fast. I don't have time for this right now. I press my shoulders back and step forward. "Sorry." I slide past Alex on my way to the car. "I'm in a hurry. Busy day."

"You look gorgeous," Alex says. "Where you headed?"

"Mom's starring in a play tonight." Ryan steps forward and offers his hand to Alex. "I'm Ryan, by the way."

"I'm Alex." She shakes his hand, but looks at me. "Really? A play. That's impressive. Where's it at? I might be able to come watch."

My smile pulls tight across my face, and I tap my watch. "I really have to get going. Don't want to be late." I yank the car door wide and sit in the driver's seat.

"Bye, B," Jake calls. "See you tonight."

"Love you, Mom," the boys say in stereo.

"You'll be amazing," my mother yells as I shut the car door.

Tears blur my eyes as I drive away, but I shake them off as soon as I reach the end of the street. I won't let anything ruin opening night for me.

"Not today," I whisper. "Today, I'm going to be amazing."

The drive to the theater is uneventful, but when I walk inside, chaos buzzes around me. Everyone has something to do and somewhere to be. And so do I. I'm part of something bigger than myself, and I'm needed backstage.

My makeup crew is anxious to get started, and it's nice to let someone else take care of me. I don't lift a finger as skilled professionals apply my makeup and style my hair. Another set of hands, just as skilled, helps me into my costume for the opening act.

I thank the costume manager for her help and step toward the black curtains separating us from the stage. When she leaves, I finally notice the quiet. I turn full circle and find I'm alone backstage. I'm about to call out to Cole when I hear Lettie's voice.

"Best friend of the leading lady in the house. I'll need three seats, please."

I part the curtain and step to stage center just as she reaches the row reserved for my family. Eric follows close behind her, which is expected, but Lettie surprises me with a much-needed gift. As I watch her slide between the rows to reach the exact center seat, my joy spills out as tears.

In her hands she carries Natalie's sunset painting.

Lettie stands before her seat, painting held high, and Eric steps next to her. Both smile up at me. I'm full to the brim with her love for me, and with the peaceful presence Natalie's painting brings.

Where will we be today? I hear Nat's voice over the sound of shuffling feet.

My mom slides into the row from the other side and walks until only one seat separates her from Lettie. She drapes a pure white cloth over the chair, and Lettie sets the painting, just so, on the smooth white surface.

My boys enter the theater next, followed by Jake, all dressed as if they're attending the Oscars. They each have a single white ribbon tied around their right arms.

In memory of my angel Nat.

From the back of the theater, Cole leads the entire cast down the aisles. Midway through their journey, they begin to sing the opening song in our play. "Another Op'nin, Another Show." I am the audience. They're performing for me.

This is another opening and another show for my life.

It's starts tonight.

"Where will I be today?" I whisper.

I stare out at a theater filled with people who care about me.

I took a chance and put myself out there. Me, a forty-one-year-old woman. Past my prime, ragged from a life of mothering, lied to and lost. And I dared to do something different. I dared to make a change. And in the process, I found the most remarkable thing.

I found me.

And I created an incredible life for myself.

I'm a singer. An actress. A hospital volunteer. I'm a friend. A daughter. A mentor. A mother. Soon-to-be a nursing student. And a stronger woman than I ever knew I could be. Each is an important part of me. And it's up to me to find balance in it all.

These past few weeks I've lived a life of my choosing and found the most important love story inside myself. The love I feel for me spills over into the love I have for others, strengthening us all.

I've realized loving myself isn't selfish, it's empowering.

I don't know exactly what my future holds, but I'm no longer looking at my life from the outside. I'm living it front and center and in complete control of my destiny. I feel the thrill of awaited excitement against my skin and the thrum of passion in my blood. Passion for my needs, my dreams, my wants. I intend to live every one of them.

And I'll paint my own happily ever after.

It's curtain time.

TWENTY-NINE

COLE AND I GET situated behind the set at stage center, and my heart is climbing up my ribcage with excitement as I lean over to pull the edge of the curtain back and peek out at the audience. Cole looks over my shoulder. Lettie's there front and center as promised, and she blows me a kiss. Mom sits next to Nat's painting, then Ryan and Robert, then Jake. But Jake isn't looking at me.

He focuses to the right side of the theater.

I follow the direction of his gaze and watch as Alex threads her way through the aisle and takes a seat next to him.

My hands clutch the curtain and squeeze, strangling the fabric in leu of Alex's neck. The sounds of the theater flicker from loud to soft and back again. Alex is sitting next to my husband on my opening night.

My nose tingles and tears begin to form. I shake my head and blink away the tears.

Robert and Ryan see me and both send me over-the-top waves and goofy smiles. I release my death grip on the curtain and wave back.

"Is that your family?" Cole asks.

"Yeah." I point to the row they're sitting in. "There's Lettie and my mom. My twin boys, Ryan and Robert. My husband, Jake, and his. . ." Even after I swallow, my voice still shakes. "His friend. Alex."

"Alex, huh?" Cole chuckles. "Tell me how you really feel."

"Stop." I turn to face him. "Nothing is going to ruin this night for me. Nothing."

Cole holds up both hands. "Perfect. Let's not ruin it. Just one question."

I raise an eyebrow.

"Why does he need her when he has you?"

I lean in and give him the biggest hug I can manage in my costume. "Exactly," I say.

"Maybe after twenty years he's forgotten how amazing you are." He touches the tip of my nose with one finger. "Maybe he's grown immune to the incredible woman he's married to."

I shrug with one shoulder. "Maybe."

The lights in the audience dim once, then twice, signaling the show is about to start.

"Well then," Cole takes my hand. "We'll just have to remind him, won't we?"

The music for the opening number cues up, and the show begins. Cole squeezes my fingers and steps out onstage. I wait behind the curtain, watching as Cole delivers his first few lines, then fades into the group of chorus members crowding the stage.

The first scene is all bright colors and flurries of motion. Twenty actresses and actors cover the stage, and when it's time for my entrance, they part down stage center. My legs shake the slightest bit as I get set.

I lift my head, take a deep breath, and step out from behind the black curtain.

Bright lights wrap me in a cocoon of strength and confidence as I make my way across the stage. My skin warms under the soft lamps above. They nourish my skills and secure my smile. This is my home, the place where I feel most alive. The reactions of the audience—a collective hush, a laugh, a sigh—nothing will ever be quite as rewarding as direct feedback from a crowd. The anticipation of my first entrance gives way to a rush I haven't experienced in twenty years. A deep void inside me fills with sureness and passion, turning the hollow shell I've become into a solid, living, breathing person once again.

Every moment of the play is a new high for me. It's an addiction. My singing, my acting, my commitment to my character, all tie together into a gift I share and receive with the audience. I tap into my inner pissed off wife and stomp around in a beautiful rage, conveying Lilli's anger with Bill. When my character begins to soften her heart, the crowd exhales together, leaning closer as arms drape around shoulders. And during our first kiss, several people watching cover their hearts with one hand and hold onto a loved one with the other.

Except for Jake.

When I chance a look into the audience, I can only make out the first few rows. But it's Jake's face that almost causes my first stumble.

He looks captivated.

By me.

Every time I glance into the audience, he's staring at me as if God himself couldn't pull his focus away. He smiles. Laughs. His eyes are bright and they never leave my face. Until Cole and I kiss. After the kiss, Jake looks as if he could happily murder Cole. His glare surprises me, and honestly, it adds to my smile.

Throughout the performance, the entire cast works together flawlessly. Each scene builds on the next. After my biggest solo, Jake and the boys clap and cheer and make me feel like a celebrity. Cole goes off book and adds in two extra kisses, making them steamier than ever by pressing his body close to mine.

By the end of the play, the audience is transported to a different time.

Their own lives placed on hold as they submerge themselves in Lilli and Fred's love story.

When the final scene ends and the curtain call begins, applause fill the theater to bursting. Cole and I are the last to come out onstage for our bow, and the moment the audience sees us, they swell to their feet in one giant wave of deafening cheers and clapping hands.

A standing ovation.

Energy surges through me. I'm on top of the world. In this moment, nothing can outshine my smile, not even the spotlight following us along the stage. This is something I'll crave for the rest of my life. The rush of applause is unlike anything else.

Cole holds my hand high as we take our bow together. He steps back and motions to me, clapping along with the audience, then puts his arm around me and kisses my cheek. When he pulls away, I wave and blow a kiss to my family. My mom whistles. The boys and Lettie cheer. And Jake glares at my hand being clasped by Cole's.

The curtain closes.

Opening night is over.

Kyle rushes behind stage and flings his arms around me. Real tears wet my cheek, and I can't tell if he's crying or laughing. "Thank you," he whispers, and then he steps back to address the cast and crew surrounding us.

"A standing ovation on opening night. It doesn't get any better than that, people," Kyle says. "Well done, everyone. Now, go take the time to greet the audience and thank them for coming. Remember, there's a short cast meeting and group picture in thirty minutes. Stage crew, you were nearly flawless tonight. Before you leave, props need to be organized and the stage reset for tomorrow night's performance. Thanks, everybody. Great job!"

As Kyle walks away, Taahira finds us and kisses Cole. When she pulls away, Cole's face shines with happiness.

Taahira grabs my hand. "You were incredible!"

"No." Cole pulls me into a hug and lifts me off the ground, spinning me in a circle. "You were perfection."

I'm laughing and smiling, with Cole's hands wrapped around me as I twirl through the air, when my entire family walks backstage. Alex is not with them. Jake stops short when he sees us, and Cole slowly lowers me down until my feet touch the stage. I walk my co-star over to meet my family, and he shakes hands with everyone.

"Mom," Ryan says. "You were great!"

"You are so talented," my mother says.

"You were amazing tonight, B," Jake adds.

Cole leans in close to me and puts his arm around my waist, pulling me tight up against him. "Bethany's a miracle. She saved the show. She's beyond incredible."

At his words, a flush paints my skin, but before I can say anything to temper his remarks, Jake steps closer to us. "You can let go of my wife now."

"What?" I laugh. "Jake, come on. He's just paying me a compliment." I'm shocked at the anger in his voice.

"Yeah, well. He can pay you a compliment without touching you." He looks Cole directly in the eye. "Seriously, take your hands off my wife."

Mom clears her throat. "Uh, maybe the boys and I should head home."

"Don't be ridiculous," I say. "Jake. Relax . . ."

"I'll relax when he gets his hands off of you."

"It's fine," Cole says, giving me a quick squeeze. He turns his gaze on me, and there's a mischievous gleam in his eyes as he smiles. "I can wait until tomorrow night to hold you again. But first . . ." He leans in and presses a quick kiss on my cheek.

"That's it," Jake says, and before I understand what he's thinking, he swings his fist through the air and hits Cole square in the face.

THIRTY

I T TAKES ME HALF a second to process. Jake just punched Cole in the eye.
"Jake!" I push him away and put my hand on Cole's shoulder. "Are you
okay?"

"What the hell, man?" Cole's hand covers his left eye, but when he looks
up at me, he's smiling.

"I told you to get away from my wife."

"Jake," I warn.

Ryan and Robert stand on either side of their father. I can't tell if they're
ready to hold him back or jump in to help him finish off my co-star.

Cole steps forward and raises one hand in surrender. "Calm down. I'll
leave." He leans over and speaks quietly to Jake. "You might want to remember
one thing. You're lucky to have her. As a man who lost his wife, trust me.
You'll always wish you had more time to make her feel like she's the center of
your world."

At Cole's kind words, warmth grows up my neck and settles onto my
cheeks.

Cole gives one last nod to Jake, reaches over to squeeze my fingers, and walks across the stage to meet up with Taahira.

"Who's that?" Jake asks.

"That's Cole's girlfriend," I hiss. "He's crazy about her."

I still can't bring myself to look at Jake. My mom steps forward to give me a hug. The boys sandwich me between them and again tell me how amazing I was onstage.

No one speaks of the awkward moment we just shared.

"Ready to go, boys?" Mom asks.

They nod and turn to walk toward the door. Mom follows. Jake does not.

"You coming?" Mom asks.

He toes at the ground. "I . . . I think I'll wait and come home with Bethany." He lifts his head to look at me. "Is that okay?"

I close my eyes and take a deep breath. "Whatever. We're taking a group picture right now. I have to go get ready."

"Sounds good. I'll wait for you," Jake says, then turns to the boys. "I'll be home when Mom's done."

Jake takes a seat at the back of the theater as the cast gathers at the front of the stage. He places himself in my line of sight, so I can't help but notice when Alex approaches him. She puts a hand on his shoulder, and he shrugs it off. She forces the issue and sits next to him.

I try to ignore them, but as it turns out, when your husband and his special friend cozy up next to each other just a few yards away, ignoring them becomes an impossibility.

While Kyle gives us all a few pointers to improve the show for the following night, Jake shakes his head and glares at Alex. The lighting crew asks for feedback while Alex points at me and says words I can't hear. We discuss the best place for our picture, and Jake rubs one hand over his face. And when Kyle asks us all to be at the theater by one o'clock the following afternoon, Alex stands up and stomps away.

I slip backstage to change into my new purple dress, then take center stage to pose for a cast photo. Cole slides in next to me and places his hand around my waist. We stand beside each other for the full cast shots, remain side by side for the main character photos, and really snuggle up for our happy couple shot.

Cole glances back to the last row of seats in the theater as we finish up our last picture. "I see he stuck around," he says with a smile.

"Yeah, he did." I shake my head and touch his swelling eye with two fingers. "I'm so sorry. I can't believe he hit you."

"It's nothing." He shrugs. "Stage makeup will cover it up, and it doesn't hurt at all. I'm actually glad it happened."

"Glad it happened? How can you be glad he hit you?"

"Because it shows he cares." He faces me and puts both hands on my shoulders. "Jake needed to be reminded what a desirable woman you are, so I nudged him a little. I figured a few punches might get thrown. But it proves he cares about you."

I lean against the wall and fold my arms across my chest. "Well, it might be too little too late. I don't know how to let go of everything that's happened. How do I forget . . ." My voice chokes to nothingness.

Cole steps directly in front of me, blocking my view of Jake. "I know he hurt you, and I'm so sorry it happened. And no one expects you to forget about it and pick up where you left off." He smiles. "Whatever you decide to do will be the right choice for you. Trust yourself."

I nod and lean forward to give him a quick hug, very aware of Jake's eyes on us. I step away from Cole and motion for Jake to join us onstage. Cole steps next to me when Jake approaches, and I brace myself for another confrontation.

But he doesn't say anything. He just stares at me in my eggplant-purple dress. His eyes glide up my body, and his heated look tells me I was right to buy it.

"You look amazing, B," he whispers. Then he surprises me yet again by holding his hand out to Cole.

Cole hesitates, looking him in the eye.

"Thanks," Jake says.

Cole grasps Jake's hand. "Don't forget again."

"I won't."

My gaze bounces back and forth between them, shocked at the conversation happening right in front of me.

As Cole walks away, he turns. "See you tomorrow."

"See you tomorrow." I don't speak to Jake as I gather up my things and walk out to the car.

Jake follows me. "Wait. Bethany. Wait."

I push open the door and step out into the cool night. "I'm not waiting, Jake. I'm going to get into my car, drive home, and try to revel in my incredible opening night."

He comes up beside me and touches my arm, but I keep walking. He matches my pace as we cross the parking lot.

"I'm sorry."

"You're sorry?" I scoff. "Sorry about Alex, or sorry you punched Cole tonight? We are so beyond you just saying sorry. You hit my co-star in the face. You're lucky he's a nice guy."

"I am lucky. But not because he's a nice guy. Because I have you in my life." He stops and turns me toward him. "I'm sorry because I should have been paying more attention to you." He looks down at his feet and clears his throat. "I told Alex our friendship was too much for you. I told her we need to take a break." He reaches for my hand and briefly touches my fingers. "I don't want to hurt you."

Tears creep up my throat and fill my eyes, but instead of wiping the moisture away, I simply turn around and keep walking. I don't know what to say, so I say nothing.

Once again, Jake follows me. When we get to the car, he holds out his hand. "Here, let me drive. You must be exhausted."

I hand him the keys and slip into the passenger's seat. Thankfully, he starts the car, turns on some quiet music, and drives home without speaking again. I stare out the window in silence. New emotions and old feelings blend together inside me, moving like the pages of a flip-book. Happiness, worry, pride, mistrust, elation, exhaustion. I flip from emotion to emotion until I'm almost numb.

Thirty minutes later we pull into the garage. It's late and Mom has gone to bed, but the boys are still awake. I say a quick goodnight to them and make my escape. I take my notebook outside to my painted garden and settle into a patio chair. The soft glow of the porch light breaks through the darkness, and for a long while I do nothing but think—and feel— and try to envision my future.

Where are we going to be tomorrow?

Nat's voice in my head shines light on my uncertainty.

Where am I going to be tomorrow? Where do I want to be?

I can't ignore all that's happened over the last twenty years, but I'm done putting my happiness on hold. I'm done being last on my priorities list. I'm going to be an amazing nurse. I'm going to help patients like Nat for the rest of my life. And I'm going to star in as many plays as I can fit into my schedule. Acting is a love I refuse to lose again.

Not everything will be decided tonight, but one thing I know for sure, I love my new life.

But what to do about Jake?

The door behind me opens, and I can tell it's my husband even before he sets a tray of lemon tea in front of me. Hot tea in the evenings is a well-established routine of mine, but on the tray next to my favorite teacup is a stem bouquet. Just like the ones I made for Nat.

"Sonia brought it over for you. She said she'd be over next week to help you plant flowers in our front gardens."

I turn to look up at him.

He's holding Nat's sunset painting in both hands.

"And Lettie dropped this off. I told her I'd make sure you got it tonight."

He hands it to me, and I hold it close to my chest. "Thank you."

Quiet tears slip down my face as he crouches in front of me to look into my eyes. "You were amazing with her, B. I mean, I've been married to you for twenty years, and I never . . . I should have seen it." He shakes his head as one hand cradles my cheek. "I'm sorry."

I see his apology in the quiver of his lip, in the way his shoulders droop, and in the pain in his eyes. His soft voice falters, full of sorrow and disappointment. Still, my heart shakes, unsteady and unsure.

"I know you're sorry. And you say you want to support me. But . . ." I swallow, hesitating, not sure how well he'll take this next bit of information. "I'm new at this. At making myself a priority. I've spent my entire married life taking care of you and the boys, and now I realize, I need to take care of myself too. I'm worried that if you're here, if we jump back into being us, I'll slip back into the old Bethany. And I don't want that."

"Okay." His hand drops away from my face. "So, what are you saying? What do you want from me?"

"I want some space."

"What does that mean?" He leans away from me, arms crossing his chest.

"I want you to move out for a while. I need some boundaries in place if we're going to have any kind of a relationship in the future. I know it's going to be hard for you, but . . ."

His eyes close, and he starts to nod, slowly. "Okay."

"What?"

"I said okay. If that's what you need. Then that's what we'll do." He sits on the edge of the chair opposite me. "Our company has a few apartments in town for when contractors come to work with us. I'll ask Phil if I can use one for a while."

"I don't know how long it will be. Or if I'll ever want to get back together."

"I get it, and I can respect that. I can't say I'm happy about it, but..." Jake pauses, lost for words for the space of one deep breath, and then he continues. "You've supported me our entire lives. Now it's my turn to support you." Even though his smile is tight, he's still smiling. "I mean it."

"Thank you," I whisper. A flicker of hope dances into my heart, and I prop Nat's picture on the table next to my tea. I can't help but think of Natalie as I look at her colorful sunset. She brought such joy into my world. "Did I ever tell you about the first time I met Nat?"

Relief seeps out in Jake's sigh, and he leans back, settling into his chair. "No. I don't know much about her."

"She called me a germaphobe, which I couldn't really argue with since I was applying hand sanitizer to my rubber gloves at the time."

"Sounds like you." Jake laughs.

I laugh too.

It feels good to laugh. To laugh with Jake.

I tell two more stories about Nat before my eyes grow heavy. But I want to keep telling her stories. I want to tell her stories to everyone I know. I glance at the ribbon-wrapped bouquet before me. And I want a fresh cut bundle of stalks in the house every day. To remember her. Always.

I'm ready to be alone, so I turn to Jake. "I'm going to be out here a while longer, and you'll want to go pack up some things from the bedroom."

Jake nods once. "Okay, that's my cue to leave. I'll grab what I'll need for the week and then arrange a time to come box up the rest of my stuff to take to the apartment." He stands. "Good night, B. You really were incredible up on that stage." He puts one hand on my shoulder and squeezes before he walks back into the house.

I sip my tea in silence, enjoying each warm, lemony drop and look out over my painted garden. It's impossible to solve all the problems in my life in a single day, but as I savor the feeling of being seen for the first time in twenty years, I realize what my next goal will be.

I open the red notebook in my lap, hold it wide, then pick up my pen and write . . .

> To paint the grass today, I will...
> Choose to forgive someone who hurt me.

For the next two minutes, I focus on breathing. Deep calming breaths to help me remind myself how strong I am.

I can do this.

It will be my most difficult goal yet, but I'm determined to figure out a way to move past the pain, no matter how long it takes me.

Finding forgiveness is going to be harder than holding onto hate. I can already feel it tearing at my chest and churning up doubting questions in my mind.

But I won't allow myself to be weighed down by anger and sadness anymore.

I have a life to live.

With one hand, I turn the page of my notebook and smooth the paper beneath my fingertips. I'm breaking tradition and penning two goals today.

For myself. For Nat.

With my purple pen I write—

> To paint the grass today, I will...
> LIVE MY BEST LIFE.

I stare at my painted grass and feel the pull to get out my stencil and start another square. Even though it's late, even though I'm tired, even though there's no way I'll chance getting paint on this dress, my fingers itch to express this pivotal moment.

But tomorrow will be soon enough. I'll get up early and paint the grass with a pale blue sky and a rising sun. An echo of Nat's sunset square to symbolize my new dawn.

When one day ends, another begins.

And tomorrow is a new day. A day to start forgiving. A day to live my best life.

A day to paint the grass.

~THE END~

BETHANY'S CHALLENGE:

- ☐ Remember what you love
- ☐ Try something new
- ☐ Show kindness to a stranger
- ☐ Do something that scares you
- ☐ Be happy being alone
- ☐ Celebrate life without romance
- ☐ Send a kind text to brighten someone's day
- ☐ Appreciate the women in your life
- ☐ Do something nice just for you
- ☐ Learn a new skill
- ☐ Share some happiness with others
- ☐ Buy something that makes you feel beautiful
- ☐ Make your life count
- ☐ Choose to forgive someone who hurt you
- ☐ Live your best life

ACKNOWLEDGEMENTS

Writing this book has been akin to prying open my chest and placing my heart on a blank page. There have been many tears as well as many laughter-filled moments. I've written on the good days with the sun skimming my cheeks. I've written on the hard days when typing felt like yelling into the void. The one constant in my efforts to get this book published has been my love of words. Writing is like breathing to me. It's how I live. But it has taken much more than my love of words to get this book into your hands. And there's no way I could have done it alone.

My village is larger than most. I have been waiting for fifteen years to write an acknowledgements page, which makes for a very long list, and an inevitable memory issue that will lead to forgotten people. If you have contributed to my life and creative pursuits in any way, please know I love you and am ever grateful, even if I forget to mention you by name.

That said, I must first start with the men in my life. All of whom now tower over me. How lucky I am to have a husband who supports me in my crazy word addiction. Thank you, David, for everything. How blessed I feel to have three boys who know who they are and are good with it. Zach, Michael, and AJ—you continue to amaze me with your kindness and drive to do what's right. I love my Boyd boys. I'm so proud of you all.

I'm ever grateful to have writing and reading loving parents and siblings. Thanks for reading multiple versions of my books. I can't even remember how many times you've encouraged me to keep going. Thank you for continuing to believe in me, even when I couldn't believe in myself.

Thanks to Ann, who's had dibs on first reading rights since version one of Paint the Grass.

Thanks to Carol-Lynn who loves me like a sister and has been cheering me on for over a decade.

Thanks to Connie who let me cry on her shoulder on the hard days.

Thanks to Jodi who, after reading Paint the Grass texted Kira and said: "Holy shit! You have to read Heidi's book!" A simple confidence boost I desperately needed at the time.

Thanks to everyone at Book Therapy and Moore for always reserving a chair for me so I could sit and write. It's the perfect place to support my word addiction.

Thanks to my early readers, who each gave me invaluable feedback. Alli, Lindsay, Lisa, Lathie, Leesa, Jodi, Karen, Kerri, Naomi, Marci, Kelsey, Kayla, Tamera, Bonnie, Debra, Connie, Kaysha, Daneesha, Ann, Tenae, Annika, Erin, Roxie, Alisa, Kira, Rebecca, Keeley, Tamara, Hillary, Tia, Carol-Lynn, Cindy, Amey, Charity, Jason, Skyler, Fast Eddie, and David.

Special thanks to Tamara Heiner for being such an amazing editor and for making me fix the hard things. You lifted my little story toward perfection.

Special thanks to Hillary Sperry for being so dang talented. My book cover is stunning and my format is so beautiful because of your dedication and sheer awesomeness. I'm so lucky to have you on my team. You truly do make gorgeous books!

And thanks to all of you, fellow word lovers. The ones who read past your bedtime, who suffer through tired days because of late nights binging on words by lamplight, and who live inside worlds created between the covers of a book. Thank you for reading. Thank you for supporting my dream to share my character's lives with you.

Now—on to the next story . . .

Coming Soon
Bethany's story continues in:

PAINT
THE TOWN

H.R. Boyd is the wife of a fly-boy, mother of three sons, and lover of words. Her mother claims she started speaking in full sentences before age two, telling stories every waking moment. After she grew up, she dedicated eight years to raising her family before her focus turned back to telling stories. She enjoyed small-town Montana life for sixteen years and still considers Three Forks to be her hometown. She now lives in Northwest Arkansas in a house full of boys, with two cats who continually compete with her computer for dominance of her lap. She has won several awards for her writing and has completed six novels. Paint the Grass is her first published work.

WWW.HRBOYD.COM

Find H.R. Boyd online:

Facebook @ H.R. Boyd, Author

Instagram @hrboydwrites

Twitter @heidi_boyd

Tiktok @hrboydwrites